P9-DNR-883

Presented to

"Sandy"

By

Nellie

On the Occasion of

Dist. 4 Meeting

Date

Oct. 6 99

Published by Barbour Publishing, Inc.
　　　　　P.O. Box 719
　　　　　Uhrichsville, OH 44683
　　　　　http://www.barbourbooks.com

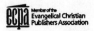
Member of the
Evangelical Christian
Publishers Association

Printed in the United States of America.

STEPPING HEAVENWARD

Elizabeth Prentiss

BARBOUR
PUBLISHING, INC.
Uhrichsville, Ohio

Introductory Note

Elizabeth Prentiss was born at Portland, Me., on the 26th of October, 1818, and died, after a brief illness, at Dorset, Vt., on the 13th of August, 1878. She was the youngest daughter of the Rev. Edward Payson, D.D., a very eminent servant of Christ, whose praise is still in all the churches. At the age of sixteen she began to write for the press: the little volume entitled *Only a Dandelion,* consisting chiefly of her early contributions to *The Youth's Companion* of Boston. The works by which she is best known are *Little Susy's Six Birthdays,* with its companions, and *Stepping Heavenward.* The latter was first published in 1869. It has passed through many editions in this country and has had a very wide circulation in Great Britain, Canada, and Australia. It was also translated into French and German, and several editions of it have been issued in those languages. It appeared at Leipsic in Tauchnitz's *Collection of British Authors.* Among Mrs. Prentiss's other works, which have been widely circulated both at home and abroad, are *The Flower of the Family, Little Lou's Sayings and Doings, Henry and Bessie, Fred and Maria and Me, The Percys, Nidworth and His Three Magic Wands, The Story Lizzie Told, The Home at Greylock, Aunt Jane's Hero, Urbane and His Friends, Pemaquid,* and *Golden Hours; or, Hymns and Songs of the Christian Life.* The aim of her writings, whether designed for young or old, is to incite to patience, fidelity, hope, and all goodness by showing how trust in God and loving obedience to His blessed will brighten the darkest paths and make a heaven upon earth.

Of her religious character the keynote is struck in her own hymn, "More Love to Thee, O Christ." That was her ruling passion in life and death. Writing to a young friend from Dorset, in 1873, she says: "To love Christ more—this is the deepest need, the constant cry of my soul. Down in the bowling alley, and out in the woods, and on my bed, and out driving, when I am happy and busy, and when I am sad and idle, the whisper keeps going up for more love, more love, more love!"

The following recollections of her by Mrs. Mary H. B. Field, now of San Jose, California, may fitly complete this sketch:

It was the first Sunday in September 1866—a quiet, perfect day among the green hills of Vermont—a sacramental Sabbath—and we had come seven miles over the mountain to go up to the house of the Lord. I had brought my little two-month-old baby in my arms, intending to leave her during the service at our brother's home, which was near the church. I knew that Mrs. Prentiss was a "summer boarder" in this home, that she was the wife of a distinguished clergyman, and a literary woman of decided ability; but it was before the "Stepping Heavenward" epoch of her life, and I had no very deep interest in the prospect of meeting her. We went in at the hospitably open door, and meeting no one, sat down in the pleasant family living room. It was about noon, and we could hear cheerful voices talking over the lunch table in the dining room. Presently the door opened, and a slight, delicate-featured woman with beautiful large dark eyes came with rapid step into the room, going across to a hall door; but her quick eye caught a glimpse of my little "bundle of flannel," and not

Introductory Note

Elizabeth Prentiss was born at Portland, Me., on the 26th of October, 1818, and died, after a brief illness, at Dorset, Vt., on the 13th of August, 1878. She was the youngest daughter of the Rev. Edward Payson, D.D., a very eminent servant of Christ, whose praise is still in all the churches. At the age of sixteen she began to write for the press: the little volume entitled *Only a Dandelion,* consisting chiefly of her early contributions to *The Youth's Companion* of Boston. The works by which she is best known are *Little Susy's Six Birthdays,* with its companions, and *Stepping Heavenward.* The latter was first published in 1869. It has passed through many editions in this country and has had a very wide circulation in Great Britain, Canada, and Australia. It was also translated into French and German, and several editions of it have been issued in those languages. It appeared at Leipsic in Tauchnitz's *Collection of British Authors.* Among Mrs. Prentiss's other works, which have been widely circulated both at home and abroad, are *The Flower of the Family, Little Lou's Sayings and Doings, Henry and Bessie, Fred and Maria and Me, The Percys, Nidworth and His Three Magic Wands, The Story Lizzie Told, The Home at Greylock, Aunt Jane's Hero, Urbane and His Friends, Pemaquid, and Golden Hours; or, Hymns and Songs of the Christian Life.* The aim of her writings, whether designed for young or old, is to incite to patience, fidelity, hope, and all goodness by showing how trust in God and loving obedience to His blessed will brighten the darkest paths and make a heaven upon earth.

Of her religious character the keynote is struck in her own hymn, "More Love to Thee, O Christ." That was her ruling passion in life and death. Writing to a young friend from Dorset, in 1873, she says: "To love Christ more—this is the deepest need, the constant cry of my soul. Down in the bowling alley, and out in the woods, and on my bed, and out driving, when I am happy and busy, and when I am sad and idle, the whisper keeps going up for more love, more love, more love!"

The following recollections of her by Mrs. Mary H. B. Field, now of San Jose, California, may fitly complete this sketch:

It was the first Sunday in September 1866—a quiet, perfect day among the green hills of Vermont—a sacramental Sabbath—and we had come seven miles over the mountain to go up to the house of the Lord. I had brought my little two-month-old baby in my arms, intending to leave her during the service at our brother's home, which was near the church. I knew that Mrs. Prentiss was a "summer boarder" in this home, that she was the wife of a distinguished clergyman, and a literary woman of decided ability; but it was before the "Stepping Heavenward" epoch of her life, and I had no very deep interest in the prospect of meeting her. We went in at the hospitably open door, and meeting no one, sat down in the pleasant family living room. It was about noon, and we could hear cheerful voices talking over the lunch table in the dining room. Presently the door opened, and a slight, delicate-featured woman with beautiful large dark eyes came with rapid step into the room, going across to a hall door; but her quick eye caught a glimpse of my little "bundle of flannel," and not pausing for an introduction or word of preparatory speech, she came towards me with a beaming face and outstretched hands.

"O, have you a baby there? How delightful! I haven't seen one for such an age! Please, may I take it? The darling tiny creature!—a girl? How lovely!"

She took the baby tenderly in her arms and went on in her eager, quick, informal way, but with a bright little blush and smile. "I'm not very polite—pray, let me introduce myself! I'm Mrs. Prentiss, and you are Mrs. Field, I know."

After a little more sweet, motherly comment and question over the baby—"a touch of nature" which at once made us "akin"—she asked, "Have you brought the baby to be christened?"

I said, "No, I thought it would be better to wait till she was a little older."

"O, no!" she pleaded. "Do let us take her over to the church now. The younger the better, I think; it is so uncertain about our keeping such treasures."

I still objected that I had not dressed the little one for so public an occasion.

"O, never mind about that," she said. "She is really lovelier in this simple fashion than to be loaded with lace and embroidery." Then, her sweet face growing more earnest, "There will be more of us here today than at the next Communion—*more of us to pray for her.*"

The little lamb was taken into the fold that day, and I was Mrs. Prentiss's warm friend forevermore. Her whole beautiful character had revealed itself to me in that little interview—the quick perception, the wholly frank, unconventional manner, the sweet motherliness, the cordial interest in even a stranger, the fervent piety that could not bear delay in duty, and even the quaint, original, forcible thought and way of expressing it—"There'll be more of us here to pray for her today."

For seven successive summers I saw more or less of her in this "Earthly Paradise," as she used to call it, and once I visited her in her city home. I have been favored with many of her sparkling, vivacious letters and have read and reread all her published writings; but that first meeting held in it for me the keynote of all her wonderfully beautiful and symmetrical character.

She brought to that little hamlet among the hills a sweet and wholesome and powerful influence. While her time was too valuable to be wasted in a general sociability, she yet found leisure for an extensive acquaintance, for a kindly interest in all her neighbors, and for Christian work of many kinds. Probably the weekly meeting for Bible-reading and prayer, which she conducted, was her closest link with the women of Dorset; but these meetings were established after I had bidden good-bye to the dear old town, and I leave others to tell how their "hearts burned within them as she opened to them the Scriptures."

She had in a remarkable degree the lovely feminine gift of homemaking. She was a true decorative artist. Her room when she was boarding and her home after it was completed were bowers of beauty. Every walk over hill and dale, every ramble by brookside or through wildwood gave to her some fresh home adornment. Some shy wildflower or fern, or brilliant tinted leaf, a bit of moss, a curious lichen, a deserted bird's nest, a strange fragment of rock, a shining pebble would catch her passing glance and reveal to her quick artistic sense possibilities of use that were quaint, original, characteristic. One saw from afar that hers was a poet's home; and, if permitted to enter its gracious portals, the first impression deepened into certainty. There was as strong an individuality about her home and especially about her own little study as there was about herself and her writings. A cheerful, sunny, hospitable Christian home! Far and wide its potent influences reached, and it was a beautiful thing to see how many another home, humble or stately, grew emulous and blossomed into a new loveliness.

Mrs. Prentiss was naturally a shy and reserved woman and necessarily a preoccupied one. Therefore she was sometimes misunderstood. But those who knew her best and were blest with her rare intimacy knew her as "a perfect woman nobly planned." Her conversation was charming. Her close study of nature taught her a thousand happy symbols and illustrations, which made both what she said and wrote a mosaic of exquisite comparisons. Her studies of character were equally constant and penetrating. Nothing escaped her; no peculiarity of mind or manner failed of her quick observation, but it was always a kindly interest. She did not ridicule that which was simply ignorance or weakness, and she saw with keen pleasure all that was quaint, original, or strong, even when it was hidden beneath the homeliest garb. She had the true artist's liking for that which was simple and genre. The common things of common life appealed to her sympathies and called out all her attention. It was a real, hearty interest, too, not feigned, even in a sense generally thought praiseworthy. Indeed, no one ever had a more intense scorn of every sort of feigning. She was honest, truthful, genuine to the highest degree It may have sometimes led her into seeming lack of courtesy, but even this was a failing that "leaned to virtue's side." I chanced to know of her once calling with a friend on a country neighbor, and finding the good housewife busy over a rag carpet, Mrs. Prentiss, who had never seen one of these bits of rural manufacture in its elementary processes, was full of questions and interest, thereby quite evidently pleasing the unassuming artist in assorted rags and home-made dyes. When the visitors were safely outside the door, Mrs. Prentiss's friend turned to her with the exclamation, "What tact you have! She really thought you were interested in her work!" The quick blood sprang into Mrs. Prentiss's face, and she turned upon her friend a look of amazement and rebuke. "Tact!" she said. "I despise such tact! Do you think I would look or act a lie?"

She was an exceedingly practical woman, not a dreamer. A systematic, thorough housekeeper, with as exalted ideals in all the affairs that pertain to good house-wifery as in those matters that are generally thought to transcend these humble occupations. Like Solomon's virtuous woman, she "looked well after the ways of her household." Methodical, careful of minutes, simple in her tastes, abstemious, and therefore enjoying evenly good health in spite of her delicate constitution—this is the secret of her accomplishing so much. Yet all this foundation of exactness and diligence was so "rounded with leafy gracefulness" that she never seemed angular or unyielding.

With her children she was a model disciplinarian, exceedingly strict, a wise lawmaker; yet withal a tender, devoted, self-sacrificing mother. I have never seen such exact obedience required and given or a more idolized mother. "Mamma's" word was indeed law, but—O happy combination!—it was also gospel.

How warm and true her friendship was! How little of selfishness in all her intercourse with other women! How well she loved to be of service to her friends! How anxious that each should reach her highest possibilities of attainment! I record with deepest sense of obligation the cordial, generous, sympathetic assistance of many kinds extended by her to me during our whole acquaintance. To every earnest worker in any field she gladly "lent a hand," rejoicing in all the successes of others as if they were her own.

But if weakness, or trouble, or sorrow of any sort or degree overtook one, she straightway became as one of God's own ministering spirits—an angel of strength and consolation. Always more eager, however, that souls should grow than that pain should cease. Volumes could be made of her letters to friends in sorrow. One tender monotone steals through them all—

"Come unto me, my kindred, I enfold you
In an embrace to sufferers only known;
Close to this heart I tenderly will hold you,
Suppress no sigh, keep back no tear, no moan.

"Thou Man of Sorrows, teach my lips that often
Have told the sacred story of my woe,
To speak of Thee till stony griefs I soften,
Till hearts that know Thee not learn Thee to know.

"Till peace takes place of storm and agitation,
Till lying on the current of Thy will
There shall be glorying in tribulation,
And Christ Himself each empty heart shall fill."

Few have the gift or the courage to deal faithfully yet lovingly with an erring soul, but she did not shrink back even from this service to those she loved. I can bear witness to the wisdom, penetration, skill, and fidelity with which she probed a terribly wounded spirit and then said with tender solemnity, "I think you need a great deal of good praying."

O, "vanished hand," still beckon to us from the Eternal Heights! O, "voice that is still," speak to us yet from the Shining Shore!

> *"Still let thy mild rebuking stand*
> *Between us and the wrong,*
> *And thy dear memory serve to make*
> *Our faith in goodness strong."*

GORDON L. PRENTISS
NEW YORK, OCTOBER 26, 1880

CHAPTER I

*H*ow dreadfully old I am getting! Sixteen! Well, I don't see as I can help it. There it is in the big Bible in Father's own hand:

"Katherine, born Jan. 15, 1815."

I meant to get up early this morning, but it looked dismally cold out of doors and felt delightfully warm in bed. So I covered myself up and made ever so many good resolutions.

I determined, in the first place, to begin this journal. To be sure, I have begun half a dozen and got tired of them after a while. Not tired of writing them, but disgusted with what I had to say of myself. But this time I mean to go on, in spite of everything. It will do me good to read it over and see what a creature I am.

Then I resolved to do more to please Mother than I have done.

And I determined to make one more effort to conquer my hasty temper. I thought, too, I would be self-denying this winter, like the people one reads about in books. I fancied how surprised and pleased everybody would be to see me so much improved!

Time passed quickly amid these agreeable thoughts, and I was quite startled to hear the bell ring for prayers. I jumped up in a great flurry and dressed as quickly as I could. Everything conspired together to plague me. I could not find a clean collar or a handkerchief. It is always just so. Mother is forever poking my things into out-of-the-way places! When at last I went down, they were all at breakfast.

"I hoped you would celebrate your birthday, dear, by coming down in good season," said Mother.

I do hate to be found fault with, so I fired up in an instant.

"If people hide my things so that I can't find them, of course I have to be late," I said. And I rather think I said it in a very cross way, for Mother sighed a little. I wish Mother wouldn't sigh. I would rather be called names out and out.

The moment breakfast was over, I had to hurry off to school. Just as I was going out, Mother said, "Have you your overshoes, dear?"

"Oh, Mother, don't slow me down! I shall be late," I said. "I don't need overshoes."

"It snowed all night and I think you do need them," Mother said.

"I don't know where they are. I hate overshoes. Do let me go, Mother," I cried. "I do wish I could ever have my own way."

"You shall have it now, my child," Mother said and went away.

Now what was the use of her calling me "my child" in such a tone, I should like to know.

I hurried off, and just as I got to the door of the school-room, it flashed into my mind that I had not said my prayers! A nice way to begin on one's birthday to be sure! Well, I had no time. And perhaps my good resolutions pleased God almost as much as one of my rambling stupid prayers could. For I must admit I can't make good prayers. I can't think of anything to say. I often wonder what Mother finds to say when she is shut up by the hour praying.

I had a pretty good time at school. My teachers praised me, and Amelia seemed so fond of me! She brought me a birthday present, a purse that she had knit for me herself and a net for my hair. Nets are just coming into fashion. It will save a good deal of time my having this one. Instead of combing and combing and combing my hair to get it glossy enough to suit Mother, I can just give it one twist and one squeeze, and the whole thing will be settled for the day.

Amelia wrote me a dear little note with her presents. I do really believe she loves me dearly. It is so nice to have people love you!

When I got home, Mother called me into her room. She looked as if she had been crying. She said I gave her a great deal of pain by my self-will and ill temper and conceit.

"Conceit!" I screamed out. "Oh Mother, if you only knew how horrid I think I am!"

Mother smiled a little. Then she went on with her list till she made me out the worst creature in the world. I burst out crying and was running off to my room, but she made me come back and hear the rest. She said my character would be essentially formed by the time I reached my twentieth year and left it to me to decide if I wished to be as a woman what I was now as a girl. I felt sulky and would not answer. I was shocked to think I had got only four years in which to improve, but after all, a good deal could be done in that time. Of course I don't want to be always exactly what I am now.

Mother went on to say that I had in me the elements of a fine character if I would only conquer some of my faults. "You are frank and truthful," she said, "and in some things conscientious. I hope you are really a child of God and are trying to please Him. And it is my daily prayer that you may become a lovely, loving, useful woman."

I made no answer. I wanted to say something, but my tongue wouldn't move. I was angry with Mother and angry with myself. At last everything came out all in a rush, mixed up with such floods of tears that I thought Mother's heart would melt and that she would take back what she had said.

"Amelia's mother never talks so to her!" I said. "She praises her and tells her what a comfort she is to her. But just as I am trying as hard as I can to be good, and making resolutions and all that, you scold me and discourage me!"

Mother's voice was very soft and gentle as she asked, "Do you call this 'scolding,' my child?"

"And I don't like to be called conceited," I went on. "I know I am perfectly horrid, and I am just as unhappy as I can be."

"I am very sorry for you, dear," Mother replied. "But you must bear with me. Other people will see your faults, but only your mother will have the courage to speak of them. Now go to your room, and wipe away the traces of your tears so the rest of the family won't know that you have been crying on your birthday." She kissed me, but I did not kiss her.

I really believe Satan himself hindered me. I ran across the hall to my room, slammed the door, and locked myself in. I was going to throw myself on the bed and cry till I was sick. Then I should look pale and tired, and they would all pity me. I do like so to be pitied! But on the table, by the window, I saw a beautiful new desk in place of the old clumsy thing I had been spattering and spoiling so many years. A little note, full of love, said it was from Mother and begged me every day of my life to read and reflect upon a few verses of a tastefully bound copy of the Bible that accompanied the desk. "A few verses," she said, "carefully read and pondered, instead of a chapter or two read for mere form's sake." I looked at my desk, which contained exactly what I wanted, plenty of paper, seals, wax, and pens. I always use wax. Wafers are vulgar. Then I opened the Bible at random and lighted on these words:

"Watch, therefore, for ye know not what hour your Lord doth come" (Matt. 24:42). There was nothing very cheering in that. I felt a real repugnance to be always on the watch, thinking I might die at any moment. I am sure I am not fit to die. Besides, I want to have a good time with nothing to worry me. I hope I shall live ever so long. Perhaps in the course of forty or fifty years I may get tired of this world and want to leave it. And I hope by that time I shall be a great deal better than I am now and fit to go to heaven.

I wrote a note to Mother on my new desk and thanked her for it. I told her she was the best mother in the world and that I was the worst daughter. When it was done, I did not like it, and so I wrote another. Then I went down to dinner and felt better. We had such a nice dinner! Everything I liked best was on the table. Mother had not forgotten one of all the dishes I like. Amelia was there, too. Mother had invited her to give me a little surprise. It is bedtime now, and I must say my prayers and go to bed. I have got all chilled through, writing here in the cold. I believe I will say my prayers in bed, just for this once. I do not feel sleepy, but I am sure I ought not to sit up another moment.

–*Jan. 30*–

Here I am at my desk once more. There is a fire in my room, and Mother is sitting by it, reading. I can't see what book it is, but I have no doubt it is Thomas à Kempis. How she can go on reading it so year after year, I cannot imagine. For my part, I like something new. But I must go back to where I left off.

That night when I stopped writing, I hurried to bed as fast as I could for I felt cold and tired. I remembered saying, "Oh, God, I am ashamed to pray," and then I began to think of all the things that had happened that day and never knew another thing till the rising bell rang and I found it was morning. I am sure I did not mean to go to sleep. I think now it was wrong of me to be such a coward that I tried to say my prayers in bed because of the cold. While I was writing I did not once think how I felt. Well, I jumped up as soon as I heard the bell, but found I had a dreadful pain in my side and a cough. Mother says I coughed all night. I remembered then that I had just such a cough and just such a pain the last time I walked in the snow without overshoes. I crept back to bed feeling about as mean as I could. Mother sent up to know why I did not come down, and I had to own that I was sick. She came up directly looking so anxious! And here I have been shut up ever since; only today I am sitting up a little. Poor Mother has had trouble enough with me; I know I have been cross and unreasonable, and it was all my own fault that I was ill. Another time I will do as Mother says.

–Jan. 31–

How easy it is to make good resolutions, and how easy it is to break them! Just as I had got so far, yesterday Mother spoke for the third time about my exerting myself so much. And just at that moment I fainted away, and she had a great time all alone there with me. I did not realize how long I had been writing nor how weak I was. I do wonder if I shall ever really learn that Mother knows more than I do!

–Feb. 17–

It is more than a month since I took that cold, and here I still am, shut up in the house. To be sure the doctor lets me go downstairs, but then he won't listen to a word about school. Oh, dear! All the girls will get ahead of me.

This is Sunday, and everybody has gone to church. I thought I ought to make a good use of the time while they were gone, so I took the *Memoir of Henry Martyn,* and read a little in that.

I am afraid I am not much like him. Then I knelt down and tried to pray. But my mind was full of all sorts of things, so I thought I would wait till I was in a better frame of mind. At noon I disputed with James about the name of an apple. He was very provoking and said he was thankful he had not got such a temper as I had. I cried, and Mother reproved him for teasing me, saying my illness had left me nervous and irritable. James replied that it had left me where it found me, then. I cried a good while, lying on the sofa, and then I fell asleep. I don't see as I am any the better for this Sunday, it has only made me feel unhappy and out of sorts. I am sure I pray to God to make me better, and why doesn't He?

–*Feb. 20*–

It has been quite a mild day for the season and the doctor said I might drive out. I enjoyed getting the air very much. I feel just as well as ever and long to get back to school. I think God has been very good to me in making me well again, and I wish I loved Him better. But, oh, I am not sure I do love Him! I hate to own it to myself and to write it down here, but I will. I do not love to pray. I am always eager to get it over with and out of the way so as to have leisure to enjoy myself. I mean that this is usually so. This morning I cried a good deal while I was on my knees and felt sorry for my quick temper and all my bad ways. If I always felt so, perhaps praying would not be such a task. I wish I knew whether anybody exactly as bad as I am ever got to heaven at last? I have read ever so many memoirs, and they were all about people who were too good to live, and so died, or else went on a mission; I am not at all like any of them.

–*March 26*–

I have been so busy that I have not said much to you, you poor old journal you, have I? Somehow I have been behaving quite nicely lately. Everything has gone on exactly to my mind. Mother has not found fault with me once, and Father has praised my drawings and seemed proud of me. He says he shall not tell me what my teachers say of me lest it should make me vain. And once or twice when he has met me singing and frisking about the house, he has kissed me and called me his dear little Flibbertigibbet, if that's the way to spell it. When he says that, I know he is very fond of me. We are all very happy together when nothing goes wrong. In the long evenings we all sit around the table with our books and our work, and one of us reads aloud. Mother chooses the books and takes her turn in reading. She reads beautifully. Of course the readings do not begin till the lessons are all learned. As to me, my lessons just take no time at all. I have only to read them over once, and there they are. So I have a good deal of time to read, and I devour all the poetry I can get hold of. I would rather read Pollok's "Course of Time," than read nothing at all.

—*April 2*—

There are three of Mother's friends living near us, each with lots of little children. It is perfectly ridiculous how much those creatures are sick. They send for Mother if so much as a pimple comes out on one of their faces. When I have children, I don't mean to have such goings-on. I shall be careful about what they eat and keep them from getting cold, and they will keep well of their own accord. Mrs. Jones has just sent for Mother to see her Tommy. It was so provoking. I had coaxed Mother into letting me have a black silk apron; they are all the fashion now, embroidered in floss silk. I had drawn a lovely vine for mine entirely out of my own hand, and Mother was going to arrange the pattern for me when that message came and she had to go. I don't believe anything ails the child! A great chubby thing!

—*April 3*—

Poor Mrs. Jones! Her dear little Tommy is dead! I stayed at home from school today and had all the other children here to get them out of their mother's way. How dreadfully she must feel! Mother cried when she told me how the dear little fellow suffered in his last moments. It reminded her of my little brothers who died in the same way just before I was born. Dear Mother! I wonder how I can ever forget what troubles she has had, and am not always sweet and loving. She has gone now, where she always goes when she feels sad, straight to God. Of course she did not say so, but I know Mother.

–*April 25*–

I have not been down in season once this week. I have persuaded Mother to let me read some of Scott's novels and have sat up late and been sleepy in the morning. I wish I could get along with Mother as nicely as James does. He is late far oftener than I am, but he never gets into such scrapes about it as I do. This is what happens. He comes down when it suits him.

Mother begins—"James, I am very much displeased with you."

James—"I should think you would be, Mother."

Mother, mollified—"I don't think you deserve any breakfast."

James, hypocritically—"No, I don't think I do, Mother."

Then Mother hurries off and gets something extra for his breakfast. Now let us see how things go on when I am late.

Mother—"Katherine" (she always calls me Katherine when she is displeased and spells it with a K), "Katherine, you are late again, how can you annoy your Father so?"

Katherine—"Of course I don't do it to annoy Father or anybody else. But if I oversleep, it is not my fault."

Mother—"I would go to bed at eight o'clock rather than be late as often as you. How should you like it if I were not down to prayers?"

Katherine, muttering—"Of course that is very different. I don't see why I should be blamed for oversleeping any more than James. I get all the scoldings."

Mother sighs and goes off.

I prowl round and get what scraps of breakfast I can.

–May 12–

The weather is getting perfectly delicious. I am sitting with my window open, and my bird is singing with all his heart. I wish I was as gay as he is.

I have been thinking lately that it was about time to begin on some of those pieces of self-denial I resolved on upon my birthday. I could not think of anything great enough for a long time. At last an idea popped into my head. Half the girls at school envy me because Amelia is so fond of me; and Jane Underhill, in particular, is just crazy to be friends with her. But I have kept Amelia all to myself. Today I said to her, "Amelia, Jane Underhill admires you above all things. I have a good mind to let you be as good friends with her as you are with me. It will be a great piece of self-denial, but I think it is my duty. She is a stranger, and nobody seems to like her much."

"You dear thing you!" cried Amelia, kissing me. "I liked Jane Underhill the moment I saw her. She has such a sweet face and such pleasant manners. But you are so jealous that I never dared to show how I like her. Don't be vexed, dearie; if you are jealous it is your only fault!"

She then rushed off, and I saw her kiss that girl exactly as she kissed me!

This was in recess. I went to my desk and made believe I was studying. Pretty soon Amelia came back.

"She is a sweet girl," she said, "and only to think! She writes poetry! Just hear this! It is a little poem addressed to me. Isn't it nice of her?"

I pretended not to hear her. I was as full of all sorts of horrid feelings as I could hold. It enraged me to think that Amelia, after all her professions of love to me, should snatch at the first chance of getting a new friend. Then I was mortified because I was enraged, and I could have torn myself to pieces for being such a fool as to let Amelia see how silly I was.

"I don't know what to make of you, Katy," she said, putting her arms around me. "Have I done anything to vex you? Come, let us make up and be friends, whatever it is. I will read you these sweet verses; I am sure you will like them."

She read them in her clear, pleasant voice.

"How can you have the vanity to read such stuff?" I cried.

Amelia colored a little.

"You have said and written much more flattering things to me," she replied. "Perhaps it has turned my head and made me too ready to believe what other people say." She folded the paper and put it into her pocket. We walked home together after school, as usual, but neither of us spoke a word. And now here I sit, unhappy enough. All my resolutions fail. But I did not think Amelia would take me at my word and rush after that stuck-up, smirking piece!

–*May 20*–

It seems this Underhill thing is here for her health,

though she looks as well as any of us. She is an orphan and has been adopted by a rich old uncle, who makes a perfect fool of her. Such dresses and such finery as she wears! Last night she had Amelia there to tea, without inviting me, though she knows I am her best friend. She gave her a bracelet made of her own hair. I wonder Amelia's mother lets her accept presents from strangers. My mother would not let me. On the whole, there is nobody like one's own mother. Amelia has been cold and distant to me of late, but no matter what I do or say to my darling, precious mother, she is always kind and loving. She noticed how I moped about today and begged me to tell her what was the matter. I was ashamed to do that. I told her that it was a little quarrel I had had with Amelia.

"Dear child," she said, "how I pity you that you have inherited my quick, irritable temper."

"Yours, Mother!" I cried out. "What can you mean?"

Mother smiled a little at my surprise.

"It is even so," she said.

"Then how did you cure yourself of it? Tell me quick, Mother, and let me cure myself of mine."

"My dear Katy," she said, "I wish I could make you see that God is just as willing and just as able to sanctify as He is to redeem us. It would save you so much weary, disappointing work. But God has opened my eyes at last."

"I wish He would open mine, then," I said, "for all I see now is that I am just as horrid as I can be and that the more I pray the worse I grow."

"That is not true, dear," she replied. "Go on praying—pray without ceasing."

I sat pulling my handkerchief this way and that and at last rolled it up into a ball and threw it across the room. I wished I could toss my bad feelings into a corner with it.

"I do wish I could make you love to pray, my darling child," Mother went on. "If you only knew the strength, and the light, and the joy you might have for the simple asking. God attaches no conditions to His gifts. He only says, 'Ask!' "

This may be true, but it is hard work to pray. It tires me. And I do wish there was some easy way of growing good. In fact, I should like to have God send a sweet temper to me just as He sent bread and meat to Elijah. I don't believe Elijah had to kneel down and pray for them.

CHAPTER II

*L*ast Sunday Dr. Cabot preached to the young. He first addressed those who knew they did not love God. It did not seem to me that I belonged to that class. Then he spoke to those who knew they did. I felt sure I was not one of those. Last of all he spoke affectionately to those who did not know what to think, and I was frightened and ashamed to feel tears running down my cheeks when he said that he believed that most of his hearers who were in this doubtful state did really love their Master, only their love was something as new and as tender and perhaps as unobserved as the tiny point of green that, forcing its way through the earth, is yet unconscious of its own existence but promises a thrifty plant. I don't suppose I express it very well, but I know what he meant. He then invited those belonging to each class to meet him on three successive Saturday afternoons. I shall certainly go.

–*July 19*–

I went to the meeting, and so did Amelia. A great many young people were there and a few children. Dr. Cabot went about from seat to seat, speaking to each one separately. When he came to us, I expected he would say something about the way in which I had been brought up and reproach me for not profiting more by the instructions and example I had at home. Instead of that he said in a cheerful voice, "Well, my dear, I cannot see into your heart and positively tell whether there is love to God there or not. But I suppose you have come today in order to let me help you find out?"

I said, "Yes"; that was all I could get out.

"Let me see, then," he went on. "Do you love your mother?"

I said, "Yes," once more.

"But prove to me that you do. How do you know it?"

I tried to think. Then I said, "I feel that I love her. I love to love her; I like to be with her. I like to hear people praise her. And I try—sometimes at least—to do things to please her. But I don't try half as hard as I ought, and I do and say a great many things to displease her."

"Yes, yes," he said, "I know."

"Has Mother told you?" I cried out.

"No, dear, no, indeed. But I know what human nature is after having one of my own fifty years and six of my children's to encounter."

Somehow I felt more courage after he said that.

"In the first place, then, you feel that you love your mother? But you never feel that you love your God and Savior?"

"I often try and try, but I never do," I said.

"Love won't be forced," he said quickly.

"Then what shall I do?"

"In the second place, you like to be with your mother. But you never like to be with the Friend who loves you so much better than she does?"

"I don't know; I never was with Him. Sometimes I think that when Mary sat at His feet and heard Him talk, she must have been very happy."

"We come to the third test, then. You like to hear people praise your mother. And have you never rejoiced to hear the Lord magnified?"

I shook my head sorrowfully enough.

"Let us then try the last test. You know you love your mother because you try to do things to please her. That is, to do what you know she wishes you to do? Very well. Have you never tried to do anything God wishes you to do?"

"Oh yes; often. But not so often as I ought."

"Of course not. No one does that. But come now, why do you try to do what you think will please Him? Because it is easy? Because you like to do what He likes rather than what you like yourself?"

I tried to think and got puzzled.

"Never mind," said Dr. Cabot. "I have come now to the point I was aiming at. You cannot prove to yourself that you love God by examining your feelings toward Him. They are indefinite and they fluctuate. But just as far as you obey Him, just so far, depend upon it, you love Him. It is not natural to us sinful, ungrateful human beings to prefer His pleasure to our own or to follow His way instead of our own way, and nothing, nothing but love of Him can or does make us obedient to Him."

"Couldn't we obey Him from fear?" Amelia now

asked. She had been listening all this time in silence.

"Yes; and so you might obey your mother from fear, but only for a season. If you had no real love for her, you would gradually cease to dread her displeasure; whereas it is in the very nature of love to grow stronger and more influential every hour."

"You mean, then, that if we want to know whether we love God, we must find out whether we are obeying Him?" Amelia asked.

"I mean exactly that. 'He that keepeth my commandments he it is that loveth me.' But I cannot talk with you any longer now. There are many others still waiting. You can come to see me some day next week if you have any more questions to ask."

When we got out into the street, Amelia and I got hold of each other's hands. We did not speak a word till we reached the door, but we knew that we were as good friends as ever.

"I understand all Dr. Cabot said," Amelia whispered as we separated. But I felt like one in a fog. I cannot see how it is possible to love God and yet feel as stupid as I do when I think of Him. Still, I am determined to do one thing, and that is to pray regularly instead of now and then, as I have got in the habit of doing lately.

–*July 25*–

School has closed for the season. I took the first prize for drawing, and my composition was read aloud on examination day, and everybody praised it. Mother could not possibly help showing, in her face, that she was very much pleased I am pleased myself. We are now getting ready to take a journey. I do not think I shall go to see Dr. Cabot again. My head is full of other things, and there is so much to do before we go. I am having four new dresses made, and I can't imagine how to have them trimmed. I mean to run down to Amelia's and ask her.

–*July 27*–

I was rushing through the hall just after I wrote that and met Mother.

"I am going to Amelia's," I said, hurrying past her.

"Stop one minute, dear. Dr. Cabot is downstairs. He says he has been expecting a visit from you, but as you did not come to him, he has come to you."

"I wish he would mind his own business," I said.

"I think he is minding it, dear," Mother answered. "His Master's business is his, and that has brought him here. Go to him, my darling child; I am sure you crave something better than prizes and compliments and new dresses and journeys."

If anybody but Mother had said that, my heart would have melted at once, and I should have gone right down to Dr. Cabot to be molded in his hands to almost any shape. But as it was, I brushed past her, ran into my room, and locked my door. Oh, what makes me act so! I hate myself for it; I don't want to do it!

Last week I dined with Mrs. Jones. Her little Tommy that died was very fond of me, and that, I suppose, makes her have me there so often. Lucy was at the table and very fractious. She cried first for one thing and then for another. At last her mother in a gentle, but very decided way put her down from the table. Then she cried louder than ever. But when her mother offered to take her back if she would be good, she screamed yet more. She wanted to come and wouldn't let herself come. I almost hated her when I saw her act so, and now I am behaving ten times worse and I am just as miserable as I can be.

–*July 29*–

Amelia has been here. She has had another talk with Dr. Cabot and is perfectly happy. She says it is so easy to be a Christian! It may be easy for her; everything is. She never has any of my dreadful feelings and does not understand them when I try to explain them to her. Well! If I am fated to be miserable, I must try to bear it.

–*Oct. 3*–

Summer is over, school has begun again, and I am so busy that I have not much time to think or to be low spirited. We had a delightful journey, and I feel well and bright and even gay. I never enjoyed my studies as I do those of this year. Everything goes on pleasantly here at home. But James has gone away to school and we miss him sadly. I do wish I had a sister. Though I dare say I should quarrel with her, if I did.

–*Oct. 23*–

I am so glad that my studies are harder this year, as I am never happy except when every moment is occupied. However, I do not study all the time, by any means. Amelia's mother, Mrs. Gordon, grows more and more fond of me and has me there to dinner or to tea continually. She has a much higher opinion of me than Mother has and is always saying the sort of things that make you feel nice. She holds me up to Amelia as an example, begging her to imitate me in my fidelity about my lessons and declaring there is nothing she so much desires as to have a daughter as bright and original like me. Amelia only laughs and goes and purrs in her mother's ears when she hears such talk. It costs her nothing to be pleasant. She was born so. For my part, I think myself lucky to have such a friend. She gets along with my odd, hateful ways better than anyone else does.

Mother, when I boast of this, says Amelia has no penetration into character and that she would be fond of almost anyone fond of her and that the fury with which I love her deserves some response. I really don't know what to make of Mother. Most people are proud of their children when they see others admire them; but she does say such poky things! Of course I know that having a gift for music and a taste for drawing and a reputation for saying witty, bright things isn't enough. But when she doesn't find fault with me and nothing happens to keep me down, I am the gayest creature on earth. I do love to get with a lot of nice girls and carry on! I have got enough fun in me to keep a houseful merry. And Mother needn't say anything. I inherited it from her.

–Evening–

I knew it was coming! Mother has been in to see what I was about and to give me a bit of her mind. She says she loves to see me gay and cheerful, as is natural at my age, but that so much levity quite upsets and disorders the mind, indisposing it for serious thoughts.

"But, Mother," I said, "didn't you carry on when you were a young girl?"

"Of course I did," she said, smiling. "But I do not think I was quite so thoughtless as you are."

"Thoughtless" indeed! I wish I were! But am I not

always full of uneasy, reproachful thoughts when the moment of excitement is over? Other girls, who seem less trifling than I, are really more so. Their heads are full of dresses and parties and beaux and all that sort of nonsense. I wonder if that ever worries their mothers, or whether mine is the only one who weeps in secret? Well, I shall be young but once, and while I am, do let me have a good time!

—*Sunday, Nov. 20*—

Oh, the difference between this day and the day I wrote that! There are no good times in this dreadful world. I have hardly courage or strength to write down the history of the past few weeks. The day after I had deliberately made up my mind to enjoy myself, cost what it might, my dear father called me to him, kissed me, pulled my ears a little, and gave me some money.

"We have had to keep you rather low on funds," he said, laughing. "But I recovered this amount yesterday, and as it was a little debt I had given up, I can spare it to you. Girls like pin money, I know, and you may spend this just as you please."

I was delighted. I want to take more drawing lessons but did not feel sure he could afford it. Besides—I am a little ashamed to write it down—I knew somebody had been praising me or Father would not have seemed so fond of me. I wondered who it was and felt a good deal puffed up. "After all," I said to myself, "some people like me even if I have got my faults." I threw my arms around his neck and kissed him, though that cost me a great effort. I never like to show what I feel. But, oh! how thankful I am for it now.

As to Mother, I know Father never goes without kissing her good-bye.

I went out with her to take a walk at three o'clock. We had just reached the corner of Orange Street, when I saw a carriage driving slowly toward us; it appeared to be full of sailors. Then I saw our friend, Mr. Freeman, among them. When he saw us, he jumped out and came up to us. I do not know what he said. I saw Mother turn pale and catch at his arm as if she were afraid of falling. But she did not speak a word.

"Oh! Mr. Freeman, what is it?" I cried out. "Has anything happened to Father? Is he hurt? Where is he?"

"He is in the carriage," he said. "We are taking him home. He has had a fall."

Then we went on in silence. The sailors were carrying Father in as we reached the house. They laid him on the sofa, and we saw his poor head—

–*Nov. 23*–

I will try to write the rest now. Father was alive but insensible. He had fallen down into the hold of the ship, and the sailors heard him groaning there. He lived three hours after they brought him home. Mr. Freeman and all our friends were very kind. But we like best to be alone, we three, Mother and James and I. Poor Mother looks twenty years older, but she is so patient and so concerned for us and has such a smile of welcome for everyone that comes in that it breaks my heart to see her.

–*Nov. 25*–

Mother spoke to me very seriously today about controlling myself more. She said she knew this was my first real sorrow and how hard it was to bear it. But that she was afraid I should become emotionally disturbed sometime if

I indulged myself in such passions of grief. And she said, too, that when friends came to see us full of sympathy and eager to say or do something for our comfort, it was our duty to receive them with as much cheerfulness as possible.

I said they, none of them, had anything to say that did not provoke me.

"It is always a trying task to visit the afflicted," Mother said, "and you make it doubly hard for your friends by putting on a gloomy, forbidding air and by refusing to talk of your dear father, as if you were resolved to keep your sorrow all to yourself."

"I can't smile when I am so unhappy," I said.

A good many people have been here today. Mother has seen them all, though she looked ready to drop. Mrs. Bates said to me in her little, weak, watery voice, "Your mother is wonderfully sustained, dear. I hope you feel reconciled to God's will. Rebellion is most displeasing to Him, dear."

I made no answer. It is very easy for people to preach. Let me see how they behave when they take their turn at losing their friends.

Mrs. Morris said this was a very mysterious dispensation. But that she was happy to see that Mother was meeting it with so much firmness. "As for myself," she went on, "I was quite broken down by my dear husband's death. I did not eat as much as would feed a bird for nearly a week. But some people have so much feeling; then again others are so firm. Your mother is so busy talking with Mrs. March that I won't interrupt her to say good-bye. Well, I came prepared to suggest several things that I thought would comfort her, but perhaps she has thought of them herself."

I could have knocked her down. Firm, indeed! Poor Mother!

After they had all gone, I made her lie down; she looked so tired and worn out. Then I could not help telling her what Mrs. Morris had said.

She only smiled a little, but said nothing.

"I wish you would flare up once in a while, Mother," I said.

She smiled again and said she had nothing to "flare up" about.

"Then I shall do it for you!" I cried. "To hear that namby-pamby woman, who is about as capable of understanding you as an old cat, talking about your being firm! You see what you get by being quiet and patient! People would like you much better if you refused to be comforted and wore a sad countenance."

"Dear Katy," said Mother, "it is not my first object in life to make people like me."

By this time she looked so pale that I was frightened. Though she is so cheerful and things go on much as they did before, I believe she has got her death blow. If she has, then I hope I have got mine. And yet I am not fit to die. I wish I was, and I wish I could die. I have lost all interest in everything and don't care what becomes of me.

–Nov. 28–

I believe I shall go crazy unless people stop coming here, hurling volleys of texts at Mother and me. When soldiers drop wounded on the battlefield, they are taken up tenderly and carried "to the rear," which means, I suppose, out of sight and sound. Is anybody mad enough to suppose it will do them any good to hear Scripture quoted—sermons launched at them before their open, bleeding wounds are staunched?

Mother assents, in a mild way, when I talk so and says, "Yes, yes, we are indeed lying wounded on the battlefield of life and in no condition to listen to any words save those of pity. But, dear Katy, we must interpret aright all the well-meant attempts of our friends to comfort us. They mean sympathy, however awkwardly they express it."

–Dec. 14–

Mother keeps saying I spend too much time in brooding over my sorrow. As for her, she seems to live in heaven. Not that she has long prosy talks about it, but little words that she lets drop now and then show where her thoughts are and where she would like to be. She seems to think everybody is as eager to go there as she is. For my part, I am not eager at all. I can't make myself feel that it will be nice to sit in rows, all the time singing, fond as I am of music. And when I say to myself, "Of course we shall not always sit in rows singing," then I fancy a multitude of shadowy, phantomlike beings, dressed in white, moving to and fro in golden streets, doing nothing in particular, and having a dreary time, without anything to look forward to.

I told Mother so. She said earnestly and yet in her sweetest, tenderest way, "Oh, my darling Katy! What you need is such a living, personal love of Christ to make the thought of being where He is so delightful as to fill your mind with the single thought!"

What is "personal love of Christ?"

Oh, dear, dear! Why need my father have been snatched away from me when so many other girls have theirs spared them? He loved me so! He indulged me much! He was so proud of me. What have I done that this dreadful thing should happen to me? I shall never be as happy as I was before. Now I shall always be expecting trouble. Yes, I dare say Mother will go next. Why shouldn't I brood over this sorrow? I like to brood over it; I like to think how wretched I am; I like to have long, furious fits of crying, lying on my face on my bed.

–Jan. 1, 1832–

People talk a great deal about the blessed effects of sorrow. But I do not see any good it has done me to lose my dear father, and as for Mother, she was good enough before.

We are going to leave our pleasant home, where all of us children were born, and move into a house in an out-of-the-way street. By selling this house and renting a smaller one, Mother hopes, with economy, to carry James through college. And I must go to Miss Higgins's school because it is less expensive than Mr. Stone's. Miss Higgins, indeed! I never could bear her! A few months ago, how I should have cried and stormed at the idea of her school. But the great sorrow swallows up the little trial.

I tried once more, this morning, as it is the first day of the year, to force myself to begin to love God.

I want to do it; I know I ought to do it; but I cannot. Every day now I go through the form of saying something that I try to pass off as praying. But I take no pleasure in it, as good people say they do and as I am sure Mother does. Nobody could live in the house with her and doubt that.

–Jan. 10–

We are in our new home now, and it is quite a cozy little place. James is at home for the long vacation, and we are together all the time I am out of school. We study and sing together, and now and then, when we forget that dear Father has gone, we are as full of fun as ever. If it is so nice to have a brother, what must it be to have a sister! Dear old Jim! He is the very pleasantest, dearest fellow in the world!

–Jan. 15–

I have come to another birthday and am seventeen. Mother has celebrated it just as usual, though I know all these anniversaries, which used to be so pleasant, must be sad days to her now my dear father has gone. She has been cheerful and loving and entered into all my pleasures exactly as if nothing had happened. I wonder at myself that I do not enter more into her sorrows, but though at times the remembrance of our loss overwhelms me, my natural elasticity soon makes me rise above and forget it. And I am absorbed with these school days that come one after another in such quick succession that I am all the time running to keep up with them. And as long as I do that, I forget that death has crossed our threshold and may do it again. But tonight, I feel very sad and as if I would give almost anything to live in a world where nothing painful could happen. Somehow Mother's pale face haunts and reproaches me. I believe I will go to bed and to sleep as quickly as possible and forget everything.

Chapter III

*M*y school days are over! I have come off with flying colors, and Mother is pleased at my success. I said to her today that I should now have time to draw and practice to my heart's content.

"You will not find your heart content with either," she said.

"Why, Mother!" I cried, "I thought you liked to see me happy!"

"And so I do," she said quietly. "But there is something better to get out of life than you have yet found."

"I am sure I hope so," I returned. On the whole I haven't got much so far.

Amelia is now on such terms with Jenny Underhill that I can hardly see one without seeing the other. After the way in which I have loved her, this seems rather hard. Sometimes I am angry about it and sometimes grieved. However, I find Jenny quite nice. She buys all the new books and lends them to me. I wish I liked more solid reading; but I don't. And I wish I were not so fond of novels; but I am. If it were not for Mother, I should read nothing else. And I am sure I often feel quite stirred up by a really good novel and admire and want to imitate every high-minded, noble character it describes.

Jenny has a miniature of her brother "Charley" in a locket, which she always wears and often shows me. According to her, he is exactly like the heroes I most admire in books. She says she knows he would like me if we should meet. But that is not probable. Very few like me. Amelia says it is because I say just what I think.

—*Wednesday*—

Mother pointed out to me this evening two lines from a book she was reading, with a significant smile that said they described me:

> *"A frank, unchastened, generous creature,*
> *Whose faults and virtues stand in bold relief."*

"Dear me!" I said. "So then I have some virtues after all!"

And I really think I must have, for Jenny's brother, who has come here for the sake of being near her, seems to like me very much. Nobody ever liked me so much before, not even Amelia. But how foolish to write that down!

—*Thursday*—

Jenny's brother has been here all the evening. He has the most perfect manners I ever saw. I am sure that Mother, who thinks so much of such things, would be charmed with him. But she happened to be out, Mrs. Jones having sent for her to see about her baby. He gave me an account of his mother's death and how he and Jenny nursed her day and night. He has a great deal of feeling. I was going to tell him about my father's death, sorrow seems to bring people together so, but I could not. Oh, if Father had only had sickness that needed our tender nursing instead of being snatched from us in that sudden way!

–*Sunday, Aug. 5*–

Jenny's brother has been at our church all day. He walked home with me this afternoon. Mother, after being up all night with Mrs. Jones and her baby, was not able to go out.

Dr. Cabot preaches as if we had all got to die pretty soon or else have something almost as bad happen to us. How can old people always try to make young people feel uncomfortable and as if things couldn't last?

–*Aug. 25*–

Jenny says her brother is perfectly fascinated with me and that I must try to like him in return. I suppose Mother would say my head was turned by my good fortune, but it is not. I am getting quite sober and serious. It is a great thing to be—to be—well—liked. I have seen some verses of his composition today that show that he is all heart and soul and would make any sacrifice for one he loved. I could not like a man who did not possess such sentiments as his.

Perhaps Mother would think I ought not to put such things into my journal.

Jenny has thought of such a splendid plan! What a dear little thing she is! She and her brother are so much alike!

The plan is for us three girls, Jenny, Amelia, and myself, to form ourselves into a little class to read and to study together. She says "Charley" will direct our readings and help us with our studies. It is perfectly delightful.

–*September 1*–

Somehow I forgot to tell Mother that Mr. Underhill was to be our teacher. So when it came my turn to have the class meet here, she was not quite pleased. I told her she could stay in the room and watch us and then she would see for herself that we all behaved ourselves.

–*Sept. 19*–

The class met at Amelia's tonight. Mother insisted on sending for me, though Mr. Underhill had proposed to see me home himself. So he stayed after I left. It was not quite the right thing, for he must see that Amelia is absolutely crazy about him.

–*Sept. 28*–

We met at Jenny's this evening. Amelia had a bad headache and could not come. Jenny idled over her lessons and at last took a book and began to read. I studied awhile with Mr. Underhill. At last he said, scribbling something on a bit of paper, "Here is a sentence I hope you can translate."

I took it and read these words:

"You are the brightest, prettiest, most warmhearted little thing in the world. And I love you more than tongue can tell. You must love me in the same way."

I felt hot and then cold and then glad and then sorry. But I pretended to laugh and said I could not translate Greek. I shall have to tell Mother, and what will she say!

—Sept. 29—

This morning Mother began thus:

"Kate, I do not like these lessons of yours. At your age, with your judgment quite unformed, it is not proper that you should spend so much time with a young man."

"Jenny is always there and Amelia," I replied.

"That makes no difference. I wish the whole thing stopped. I do not know what I have been thinking of to let it go on so long. Mrs. Gordon says—"

"Mrs. Gordon! Ha!" I burst out. "I knew Amelia was at the bottom of it! Amelia is in love with him up to her very ears, and because he does not entirely neglect me, she has put her mother up to coming here, meddling and making—"

"If what you say of Amelia is true, it is most ungenerous in you to tell of it. But I do not believe it. Amelia Gordon has too much good sense to be carried away by a handsome face and agreeable manners."

I began to cry.

"He likes me," I got out. "He likes me ever so much. Nobody ever was so kind to me before. Nobody ever said such nice things to me. And I don't want such horrid things said about him."

"Has it really come to this?" said Mother, quite shocked. "Oh, my poor child, how my selfish sorrow has made me neglect you."

I kept on crying.

"Is it possible," she went on, "that with your good sense and the education you have had, you are captivated by this mere boy?"

"He's not a boy," I said. "He is a man. He is twenty years old; or at least he will be on the fifteenth of next October."

"The child actually keeps his birthdays!" cried Mother.

"Oh, my wicked, shameful carelessness."

"It's done now," I said, desperately. "It is too late to help it now."

"You don't mean that he has dared to say anything without consulting me?" asked Mother. "And that you have allowed it! Oh, Katherine!"

By this time my mouth shut itself up, and no mortal force could open it. I stopped crying and sat with folded arms. Mother said what she had to say, and then I came to you, my dear old Journal.

> *Yes, he likes me and I like him.*
>> *Come now, let's out with it once for all.*
> *He loves me and I love him.*
>> *You are just a little bit too late, Mother.*

—Oct. 1—

I never can write down all the things that have happened. The very day after I wrote Jenny that Mother had forbidden my going to the class, Charley came to see Mother, and they had a regular fight together. He has told me about it since. Then, as he could not prevail, his uncle wrote, told her it would be the making of Charley to be settled down on one young lady instead of hovering from flower to flower, as he was doing now. Then Jenny came with her pretty ways and cried and told Mother what a darling brother Charley was. She made a good deal, too, out of his having lost both father and mother and needing my affection so much. Mother shut herself up and, I have no doubt, prayed over it. I really believe she prays over every new dress she buys. Then she sent for me and talked beautifully, and I behaved abominably.

At last she said she would put us on one year's proba-tion. Charley might spend one evening here every two weeks, when she should always be present. We were never to be seen together in public, nor would she allow us to cor-respond. If, at the end of the year, we were both as eager for it as we are now, she would consent to our engagement. Of course we shall be, so I consider myself as good as engaged now. Dear me! How funny it seems.

–*Oct. 2*–

Charley is not at all pleased with Mother's terms, but no one would guess it from his manner to her. His coming is always the signal for her trotting downstairs; he goes to meet her and offers her a chair as if he was delighted to see her. We go on with the lessons, as this gives us a chance to sit pretty close together; and when I am writing my exer-cises and he corrects them, I rather think a few little things get on to the paper that sound nice to us but would not strike Mother very agreeably. For instance, last night Charley wrote:

"Is your mother never sick? A nice little headache or two would be so convenient to us!"

And I wrote back: "You dear old horrid thing! How can you be so selfish?"

–*Jan. 15, 1883*–

I have been trying to think whether I am any happier today than I was at this time a year ago. If I am not, I sup-pose it is the tantalizing way in which I am placed in regard to Charley. We have so much to say to each other that we can't say before Mother and that we cannot say in writing, because a correspondence is one of the forbidden things.

He says he entered into no contract not to write and keeps slipping little notes into my hand; but I don't think that quite right. Mother hears us arguing and disputing about it, though she does not know the subject under discussion, and today she said to me:

"I would not argue with him if I were you. He never will yield."

"But it is a case of conscience," I said, "and he ought to yield."

"There is no obstinacy like that of a f—," she began and stopped short.

"Oh, you may as well finish it!" I cried. "I know you think him a fool."

Then Mother burst out. "Oh, my child," she said, "before it is too late, do be persuaded by me to give up this whole thing. I shrink from paining or offending you, but it is my duty as your mother to warn you against a marriage that will make shipwreck of your happiness."

"Marriage!" I fairly shrieked out. That is the last thing I have ever thought of. I felt a chill creep over me. All I had wanted was to have Charley come here every day, take me out now and then, and care for nobody else.

"Yes, marriage!" Mother repeated. "For what is the meaning of an engagement if marriage is not to follow? How can you fail to see what I see, oh! so plainly, that Charley Underhill never, never can meet the requirements of your soul. You are captivated by what girls of your age call beauty, regular features, a fair complexion, and soft eyes. His flatteries delude, and his professions of affection gratify you. You do not see that he is shallow and conceited and selfish and—"

"Oh, Mother! How can you be so unjust? His whole

study seems to be to please others."

"Seems to be—that is true," she replied. "His ruling passion is love of admiration. The little pleasing acts that attract you are so many traps set to catch the attention and the favorable opinion of those about him. He has not one honest desire to please because it is right to be pleasing. Oh, my precious child, what a fatal mistake you are making in relying on your own judgment in this, the most important of earthly decisions!"

I felt very angry.

"I thought the Bible forbade backbiting," I said.

Mother made no reply except by a look that said about a hundred and forty different things. And then I came up here and wrote some poetry, which was very good (for me), though I don't suppose she would think so.

–Oct. 1–

The year of probation is over, and I have nothing to do now but to be happy. But being engaged is not half so nice as I expected it would be. I suppose it is owing to my being obliged to defy Mother's judgment in order to gratify my own. People say she has great insight into character and sees, at a glance, what others only learn after much study.

–Oct. 10–

I have taken a dreadful cold. It is too bad. I dare say I shall be coughing all winter and, instead of going out with Charley, be shut up at home.

–Oct. 12–

Charley says he did not know that I was subject to a cough and that he hopes I am not consumptive, because his father and mother both died of consumption, and it makes him nervous to hear people cough. I nearly strangled myself all the evening trying not to annoy him with mine.

CHAPTER IV

J really think I am sick and going to die. Last night I raised a little blood. I dare not tell Mother; it would distress her so; but I am sure it came from my lungs. Charley said last week he really must stay away till I got better, for my cough sounded like his mother's. I have been very lonely and have shed some tears, but most of the time have been too sorrowful to cry. If we were married and I had a cough, would he go and leave me, I wonder?

—Sunday, 18th—

Poor Mother is dreadfully anxious about me. But I don't see how she can love me so after the way I have behaved. I wonder if, after all, mothers are not the best friends there are! I keep her awake with my cough all night and am mopey and cross all day, but she is just as kind and affectionate as she can be.

–Nov. 25–

The day I wrote that was Sunday. I could not go to church, and I felt very forlorn and desolate. I tried to get some comfort by praying; but when I got on my knees, I just burst out crying and could not say a word. For I have not seen Charley for ten days. As I knelt there I began to think myself a perfect monster of selfishness for wanting him to spend his evenings with me now that I am so unwell and annoy him so with my cough, and I asked myself if I ought not to break off the engagement altogether, if I was really in a consumption, the very disease Charley dreaded most of all. It seemed such a proper sacrifice to make of myself. Then I prayed—yes, I am sure I really prayed as I had not done for more than a year—and the idea of self-sacrifice grew every moment more beautiful in my eyes till at last I felt an almost joyful triumph in writing to poor Charley and telling him what I had resolved to do.

This is my letter:

MY DEAR, DEAR CHARLEY:—I dare not tell you what it costs me to say what I am about to do; but I am sure you know me well enough by this time to believe that it is only because your happiness is far more precious to me than my own that I have decided to write you this letter. When you first told me that you loved me, you said, and you have often said so since then, that it was my "brightness and gaiety" that attracted you. I knew there was something underneath my gaiety better worth your love and was glad I could give you more than you asked for. I knew I was not a mere thoughtless, laughing girl, but that I had a heart as wide as the ocean to give you—as wide and as deep.

But now my "brightness and gaiety" have gone; I am

sick and perhaps am going to die. If this is so, it would be very sweet to have your love go with me to the very gates of death and beautify and glorify my path thither. But what a weary task this would be for you, my poor Charley! And so, if you think it best and it would relieve you of any care and pain, I will release you from our engagement and set you free.

YOUR LITTLE KATY.

I did not sleep at all that night. Early on Monday I sent off my letter, and my heart beat so hard all day that I was tired and faint. Just at dark his answer came; I can copy it from memory.

DEAR KATE:—What a generous, self-sacrificing little thing you are! I always thought so, but now you have given me a noble proof of it. I will own that I have been disappointed to find your constitution so poor and that it has been very dull sitting and hearing you cough, especially as I was reminded of the long and tedious illness through which poor Jenny and myself had to nurse our mother. I vowed then never to marry a consumptive woman, and I thank you for making it so easy for me to bring our engagement to an end. My bright hopes are blighted, and it will be long before I shall find another to fill your place. I need not say how much I sympathize with you in this disappointment. I hope the consolations of religion will now be yours. Your notes, the lock of your hair, etc., I return with this. I will not reproach you for the pain you have cost me; I know it is not your fault that your health has become so frail.

I remain your sincere friend,

CHARLES UNDERHILL.

–*Jan. 1, 1834*–

Let me finish this story if I can.

My first impulse after reading his letter was to fly to Mother and hide away forever in her dear, loving arms.

But I restrained myself, and with my heart beating so that I could hardly hold my pen, I wrote this:

MR. UNDERHILL: Sir—The scales have fallen from my eyes, and I see you at last just as you are. Since my note to you on Sunday last I have had a consultation of physicians, and they all agree that my disease is not of an alarming character and that I shall soon recover. But I thank God that before it was too late, you have been revealed to me just as you are—a heartless, selfish, shallow creature, unworthy of the love of a true-hearted woman, unworthy even of your own self-respect. I gave you an opportunity to withdraw from our engagement in full faith, loving you so truly that I was ready to go trembling to my grave alone if you shrank from sustaining me to it. But I see now that I did not dream for one moment that you would take me at my word and leave me to my fate. I thought I loved a man and could lean on him when strength failed me. I know now that I loved a mere creature of my imagination. Take back your letters; I loathe the sight of them. Take back the ring and find, if you can, a woman who will never be sick, never out of spirits, and who never will die.

KATHERINE MORTIMER.

These lines came to me in reply:

Thank God it is not Kate Mortimer. I want an angel for my wife, not a vixen. C.U.

–Jan. 15–

What a tempest-tossed creature this birthday finds me! But let me finish this wretched, disgraceful story, if I can, before I quite lose my senses.

I showed Mother the letters. She burst into tears and opened her arms, and I ran into them as a wounded bird flies into the ark. We cried together. Mother never said, never looked, "I told you so." All she did say was this:

"God has heard my prayers! He is reserving better things for my child!"

Dear Mother's are not the only arms I have flown to. But it does not seem as if God ought to take me in because I am in trouble, when I would not go to Him when I was happy in something else. But even in the midst of my greatest felicity I had many and many a misgiving; many a season when my conscience upbraided me for my willfulness towards my dear mother and my whole soul yearned for something higher and better even than Charley's love, precious as it was.

–Jan. 26–

I have shut myself up in my room today to think over things. The end of it is that I am full of mortification and confusion of face. If I had only had confidence in Mother's judgment I should never have got entangled in this silly engagement. I see now that Charley never could have made me happy, and I know there is a good deal in my heart he never called out. I wish, however, I had not written him when I was in such a passion. No wonder he is thankful that he has got free from such a vixen. But, oh! the provocation was terrible!

I have made up my mind never to tell a human soul

about this affair. It will be so high-minded and honorable to shield him thus from the contempt he deserves. With all my faults I am glad that there is nothing mean or little about me!

–*Jan. 27*–

I can't bear to write it down, but I will. The ink was hardly dry yesterday on the above self-laudation when Amelia came. She had been out of town and had only just learned what had happened. Of course she was curious to know the whole story.

And I told it to her, every word of it! Oh, Kate Mortimer, how "high-minded" you are! How free from all that is "mean and little!" I could tear my hair if it would do any good!

Amelia defended Charley, and I was thus led on to say every harsh thing of him I could think of. She said he was of so sensitive a nature, had so much sensibility, and such a constitutional aversion to seeing suffering that for her part she could not blame him.

"It is such a pity you had not had your lungs examined before you wrote that first letter," she went on. "But you are so impulsive! If you had only waited, you would be engaged to Charley, still!"

"I am thankful I did not wait," I cried angrily. "Do, Amelia, drop the subject forever. You and I shall never agree upon it. The truth is, you are two-thirds in love with him and have been all along."

She colored and laughed and actually looked pleased. If anyone had made such an outrageous speech to me, I should have been furious.

"I suppose you know," said she, "that old Mr. Underhill has taken such a fancy to him that he has made him his heir; and he will be ever so rich."

"Indeed!" I said dryly.

I wonder if Mother knew it when she opposed our engagement so strenuously.

–Jan. 31–

I have asked her, and she said she did. Mr. Underhill told her his intentions when he urged her consent to the engagement. Dear Mother! How unworldly, how unselfish she is!

–Feb. 4–

The name of Charley Underhill appears on these pages for the last time. He is engaged to Amelia! From this moment she is lost to me forever. How desolate, how mortified, how miserable I am! Who could have thought this of Amelia? She came to see me, radiant with joy. I concealed my disgust until she said that Charley felt now that he had never really loved me but had preferred her all along. Then I burst out. What I said I do not know and do not care. The whole thing is so disgraceful that I should be a stock or a stone not to resent it.

–Feb. 5–

After yesterday's passion of grief, shame, and anger, I feel perfectly stupid and languid. Oh, that I was prepared for a better world and could fly to it and be at rest!

–Feb. 6–

Now that it is all over, how ashamed I am of the fury I have been in and which has given Amelia such advantage over me! I was beginning to believe that I was really living a feeble and fluttering but real Christian life and finding some satisfaction in it. But that is all over now. I am doomed to be a victim of my own unstable, passionate, wayward nature; and the sooner I settle down into that conviction, the better. And yet how my very soul craves the highest happiness and refuses to be comforted while that is wanting.

–*Feb. 7*–

After writing that, I do not know what made me go to see Dr. Cabot. He received me in that cheerful way of his that seems to promise he will take one's burden right off one's back.

"I am very glad to see you, my dear child," he said.

I intended to be very dignified and cold. As if I was going to have any Dr. Cabots undertaking to sympathize with me! But those few kind words just upset me, and I began to cry.

"You would not speak so kindly," I got out at last, "if you knew what a dreadful creature I am. I am angry with myself and angry with everybody and angry with God. I can't be good two minutes at a time. I do everything I do not want to do and do nothing I try and pray to do. Everybody plagues me and tempts me. And God does not answer any of my prayers, and I am just desperate."

"Poor child!" he said in a low voice, as if to himself. "Poor, heartsick, tired child that cannot see what I can see, that its Father's loving arms are all about it!"

I stopped crying to strain my ears to listen. He went on.

"Katy, all that you say may be true. I dare say it is. But God loves you. He loves you."

He loves me, I repeated to myself. He loves me. "Oh, Dr. Cabot, if I could believe that! If I could believe that, after all the promises I have broken, all the foolish, wrong things I have done and shall always be doing, God perhaps still loves me!"

"You may be sure of it," he said solemnly. "I, His minister, bring the gospel to you today. Go home and say over and over to yourself, 'I am a wayward, foolish child. But He loves me! I have disobeyed and grieved Him ten thousand times. But He loves me! I have lost faith in some of my dearest friends and am very desolate. But He loves me! I do not love Him; I am even angry with Him! But He loves me!'"

I came away; and all the way home I fought this battle with myself, saying, "He loves me!" I knelt down to pray, and all my wasted, childish, wicked life came and stared me in the face. I looked at it and said with tears of joy, "But He loves me!" Never in my life did I feel so rested, so quieted, so sorrowful, and yet so satisfied.

–*Feb. 10*–

What a beautiful world this is and how full it is of truly kind, good people. Mrs. Morris was here this morning, and just one squeeze of that long, yellow old hand of hers seemed to speak a bookfull! I wonder why I have always disliked her so, for she is really an excellent woman. I gave her a good kiss to pay her for the sympathy she had sense enough not to put into canting words; and if you will believe it, dear old Journal, the tears came into her eyes, and she said, "You are one of the Lord's beloved ones, though perhaps you do not know it."

I repeated again to myself those sweet, mysterious words; and then I tried to think what I could do for Him. But I could not think of anything great or good enough. I went into Mother's room and put my arms round her and told her how I loved her. She looked surprised and pleased.

"Ah, I knew it would come!" she said, laying her hand on her Bible.

"Knew what would come, Mother?"

"Peace," she said.

I came back here and wrote a little note to Amelia, telling her how ashamed and sorry I was that I could not control myself the other day. Then I wrote a long letter to James. I have been very careless about writing to him.

Then I began to hem those handkerchiefs Mother asked me to finish a month ago. But I could not think of anything to do for God. I wish I could. It makes me happy to think, that all this time, while I was caring for nobody but myself and fancying He must almost hate me, He was loving and pitying me.

–Feb. 15–

I went to see Dr. Cabot again today. He came down from his study with his pen in his hand.

"How dare you come and spoil my sermon on Saturday?" he asked good-humoredly.

Though he seemed full of lovingkindness, I was ashamed of my thoughtlessness. Though I did not know he was particularly busy on Saturdays. If I were a minister, I am sure I would get my sermons done early in the week.

"I only wanted to ask one thing," I said. "I want to do something for God. And I cannot think of anything unless it is to go on a mission. And Mother would never let me do that. She thinks girls with delicate health are not fit for such work."

"At all events I would not go today," he replied. "Meanwhile do everything you do for Him who has loved you and given Himself for you."

I did not dare to stay any longer and so came away quite puzzled. Dinner was ready, and as I sat down to the table, I said to myself, "I eat this dinner for myself, not for God. What can Dr. Cabot mean?" Then I remembered the text about doing all for the glory of God, even in eating and drinking; but I do not understand it at all.

–Feb. 19–

It has seemed to me for several days that it must be that I really do love God, though ever so little. But it shot through my mind today like a knife that it is a miserable, selfish love at the best, not worth my giving, not worth God's accepting. All my old misery has come back with seven other miseries more miserable than itself. I wish I had never been born! I wish I were thoughtless and careless like so many other girls of my age, who seem to get along very well and to enjoy themselves far more than I do.

–Feb. 21–

Dr. Cabot came to see me today. I told him about it. He could not help smiling as he said:

"When I see a little infant caressing its mother, would you have me to say to it, 'You selfish child, how dare you pretend to caress your mother in that way? You are quite unable to appreciate her character; you love her merely because she loves you, treats you kindly?' "

It was my turn to smile now at my own folly.

"You are as yet but a babe in Christ," Dr. Cabot continued. "You love your God and Savior because He first loved you. The time will come when the character of your love will become changed into one which sees and feels the beauty and the perfection of its object; and if you could be assured that He no longer looked on you with favor, you would still cling to Him with devoted affection."

"There is one thing more that troubles me," I said. "Most persons know the exact moment when they begin real Christian lives. But I do not know of any such time in my history. This causes me many uneasy moments."

"You are wrong in thinking that most persons have this advantage over you. I believe that the children of Christian parents, who have been judiciously trained, rarely can point to any day or hour when they began to live this new life. The question is not, Do you remember, my child, when you entered this world and how? It is simply this: Are you now alive and an inhabitant thereof? And now it is my turn to ask you a question. How happens it that you, who have a mother of rich and varied experience, allow yourself to be tormented with these petty anxieties that she is as capable of dispelling as I am?"

"I do not know," I answered. "But we girls can't talk to our mothers about any of our sacred feelings, and we hate to have them talk to us."

Dr. Cabot shook his head.

"There is something wrong somewhere," he said. "A young girl's mother is her natural refuge in every per-plexity. I hoped that you, who have rather more sense than most girls of your age, could give me some idea what the difficulty is."

After he had gone, I am ashamed to own that I was in a perfect flutter of delight at what he had said about my hav-ing more sense than most girls. Meeting poor Mother on the stairs while in this exalted state of mind, I gave her a very short answer to a kind question and made her unhappy, as I have made myself.

It is just a year ago today that I got frightened at my novel-reading propensities and resolved not to look into one for twelve months. I was getting to dislike all other books and night after night sat up late, devouring everything exciting I could get hold of. One Saturday night I sat up till the clock struck twelve to finish one, and the next morning I was so sleepy that I had to stay at home from church. Now I hope and believe the back of this taste is broken and that I shall never be a slave to it again. Indeed it does not seem to me now that I shall ever care for such books again.

—*Feb. 24*—

Mother spoke to me this morning for the fiftieth time, I really believe, about my disorderly habits. I don't think I am careless because I like confusion, but the trouble is I am always in a hurry and a ferment about something. If I want anything, I want it very much and right away. So if I am looking for a book or a piece of music or a pattern, I tumble everything around and can't stop to put them to rights. I wish I were not so eager and impatient. But I mean to try to keep my room and my drawers in order to please Mother.

She says, too, that I am growing careless about my hair and my dress. But that is because my mind is so full of graver, more important things. I thought I ought to be wholly occupied with my duty to God. But Mother says duty to God includes duty to one's neighbor and that untidy hair, put up in all sorts of rough bunches, rumpled cuffs and collars, and all that sort of thing make one offensive to all one meets. I am sorry she thinks so, for I find it very convenient to twist up my hair almost any how, and it takes a good deal of time to look after collars and cuffs.

–*March 14*–

Today I feel discouraged and disappointed. I certainly thought that if God really loved me and I really loved Him, I should find myself growing better day by day. But I am not improved in the least. Most of the time I spend on my knees I am either stupid, feeling nothing at all, or else my head is full of what I was doing before I began to pray or what I am going to do as soon as I get through. I do not believe anybody else in the world is like me in this respect. Then when I feel differently and can make a nice, glib prayer, with floods of tears running down my cheeks, I get all puffed up and think how much pleased God must be to see me so fervent in spirit. I go downstairs in this frame and begin to complain to our maid, Susan, for misplacing my music till all of a sudden I catch myself doing it and stop short, crestfallen and confounded. I have so many such experiences that I feel like a baby just learning to walk, who is so afraid of falling that it has half a mind to sit down once for all.

Then there is another thing. Seeing Mother so fond of Thomas à Kempis. I have been reading it, now and then, and am not fond of it at all. From beginning to end it exhorts to self-denial in every form and shape. Must I then give up all hope of happiness in this world and modify all my natural tastes and desires? Oh, I do love so to be happy! And I do so hate to suffer! The very thought of being sick or of being forced to nurse sick people with all their cross way, and of losing my friends or of having to live with disagreeable people, makes me shudder. I want to please God and to be like Him. I certainly do. But I am so young, and it is so natural to want to have a good time! And now I am in for it, I may as well tell the whole story. When I read the lives of good men and women who have died and gone to heaven, I find they all like to sit and think about God and about Christ. Now I don't. I often try, but my mind flies off in a tangent. The truth is I am perfectly discouraged.

–*March 17*–

I went to see Dr. Cabot today, but he was out, so I thought I would ask for Mrs. Cabot, though I was determined not to tell her any of my troubles. But somehow she got the whole story out of me, and instead of being shocked, as I expected she would be, she actually burst out laughing! She recovered herself immediately, however.

"Do excuse me for laughing at you, you dear child you!" she said. "But I remember so well how I used to flounder through just such needless anxieties; and life looks so different, so very different, to me now from what it did then! What should you think of a man, who having just sowed his field, was astonished not to see it at once ripe for the harvest because his neighbor's, after long months of waiting, was just being gathered in?"

"Do you mean," I asked, "that by and by I shall naturally come to feel and think as other good people do?"

"Yes, I do. You must make the most of what little Christian life you have; be thankful God has given you so much, cherish it, pray over it, and guard it like the apple of your eye. Imperceptibly, but surely it will grow and keep on growing, for this is its nature."

"But I don't want to wait," I said despondently. "I have just been reading a delightful book, full of stories of heroic deeds—not fables, but histories of real events and real people. It has quite stirred me up and made me wish to possess such beautiful heroism that I might have a chance to perform some truly noble, self-sacrificing acts."

"I dare say your chance will come," she replied. "I fancy we all get, more or less, what we want."

"Do you really think so? Let me see, then, what I want most. But am I staying too long? Were you particularly busy?"

"No," she returned smilingly, "I am learning 'that the man who wants me is the man I want.' "

"You are very good to say so. Well, in the first place, I do really and truly want to be good. Not with common goodness, you know, but—"

"But uncommon goodness, " she put in.

"I mean that I want to be very, very good. I should like next best to be learned and accomplished. Then I should want to be perfectly well and perfectly happy. And a pleasant home, of course, I must have with friends to love me and like me, too. And I can't get along without some pretty, tasteful things about me. But you are laughing at me! Have I said anything foolish?"

"If I laughed, it was not at you but at poor human nature that would fain grasp everything at once. Allowing that you should possess all you have just described, where is the heroism you so much admire to find room for exercise?"

"That's just what I was saying. That is just what troubles me."

"To be sure, while perfectly well and happy in a pleasant home with friends to love and admire you—"

"Oh, I did not say admire," I interrupted.

"That was just what you meant, my dear."

I am afraid it was, now I come to think it over.

"Well, with plenty of friends, good in an uncommon way, accomplished, learned, and surrounded with pretty and tasteful objects, your life will certainly be in danger of not proving very sublime."

"It is a great pity," I said musingly.

"Suppose, then, you content yourself for the present with doing in a faithful, quiet, persistent way all the little, homely tasks that return with each returning day, each one as unto God, and perhaps by and by you will thus have gained strength for a more heroic life."

"But I don't know how."

"You have some little home duties, I suppose?"

"Yes; I have the care of my own room, and Mother wants me to have a general oversight of the parlor."

"Is that all you have to do?"

"Why, my music and drawing take up a good deal of my time, and I read and study more or less and go out some, and we have a good many visitors."

"I suppose, then, you keep your room in nice, ladylike order and that the parlor is dusted every morning, loose music put out of the way, books restored to their places—"

"Now I know Mother has been telling you."

"Your mother has told me nothing at all."

"Well, then," I said, laughing but a little ashamed, "I don't keep my room in nice order, and Mother really sees to the parlor herself, though I pretend to do it."

"And is she never annoyed by this neglect?"

"Oh, yes, very much annoyed."

"Then, dear Katy, suppose your first act of heroism tomorrow should be gratifying your mother in these little things, little though they are. Surely your first duty, next to pleasing God, is to please your mother and in every possible way to sweeten and beautify her life. You may depend upon it that a life of real heroism and self-sacrifice must begin and lay its foundation in this little world wherein it learns its first lesson and takes its first steps."

"And do you really think that God notices such little things?"

"My dear child, what a question! If there is any one truth I would gladly impress on the mind of a young Christian, it is just this, that God notices the most trivial act, accepts the poorest, most threadbare little service, listens to the coldest, feeblest petition, and gathers up with parental fondness all our fragmentary desires and attempts at good works. Oh, if we could only begin to conceive how He loves us, what different creatures we should be!"

I felt inspired by her enthusiasm, though I don't think I quite understand what she means. I did not dare to stay any longer for, with her great host of children, she must have her hands full.

–*March 25*–

Mother is very much astonished to see how nicely I am keeping things in order. I was flying about this morning, singing and dusting the furniture, when she came in and began, "He that is faithful in that which is least"—but I ran at her with my brush and would not let her finish. I really, really don't deserve to be praised. For I have been thinking that, if it is true that God notices every little thing we do to please Him, He must also notice every cross word we speak, every shrug of the shoulders, every ungracious look, and that they displease Him. And my list of such offenses is as long as my life!

–March 29–

Yesterday for the first time since that dreadful blow, I felt some return of my natural gaiety and cheerfulness. It seemed to come hand in hand with my first real effort to go so far out of myself as to try to do exactly what would gratify dear Mother.

But today I am all down again. I miss Amelia's friendship, for one thing. To be sure, I wonder how I ever came to love such a superficial character so devotedly; but I must have somebody to love, and perhaps I invented a lovely creature and called it by her name and bowed down to it and worshipped it. I certainly did so in regard to him whose heartless cruelty has left me so sad, so desolate.

–Evening–

Mother has been very patient and forbearing with me all day. Tonight, after tea, she said in her gentlest, tenderest way, "Dear Katy, I feel very sorry for you. But I see one path which you have not yet tried, which can lead you out of these sore straits. You have tried living for yourself a good many years, and the result is great weariness and heaviness of soul. Try now to live for others. Take a class in the Sunday school. Go with me to visit my poor people. You will be astonished to find how much suffering and sickness there is in the world and how delightful it is to sympathize with and try to relieve it."

This advice was very repugnant to me. My time is pretty fully occupied with my books, my music, and my drawing. And of all places in the world I hate a sickroom. But, on the whole, I will take a class in the Sunday school.

CHAPTER V

I have taken it at last. I would not take one before, because I knew I could not teach little children how to love God unless I loved Him myself. My class is perfectly delightful. There are twelve dear little things in it of all ages between eight and nine. Eleven are girls, and the one boy makes me more trouble than all of them put together. When I get them all about me and their sweet innocent faces look up into mine, I am so happy that I can hardly help stopping every now and then to kiss them. They ask the very strangest questions! I mean to spend a great deal of time in preparing the lesson and in hunting up stories to illustrate it. Oh, I am so glad I was ever born into this beautiful world, where there will always be dear little children to love!

–April 13–

Sunday has come again and with it my darling little class! Dr. Cabot has preached delightfully all day, and I feel that I begin to understand his preaching better and that it must do me good. I long, I truly long to please God; I long to feel as the best Christians feel and to live as they live.

–April 20–

Now that I have these twelve little ones to instruct, I am more than ever in earnest about setting them a good example through the week. It is true they do not, most of them, know how I spend my time nor how I act. But I know; and whenever I am conscious of not practicing what I preach, I am bitterly ashamed and grieved. How much work, badly done, I am now having to undo! If I had begun in earnest to serve God when I was as young as these children are, how many wrong habits I should have avoided, habits that entangle me now as in so many nets. I am trying to take each of these little gentle girls by the hand and to lead her to Christ. Poor Johnny Ross is not so docile as they are and tries my patience to the last degree.

–April 27–

This morning I had all my little flock about me and talked to them out of the very bottom of my heart about Jesus. They left their seats and got close to me in a circle, leaning on my lap and drinking in every word. All of a sudden I was aware, as by a magnetic influence, that a great lumbering man in the next seat was looking at me out of two of the blackest eyes I ever saw and evidently listening to what I was saying. I was disconcerted first, then angry. What impertinence. What rudeness! I am sure he must have seen my displeasure in my face for he got up what I suppose he meant for a blush, that is he turned several shades darker than he was before, giving one the idea that he is full of black rather than red blood. I should not have remembered it, however—by it I mean his impertinence—if he had not shortly after made a really excellent address to the children. Perhaps it was a little above their comprehension, but it showed a good deal of thought and earnestness. I meant to ask who he was but forgot it.

This has been a delightful Sunday. I have really feasted on Dr. Cabot's preaching. But I am satisfied that there is something in religion I do not yet apprehend. I do wish I positively knew that God had forgiven and accepted me.

–*May 6*–

Last evening Clara Ray had a little party and I was there. She has a great knack at getting the right sort of people together and of making them enjoy themselves.

I sang several songs and so did Clara, but they all said my voice was finer and in better training than hers. It is delightful to be with cultivated, agreeable people. I could have stayed all night, but Mother sent for me before anyone else had thought of going.

–*May 7*–

I have been on a charming excursion today with Clara Ray and all her set. I was rather tired but had an invitation to a concert this evening, which I could not resist.

–*July 21*–

So much has been going on that I have not had time to write. There is no end to the picnics, drives, parties, etc., this summer. I am afraid that I am not getting on at all. My prayers are dull and short and full of wandering thoughts. I am brimful of vivacity and good humor in company and as soon as I get home am stupid and peevish. I suppose this will always be so, as it always has been; and I declare I would rather be so than such a vapid, flat creature as Mary Jones or such a dull, heavy one as big Lucy Merrill.

–*July 24*–

Clara Ray says the girls think me reckless and imprudent in speech. I've a good mind not to go with her set anymore. I am afraid I have been a good deal dazzled by the attentions I have received of late; and now comes this blow at my vanity.

On the whole, I feel greatly out of sorts this evening.

–*July 28*–

People talk about happiness to be found in a Christian life. I wonder why I do not find more! On Sundays I am pretty good and always seem to start afresh; but on weekdays I am drawn along with those about me. All my pleasures are innocent ones; there is surely no harm in going to concerts, driving out, singing, and making little visits! But these things distract me; they absorb me; they make religious duties irksome. I almost wish I could shut myself up in a cell and so get out of the reach of temptation.

The truth is, the journey heavenward is all uphill. I have to force myself to keep on. The wonder is that anybody gets there with so much to oppose—so little to help one!

–*July 29*–

It is high time to stop and think. I have been like one running a race and am stopping to take breath. I do not like the way in which things have been going on of late. I feel restless and ill at ease. I see that if I would be happy in God, I must give Him all. And there is a wicked reluctance to do that. I want Him—but I want to have my own way, too. I want to walk humbly and softly before Him and I want to go where I shall be admired and applauded. To whom shall I yield? To God? Or to myself?

—*July 30*—

I met Dr. Cabot today and could not help asking the question:

"Is it right for me to sing and play in company when all I do it for is to be admired?"

"Are you sure it is all you do it for?" he returned.

"Oh," I said, "I suppose there may be a sprinkling of desire to entertain and please mixed with the love of display."

"Do you suppose that your love of display, allowing you have it, would be forever slain by your merely refusing to sing in company?"

"I thought that might give it a pretty hard blow," I said, "if not its death blow."

"Meanwhile, in punishing yourself, you punish your poor innocent friends," he said laughing. "No, child, go on singing; God has given you this power of entertaining and gratifying your friends. But pray without ceasing that you may sing from pure benevolence and not from pure self-love."

"Why, do people pray about such things as that?" I cried.

"Of course they do. Why, I would pray about my little finger if my little finger went astray."

I looked at his little finger but saw no signs of its becoming schismatic.

–Aug. 3–

This morning I took great delight in praying for my little scholars and went to Sunday school as on wings. But on reaching my seat, what was my horror to find Maria Perry there!

"O, your seat is changed," said she. "I am to have half your class, and I like this seat better than those higher up. I suppose you don't care?"

"But I do care," I returned, "and you have taken my very best children—the very sweetest and the very prettiest. I shall speak to Mr. Williams about it directly."

"At any rate I would not fly into such a fury," she said. "It is just as pleasant to me to have pretty children to teach as it is to you. Mr. Williams said he had no doubt you would be glad to divide your class with me, as it is so large; and I doubt if you gain anything by speaking to him."

There was not time for further discussion as school was about to begin. I went to my new seat with great disgust and found it very inconvenient. The children could not cluster around me as they did before, and I got on with the lesson very badly. I am sure Maria Perry has no gift at teaching little children, and I feel quite vexed and disappointed. This has not been a profitable Sunday, and I am now going to bed cheerless and uneasy.

–Aug. 9–

Mr. Williams called this evening to say that I am to have my old seat and all the children again. All the mothers had been to see him or had written him notes about it and requested that I might continue to teach them. Mr. Williams said he hoped I would go on teaching for twenty years and that as fast as his little girls grew old enough to come to Sunday school, he should want me to take charge of them. I should have been greatly elated by these compliments but for the display I made of myself to Maria Perry on Sunday. Oh, that I could learn to bridle my unlucky tongue!

–Jan. 15, 1835–

Today I am twenty. That sounds very old, yet I feel pretty much as I did before. I have begun to visit some of Mother's poor folks with her and am astonished to see how they love her and how plainly they let her talk to them. As a general rule I do not think poor people are very interesting, and they are always ungrateful.

We went first to see old Jacob Stone. I have been there a good many times with the baskets of nice things Mother takes such comfort in sending him, but I never would go in. I was shocked to see how worn away he was. He seemed in great distress of mind and begged Mother to pray with him. I do not see how she could. I am perfectly sure that no earthly power could ever induce me to go round praying on bare floors, with people sitting, rocking, and staring all the time as the two Stone girls stared at Mother. How tenderly she prayed for him!

We then went to see Susan Green. She had made a carpet for her room by sewing together little bits of pieces given her, I suppose, by persons for whom she works, for she goes about fitting and making carpets. It looked bright and cheerful. She had a nice bed in the corner, covered with a white quilt, and some little ornaments were arranged about the room. Mother complimented her on her neatness and said a queen might sleep in such a bed as that and hoped she found it as comfortable as it looked.

"Mercy on us!" she cried out. "It ain't to sleep in! I sleep up in the loft that I climb to by a ladder every night."

Mother looked a little amused, and then she sat and listened patiently to a long account of how the poor old thing had invested her money, how Mr. Jones did not pay the interest regularly, and how Mr. Stevens haggled about the percentage. After we came away, I asked Mother how she could listen to such a rigmarole in patience and what good she supposed she had done by her visit.

"Why the poor creature likes to show off her bright carpet and nice bed, her chairs, her vases, and her knick-knacks, and she likes to talk about her beloved money and her bank stock. I may not have done her any good, but I have given her a pleasure, and so have you."

"Why, I hardly spoke a word."

"Yes, but your mere presence gratified her. And if she ever gets into trouble, she will feel kindly toward us for the sake of our sympathy with her pleasures and will let us sympathize with her sorrows."

I confess this did not seem a privilege to be coveted. She is not nice at all and takes snuff.

We went next to see Bridget Shannon. Mother had lost sight of her for some years and had just heard that she was sick and in great want. We found her in bed; there was no furniture in the room, and three little half-naked children sat with their bare feet in some ashes where there had been a little fire. Three such disconsolate faces I never saw. Mother sent me to the nearest baker's for bread; I nearly ran all the way, and I hardly know which I enjoyed most, Mother's eagerness in distributing or the children's in clutching at and devouring it. I am going to cut up one or two old dresses to make the poor things something to cover them. One of them has lovely hair that would curl beautifully if it were only brushed out. I told her to come to see me tomorrow; she is so very pretty.

Those few visits used up the very time I usually spend in drawing. But on the whole I am glad I went with Mother because it has gratified her. Besides, one must either stop reading the Bible altogether or else leave off spending one's whole time in just doing easy, pleasant things one likes to do.

–*Jan. 20*–

The little Shannon girl came, and I washed her face and hands, brushed out her hair, made it curl in lovely golden ringlets all round her sweet face, and carried her in great triumph to Mother.

"Look at the dear little thing, Mother!" I cried. "Doesn't she look like a line of poetry?"

"You foolish, romantic child!" Mother said. "She looks to me like a very ordinary line of prose. A slice of bread with butter and a piece of gingerbread mean more to her than these elaborate ringlets possibly can. They get in her eyes and make her neck cold; see, they are dripping with water, and the child is all in a shiver."

So saying, Mother folded a towel round her neck to catch the falling drops and went for bread and butter, of which the child consumed a quantity that was absolutely appalling. To crown all, the ungrateful little thing would not so much as look at me from that moment but clung to Mother, turning her back upon me in supreme contempt.

Moral—Mothers occasionally know more than their daughters do.

CHAPTER VI

A message came yesterday morning from Susan Green to the effect that she had had a dreadful fall and was half-killed. Mother wanted to set off at once to see her, but I would not let her go, as she has one of her worst colds. She then asked me to go in her place. I turned up my nose at the bare thought, though I dare say it turns up enough on its own account.

"Oh, Mother!" I said, reproachfully, "that dirty old woman!"

Mother made no answer, and I sat down at the piano and played a little. But I only played discords.

"Do you think it is my duty to run after such horrid old women?" I asked Mother at last.

"I think, dear, you must make your own duties," she said kindly. "I dare say that at your age I should have made a great deal out of my personal repugnance to such a woman as Susan and very little out of her sufferings."

I believe I am the most fastidious creature in the world.

Sickrooms with their intolerable smells of camphor and vinegar and mustard, their gloom and their whines and their groans, actually make me shudder. But was it now just such fastidiousness that made Cha—no, I won't utter his name—that made somebody weary of my possibilities? And has that terrible lesson really done me no good?

–*Jan. 26*–

No sooner had I written the above than I scrambled into my cloak and bonnet and flew, on the wings of holy indignation, to Susan Green. Such wings fly fast and got me a little out of breath. I found her lying on that nice white bed of hers in a frilled cap and nightgown. It seems she fell from her ladder in climbing to the dismal den where she sleeps and lay all night in great distress with some serious internal injury. I found her groaning and complaining in a fearful way.

"Are you in such pain?" I asked as kindly as I could.

"It isn't the pain," she said. "It isn't the pain. It's the way my nice bed is going to wreck and ruin and the starch all getting out of my frills that I fluted with my own hands. And the doctor's bill and the medicines, oh, dear, dear, dear!"

Just then the doctor came in. After examining her, he said to a woman who seemed to have charge of her, "Are you the nurse?"

"Oh, no, I only stepped in to see what I could do for her."

"Who is to be with her tonight, then?"

Nobody knew.

"I will send a nurse, then," he said. "But someone else will be needed also," he added, looking at me.

"I will stay," I said. But my heart died within me.

The doctor took me aside. "Her injuries are very

serious," he said. "If she has any friends, they ought to be sent for."

"You don't mean that she is going to die?" I asked.

"I fear she is. But not immediately." He took leave, and I went back to the bedside. I saw there no longer a snuffy, repulsive old woman, but a human being about to make that mysterious journey to a far country whence there is no return. Oh, how I wished Mother were there!

"Susan," I said, "have you any relatives?"

"No, I haven't," she answered sharply. "And if I had, they needn't come prowling around me. I don't want to have relations about my body."

"Would you like to see Dr. Cabot?"

"What should I want of Dr. Cabot? Don't tease, child."

Considering the deference with which she had heretofore treated me, this was quite a new order of things.

I sat down and tried to pray for her silently in my heart. Who was to go with her on that long journey, and where was it to end?

The woman who had been caring for her now went away, and it was growing dark. I sat still, listening to my own heart, which beat till it half-choked me.

"What were you and the doctor whispering about?" she suddenly burst out.

"He asked me, for one thing, if you had any friends that could be sent for?"

"I've been my own best friend," she returned. "Who'd have raked and scraped and hoarded and counted for Susan Green if I hadn't ha' done it? I've got enough to make me comfortable as long as I live and when I lie on my lying bed."

"But you can't carry it with you," I said. This highly original remark was all I had courage to utter.

"I wish I could," she cried. "I suppose you think I talk awful. They say you are getting most to be as much of a saint as your ma. It's born in some, and in some it ain't. Do get a light. It's lonesome here in the dark, and cold."

I was thankful enough to enliven the dark room with light and fire. But I saw now that the thin, yellow, hard face had changed sadly. She fixed her two little black eyes on me, evidently startled by the expression of my face.

"Look here, child, I ain't hurt to speak of, am I?"

"The doctor says you are hurt seriously."

My tone must have said more than my words did, for she caught me by the wrist and held me fast.

"He didn't say nothing about my—about it's being dangerous? I ain't dangerous, am I?" I felt ready to sink.

"Oh, Susan," I gasped out, "you haven't any time to lose. You're going, you're going!"

"Going!" she cried. "Going where? You don't mean to say I'm a-dying? Why, it beats all my calculations. I was going to live ever so many years and save up ever so much money, and then, when my time come, I was going to put on my best fluted nightgown and nightcap and lay my head on my handsome pillow and draw the clothes up over me, neat and tidy, and die decent. But here's my bed all in a toss, and my frills all in a crumple, and my room all upside down, and bottles of medicine setting around alongside of my vases, and nobody here but you, just a girl, and nothing else!"

All this came out by jerks, as it were, and at intervals.

"Don't talk so!" I fairly screamed. "Pray, pray to God to have mercy on you!"

She looked at me, bewildered, but yet as if the truth had reached her at last.

"Pray yourself!" she said eagerly. "I don't know how. I can't think. Oh, my time's come! My time's come! And I ain't ready! I ain't ready! Get down on your knees and pray with all your might and main."

And I did, she holding my wrist tightly in her hand. All at once I felt her hold relax. After that the next thing I knew, I was lying on the floor and somebody was dashing water in my face.

It was the nurse. She had come at last and found me by the side of the bed, where I had fallen, and had been trying to revive me ever since. I started up and looked about me. The nurse was closing Susan's eyes in a professional way and performing other little services of the sort. The room wore an air of perfect desolation. The clothes Susan had on when she fell lay in a forlorn heap on a chair; her shoes and stockings were thrown hither and thither; the mahogany bureau, in which she had taken so much pride, was covered with vials, to make room for which some pretty trifles had been hastily thrust aside. With a sort of shudder, I remembered what I had once said to Mrs. Cabot, about having tasteful things about me. What a mockery they are in the awful presence of death.

Mother met me with open arms when I reached home. She was much shocked at what I had to tell and at my having encountered such a scene alone. I should have felt myself quite a heroine under her caresses if I had not been overcome with bitter regret that I had not, with firmness and dignity, turned poor Susan's last thoughts to her Savior. Oh, how could I, through miserable cowardice, let those precious moments slip by!

–*Feb. 27*–

I have learned one thing, by yesterday's experience, that is worth knowing. It is this: Duty looks more repelling at a distance than when fairly faced and met. Of course I have read the lines,

> *Nor know we anything so fair*
> *As is the smile upon thy face;*

but I seem to be one of the stupid sort who never apprehend a thing till they experience it. Now, however, I have seen the smile and find it so "fair" that I shall gladly plod through many a hardship and trial to meet it again.

Poor Susan! Perhaps God heard my eager prayer for her soul and revealed Himself to her at the very last moment.

–*March 2*–

Such a strange thing has happened! Susan Green left a will bequeathing her precious savings to whoever offered the last prayer in her hearing! I do not want, I never could touch a penny of that hardly earned store; and if I did want it, no earthly motive would tempt me to tell a human being that that last prayer was offered by me, an inexperienced, trembling girl, driven to it by mere desperation! So it has gone to Dr. Cabot, who will not use it for himself, I am sure, but will be delighted to have it to give to poor people, who really besiege him. The last time he called to see Susan, he talked and prayed with her and says she seemed pleased and grateful and promised to be more regular at church, which she had been, ever since.

I feel all out of sorts. Mother says it is owing to the strain I went through at Susan's dying bed. She wants me to go to visit my Aunt Mary, who is always urging me to come. But I do not like to leave my little Sunday scholars nor to give Mother the occasion to deny herself in order to meet the expense of such a long journey. Besides, I should have to have some new dresses, a new bonnet, and lots of things.

Today Dr. Cabot has sent me some directions for which I have been begging him a long time. Lest I should wear out this precious letter by reading it over, I will copy it here. After alluding to my complaint that I still "saw men as trees walking," he says:

Yet he who first uttered this complaint had had his eyes opened by the Son of God, and so have you. Now He never leaves His work incomplete, and He will gradually lead you into clear and open vision if you will allow Him to do it. I say gradually, because I believe this to be His usual method, while I do not deny that there are cases where light suddenly bursts in like a flood. To return to the blind man. When Jesus found that his cure was not complete, He put His hands again upon his eyes and made him look up; and he was restored and saw every man clearly. Now this must be done for you; and in order to have it done, you must go to Christ Himself, not to one of His servants. Make your complaint, tell Him how obscure everything still looks to you, and beg Him to complete your cure. He may see fit to try your faith and patience by delaying this completion; but meanwhile you are safe in His presence, and while led by His hand, He will excuse the mistakes you make and pity your falls. But you will imagine that it is best that He should at once enable you to see clearly. If it is, you may be sure He will do it. He never makes mistakes. But He often deals far differently with His disciples. He lets them grope their way in the dark until they fully learn how blind they are, how helpless, how absolutely in need of Him.

What His methods will be with you I cannot foretell. But you may be sure that He never works in an arbitrary way. He has a reason for everything He does. You may not understand why He leads you now in this way and now in that, but you may, nay, you must believe that perfection is stamped on His every act.

I am afraid that you are in danger of falling into an error only too common among young Christians. You acknowledge that there has been enmity toward God in your secret soul and that one of the first steps toward peace is to become reconciled to Him and to have your sins forgiven for Christ's sake. This done, you settle down with the feeling that the great work of life is done and that your salvation is sure. Or, if not sure, that your whole business is to study your own case to see whether you are really in a state of grace. Many persons never get beyond this point. They spend their whole time in asking the question:

> *Do I love the Lord or no?*
> *Am I His or am I not?*

I beg you, my dear child, if you are doing this aimless, useless work, to stop short at once. Life is too precious to spend in a treadmill. Having been pardoned by your God and Savior, the next thing you have to do is to show your gratitude for this infinite favor by consecrating your self entirely to Him, body, soul, and spirit. This is the least you can do. He has bought you with a price, and you are no longer your own. "But," you may reply, "this is contrary to my nature. I love my own way. I desire ease and pleasure; I desire to go to heaven, but I want to be carried thither on a bed of flowers. Can I not give myself so far to God as to feel a sweet sense of peace with Him, and be sure of final salvation, and yet, to a certain extent, indulge and gratify myself? If I give myself entirely away to Him and lose all ownership in myself, He may deny me many things I greatly desire. He may make my life hard and wearisome, depriving me of all that now makes it agreeable." But, I reply, this is no matter of parley and discussion; it is not optional with God's children whether they will pay Him a part of the price they owe Him and keep back the rest. He asks, and He has a right to ask, for all you have and all you are. And if you shrink from what is involved in such a surrender, you should fly to Him at once and never rest till He has conquered this secret disinclination to give to Him as freely and as fully as He has given to you. It is true that such an act of consecration on your part may involve a great deal of future discipline and correction. But as soon as you become the Lord's by your own deliberate and conscious act, He will begin that process of sanctification which is to make you holy as He is holy, perfect as He is perfect. He becomes at once your Physician as well as your dearest and best Friend, but He will use no painful remedy that can be avoided. Remember that it is His will that you should be sanctified and that the work of making you holy is His, not yours. At the same time you are not to sit with folded hands, waiting for this blessing. You are to avoid laying hindrances in His way, and you are to exercise faith in Him as just as able and just as willing to give you sanctification as He was to give you redemption. And now if you ask how you may know that you have truly consecrated yourself to Him, I reply, observe every indication of His will concerning you, no matter how trivial, and see whether you at once close in with that will. Lay down this principle as a law—God does nothing arbitrary. If He takes away your health, for instance, it is because He has some reason for doing so; and this is true of everything you value; and if you have real faith in Him, you will not insist on knowing the reason. If you find, in the course of daily events, that your self-consecration was not perfect—that is, that your will revolts at His will—do not be discouraged, but fly to your Savior and stay in His presence till you obtain the spirit in which He cried in His hour of anguish, "Father, if Thou be willing, remove this cup from me: nevertheless not my will but Thine be done" (Luke 22:42). Every time you do this it will be easier to do it; every such consent to suffer will bring you nearer and nearer to Him; and in this nearness to Him you will find such peace such blessed, sweet peace as will make your life infinitely happy, no matter what may be its mere outside conditions. Just think, my dear Katy, of the honor and the joy of having your will one with the Divine will and so becoming changed into Christ's image from glory to glory!

But I cannot say, in a letter, the tithe of what I want to say. Listen to my sermons from week to week, and glean from them all the instruction you can, remembering that they are preached to you.

In reading the Bible I advise you to choose detached passages, or even one verse a day, rather than whole chapters. Study every word; ponder and pray over it till you have got from it all the truth it contains.

As to the other devotional reading, it is better to settle down on a few favorite authors and read their works over and over and over until you have digested their thoughts and made them your own.

It has been said "that a fixed, inflexible will is a great assistance in a holy life."

You can will to choose for your associates those who are most devout and holy.

You can will to read books that will stimulate you in your Christian life rather than those that merely amuse.

You can will to use every means of grace appointed by God.

You can will to spend much time in prayer without regard to your frame at the moment.

You can will to prefer a religion of principle to one of mere feeling; in other words, to obey the will of God when no comfortable glow of emotion accompanies your obedience.

You cannot will to possess the spirit of Christ; that must come as His gift; but you can choose to study His life and to imitate it. This will infallibly lead to such self-denying work as visiting the poor, nursing the sick, giving of your time and money to the needy, and the like.

If the thought of such self-denial is repugnant to you, remember that it is enough for the disciple to be as his Lord. And let me assure you that as you penetrate the labyrinth of life in pursuit of Christian duty, you will often be surprised and charmed by meeting your Master Himself amid its windings and turnings and receive His soul-inspiring smile. Or, I should rather say, you will always meet Him, wherever you go.

I have read this letter again and again. It has taken such hold of me that I can think of nothing else. The idea of seeking holiness had never so much as crossed my mind. And even now it seems like presumption for such a one as I to utter so sacred a word. And I shrink from committing myself to such a pursuit, lest after a time I should fall back into the old routine. And I have an undefined, wicked dread of being singular, as well as a certain terror of self-denial and loss of all liberty. But no choice seems left to me. Now that my duty has been clearly pointed out to me, I do not stand where I did before. And I feel, mingled with my indolence and love of ease and pleasure, some drawings toward a higher and better life. There is one thing I can do, and that is to pray that Jesus would do for me what He did for the blind man—put His hands yet again upon my eyes and make me to see clearly. And I will.

–March 30–

Yes, I have prayed, and He has heard me. I see that I have no right to live for myself and that I must live for Him. I have given myself to Him as I never did before and have entered, as it were, a new world. I was very happy when I first began to believe in His love for me and that He had redeemed me. But this new happiness is deeper; it involves something higher than getting to heaven at last, which has, hitherto, been my great aim.

–March 31–

The more I pray and the more I read the Bible, the more I feel my ignorance. And the more earnestly I desire holiness, the more utterly unholy I see myself to be. But I have pledged myself to the Lord, and I must pay my vows, cost what it may.

I have begun to read Taylor's *Holy Living and Dying.* A month ago I should have found it a tedious, dry book. But I am reading it with a sort of avidity, like one seeking after hid treasure. Mother, observing what I was doing, advised me not to read it straight through but to mingle a passage now and then with chapters from other books. She suggested my beginning on Baxter's *Saints' Rest,* and of that I have read every word. I shall read it over, as Dr. Cabot advised, till I have fully caught its spirit. Even this one reading has taken away my lingering fear of death and made heaven wonderfully attractive. I never mean to read worldly books again, and my music and drawing I have given up forever.

CHAPTER VII

*M*other asked me last evening to sing and play for her. I was embarrassed to know how to excuse myself without telling her my real reason for declining. But somehow she got it out of me.

"One need not be fanatical in order to be religious," she said.

"Is it fanatical to give up all for God?" I asked.

"What is it to give up all?" she asked in reply.

"Why, to deny one's self every gratification and indulgence in order to mortify one's natural inclinations and to live entirely for Him."

"God is then a hard Master who allows His children no liberty," she replied. "Now let us see where this theory will lead you. In the first place, you must shut your eyes to all the beautiful things He has made. You must shut your ears to all the harmonies He has ordained. You must shut your heart against all sweet, human affections. You have a body, it is true, and it may revolt at such bondage—"

"We are told to keep under the body," I interrupted.

"Oh, Mother, don't hinder me! You know that my love for music is a passion and that it is my snare and temptation. And how can I spend my whole time in reading the Bible and praying if I go on with my drawing? It may do for other people to serve both God and Mammon, but not for me. I must belong wholly to the world or wholly to Christ."

Mother said no more, and I went on with my reading. But somehow my book seemed to have lost its flavor. Besides, it was time to retire for my evening devotions, which I never put off now till the last thing at night, as I used to do. When I came down, Mother was lying on the sofa, by which I knew she was not well. I felt troubled that I had refused to sing to her. Think of the money she has spent on that part of my education! I went to her and kissed her with a pang of terror. What if she were going to be very sick and to die?

"It is nothing, darling," she said, "nothing at all. I am tired and felt a little faint."

I looked at her anxiously, and the bare thought that she might die and leave me alone was so terrible that I could hardly help crying out. And I saw, as by a flash of lightning, that if God took her from me, I could not, would not say: Thy will be done.

But she was better after taking a few drops of lavender, and what color she has came back to her dear, sweet face.

—April 12—

Dr. Cabot's letter has lost all its power over me. A stone has more feeling than I. I don't love to pray. I am sick and tired of this dreadful struggle after holiness; good books are all alike, flat and meaningless. But I must have something to absorb and carry me away, and I have come back to my music and my drawing with new zest. Mother was right in warning me against giving them up. Maria Kelley is teaching me to paint in oil colors and says I have a natural gift for it.

–*April 13*–

Mother asked me to go to church with her last evening, and I said I did not want to go. She looked surprised and troubled.

"Are you well, dear?" she asked.

"I don't know. Yes, I suppose I am. But I could not be still at church five minutes. I am so nervous that I feel as if I should fly."

"I see how it is," she said. "You have forgotten that body of yours, of which I reminded you, and have been trying to live as if you were all soul and spirit. You have been straining every nerve to acquire perfection, whereas this is God's gift and one that He is willing to give you, fully and freely."

"I have done seeking for that or anything else that is good," I said despondently. "And so I have gone back to my music and everything else."

"Here is just the rock upon which you split," she returned. "You speak of going back to your music as if that implied going away from God. You rush from one extreme to another. The only true way to live in this world, constituted just as we are, is to make all our employments subserve the one great end and aim of existence, namely, to glorify God and to enjoy Him forever. But in order to do this we must be wise taskmasters and not require of ourselves what we cannot possibly perform. Recreation we must have. Otherwise, the strings of our soul, wound up to an unnatural tension, will break."

"Oh, I do wish," I cried, "that God had given us plain rules about which we could make no mistake."

"I think His rules are plain," she replied. "And some liberty of action He must leave us or we should become mere machines. I think that those who love Him and wait upon Him day by day learn His will almost imperceptibly and need not go astray."

"But, Mother, music and drawing are sharp-edged tools in such hands as mine. I cannot be moderate in my use of them. And the more I delight in them, the less I delight in God."

"Yes, this is human nature. But God's divine nature will supplant it if we only consent to let Him work in us of His own good pleasure."

–New York, April 16–

After all, Mother has come off conqueror, and here I am at Aunty's. After our quiet, plain little home in our quiet little town, this seems like a new world. The house is large, but it is as full as it can hold. Aunty has six children of her own and had adopted two. She says she always meant to imitate the old woman who lived in a shoe. She reminds me of Mother, and yet she is very different: full of fun and energy; flying about the house as on wings, with a kind, bright word for everybody. All her household affairs go on like clockwork; the children are always nicely dressed; nobody ever seems out of humor; nobody is ever sick. Aunty is the central object round which everybody revolves; you can't forget her a moment for she is always doing something for you, and then her unflagging good humor and cheerfulness keep you good-humored and cheerful. I don't wonder Uncle Alfred loves her so!

I hope I shall have just such a home. I mean this is the sort of home I should like if I were married, which I never mean to be. I should like to be just such a bright, loving wife as Aunty is; to have my husband lean on me as Uncle leans on her; to have just as many children and to train them as wisely and kindly as she does hers. Then, indeed, I should feel that I had not been born in vain but had a high and sacred mission on earth. But as it is, I must just pick up what scraps of usefulness I can and let the rest go.

—*April 18*—

Aunty says I sit writing and reading and thinking too much and wants me to go out more. I tell her I don't feel strong enough to go out much. She says that is all nonsense and drags me out. I get tired, and hungry, and sleep like a baby a month old. I see now Mother's wisdom and kindness in making me leave home when I did. I had veered about from point to point till I was nearly ill. Now Aunty keeps me well by making me go out, and dear Dr. Cabot's precious letter can work a true and not a morbid work in my soul. I am very happy. I have delightful talks with Aunty, who sets me right at this point and at that; and it is beautiful to watch her homelife and to see with what sweet unconsciousness she carries her religion into every detail. I am sure it must do me good to be here; and yet, if I am growing better, how slowly it is! Somebody has said that "our course heavenward is like the plan of the zealous pilgrim of old, who for every three steps forward, took one backward."

—*April 30*—

Aunty's baby, my dear father's namesake and hitherto

the merriest little fellow I ever saw, was taken sick last night very suddenly. She sent for the doctor at once, who would not say positively what was the matter but this morning pronounced it scarlet fever. The three youngest have all come down with it today. If they were my children, I should be in a perfect worry and flurry. Indeed, I am as it is. But Aunty is as bright and cheerful as ever. She flies from one to another and keeps up their spirits with her own gaiety. I am mortified to find that at such a time as this I can think of myself and that I find it irksome to be shut up in sickrooms instead of walking, driving, visiting, and the like. But, as Dr. Cabot says, I can now choose to imitate my Master, who spent His whole life in doing good; and I do hope, too, to be of some little use to Aunty after her kindness to me.

–*May 1*–

The doctor says the children are doing as well as could be expected. He made a short visit this morning as it is Sunday. If I had seen him before, I should say I had some unpleasant association with him. I wonder Aunty employs such a great clumsy man. But she says he is very good and very skillful. I wish I did not take such violent likes and dislikes to people. I want my religion to change me in every respect.

–*May 2*–

Oh, I know now! This is the very man who was so rude at Sunday school and afterwards made such a nice address to the children. Well, he may know how to speak in public, but I am sure he doesn't in private. I never knew such a shut-up man.

—May 4—

I have my hands as full as they can hold. The children have got so fond of me, and one or the other is in my lap nearly all the time. I sing to them, tell them stories, build blockhouses, and relieve Aunty all I can. Dull and poky as the doctor is, I am not afraid of him for he never notices anything I say or do; so while he is holding solemn consultations with Aunty in one corner, I can sing and talk all sorts of nonsense to my little pets in mine. What fearful black eyes he has and what masses of black hair!

This busy life quite suits me now I have got used to it. And it sweetens every bit of work to think that I am doing it in humble, far-off, yet real imitation of Jesus. I am indeed really and truly happy.

—May 14—

It is now two weeks since little Raymond was taken sick and I have just lived in the nursery all the time, though Aunty has tried to make me go out. Little Emma was taken down today, though she has been kept on the third floor all the time. I feel dreadfully myself. But this hard, cold doctor of Aunty's is so taken up with the children that he never so much as looks at me. I have been in a perfect shiver all day, but these merciless little folks call for stories as eagerly as ever. Well, let me be a comfort to them if I can! I hate selfishness more and more and am shocked to see how selfish I have been.

—May 15—

I was in a burning fever all night, and my head ached, and my throat was and is very sore. If I knew I was going to die, I would burn up this journal first. I would not have anyone see it for the world.

–May 24–

Dr. Elliott asked me on Sunday morning a week ago if I still felt well. For answer I behaved like a goose and burst out crying. Aunty looked more anxious than I have seen her look yet and reproached herself for having allowed me to be with the children. She took me by one elbow and the doctor by the other, and they marched me to my own room, where I was put through the usual routine on such occasions and then ordered to bed. I fell asleep immediately and slept all day. The doctor came to see me in the evening and made me a short, stiff little visit, gave me a powder, and said he thought I should soon be better.

I had two such visits from him the next day, when I began to feel quite like myself again, and in spite of his grave, stayed deportment, could not help letting my good spirits run away with me in a style that evidently shocked him. He says persons nursing in scarlet fever often have such little attacks as mine; indeed, every one of the servants have had a touch of sore throat and headache.

–May 25–

This morning, just as the doctor shuffled in on his big feet, it came over me how ridiculously I must have looked the day I was taken sick, being walked off between Aunty and himself, crying like a baby. I burst out laughing, and no consideration I could make to myself would stop me. I pinched myself, asked myself how I should feel if one of the children should die, and used other kindred devices all to no purpose. At last the doctor, gravity personified as he is, joined in, though not knowing in the least what he was laughing at. Then he said, "After this, I suppose, I shall have to pronounce you convalescent."

"Oh, no!" I cried. "I am very sick indeed."

"I suppose this will be your last visit, Dr. Elliott," I went on, "and I am glad of it. After the way I behaved the day I was taken sick, I have been ashamed to look you in the face. But I really felt dreadfully."

He made no answer whatever. I don't suppose he would speak a little flattering word by way of putting one in good humor with one's self for the whole world!

–*June 1*–

We are all as well as ever, but the doctor keeps some of the children still confined to the house for fear of bad consequences following the fever. He visits them twice a day for the same reason, or at least under that pretense, but I really believe he comes because he has got the habit of coming and because he admires Aunty so much. She has a real affection for him and is continually asking me if I don't like this and that quality in him, which I can't see at all. We begin to drive out again. The weather is very warm, but I feel perfectly well.

–*June 2*–

After the children's dinner today, I took care of them while their nurse got hers and Aunty went to lie down, as she was all tired out. We were all full of life and fun, and some of the little ones wanted me to play a play of their own invention, which was to lie down on the floor, cover my face with a handkerchief, and make believe I was dead. They were to gather about me, and I was suddenly to come to life and jump up and try to catch them as they all ran scampering and screaming about. We had played in this interesting way for some time, and my hair, which I keep in nice order nowadays, was pulled down and flying every way when in marched the doctor. I started up and came to life quickly enough when I heard his step, looking red and angry, no doubt.

"I shouldn't think you might have knocked, Dr. Elliott," I said with much displeasure.

"I ask your pardon; I knocked several times," he returned. "I need hardly ask how my little patients are."

"No," I replied, still ruffled and making desperate efforts to get my hair into some sort of order. "They are as well as possible."

"I came a little earlier than usual today," he went on, "because I am called to visit my uncle, Dr. Cabot, who is in a very critical state of health."

"Dr. Cabot!" I repeated, bursting into tears.

"Compose yourself, I entreat," he said. "I hope that I may be able to relieve him. At all events—"

"At all events, if you let him die it will break my heart," I cried, passionately. "Don't wait another moment; go this instant."

"I cannot go this instant," he replied. "The boat does not leave until four o'clock. And if I may be allowed, as a physician, to say one word, that my brief acquaintance hardly justifies, I do wish to warn you that unless you acquire more self-control—"

"Oh, I know that I have a quick temper and that I spoke very rudely to you just now," I interrupted, not a little startled by the seriousness of his manner.

"I did not refer to your temper," he said. "I meant your whole passionate nature. Your vehement loves and hates, your ecstasies and your despondencies, your disposition to throw yourself headlong into whatever interests you."

"I would rather have too little self-control," I retorted resentfully, "than to be as cold as a stone, and as hard as a rock, and as silent as the grave, like some people I know."

His countenance fell; he looked disappointed, even pained.

"I shall probably see your mother," he said, turning to go. "Your aunt wishes me to call on her; have you any message?"

"No," I said.

Another pained, disappointed look made me begin to recollect myself. I was sorry, oh! so sorry, for my anger and rudeness. I ran after him into the hall, my eyes full of tears, holding out both hands, which he took in both of his.

"Don't go until you have forgiven me for being so angry!" I cried. "Indeed, Dr. Elliott, though you may not be able to believe it, I am trying to do right all the time!"

"I do believe it," he said earnestly.

"Then tell me that you forgive me!"

"If I once begin, I shall be tempted to tell something else," he said, looking me through and through with those great dusky eyes. "And I will tell it," he went on, his grasp on my hands growing firmer. "It is easy to forgive when one loves." I pulled my hands away and burst out crying again.

"Oh, Dr. Elliott, this is dreadful!" I said. "You do not, you cannot love me! You are so much older than I am! So grave and silent! You are not in earnest!"

"I am only too much so," he said and went quietly out.

I went back to the nursery. The children rushed upon me and insisted that I should "play die." I let them pull me about as they pleased. I only wished I could play it in earnest.

CHAPTER VIII

June 28

Mother writes me that Dr. Cabot is out of danger, Dr. Elliott having thrown new light on his case and performed some sort of an operation that relieved him at once. I am going home. Nothing would tempt me to encounter those black eyes again. Besides, the weather is growing warm, and Aunty is getting ready to go out of town with the children.

—June 29—

Aunty insisted on knowing why I was hurrying home so suddenly and at last got it out of me inch by inch. On the whole it was a relief to have someone to speak to.

"Well!" she said and leaned back in her chair in a fit of musing.

"Is that all you are going to say, Aunty?" I ventured to ask at last.

"No, I have one more remark to add," she said, "and it is this: I don't know which of you has behaved most ridiculously. It would relieve me to give you each a good shaking."

"I think Dr. Elliott has behaved ridiculously," I said, "and he has made me most unhappy."

"Unhappy!" she repeated. "I don't wonder you are unhappy. You have pained and wounded one of the noblest men that walks the earth."

"It is not my fault. I never tried to make him like me."

"Yes, you did. You were perfectly bewitching whenever he came here. No mortal man could help being fascinated."

I knew this was not true, and I bitterly resented Aunty's injustice.

"If I wanted to 'fascinate' or 'bewitch' a man," I cried, "I should not choose one old enough to be my father nor one who was as uninteresting, awkward, and stiff as Dr. Elliott. Besides, how should I know he was not married? If I thought anything about it at all, I certainly thought of him as a middle-aged man settled down with a wife long ago."

"In the first place, he is not old or even middle-aged. He is not more than twenty-seven or eight. As to his being uninteresting, perhaps he is to you, who doesn't know him. And if he were a married man, what business had he to come here to see you as he had done?"

"I did not know he came to see me; he never spoke to me. And I always said I would never marry a doctor."

"We all say scores of things we live to repent," she replied. "But I must own that the doctor acted quite out of character when he expected you to take a fancy to him on such short notice, you romantic little thing. Of course knowing him as little as you do and only seeing him in sickrooms, you could not have done otherwise than as you did."

"Thank you, Aunty," I said, running and throwing my arms around her. "Thank you with all my heart. And now won't you take back what you said about my trying to fascinate him?"

"I suppose I must, you dear child," she said. "I was not half in earnest. The truth is I am so fond of you both that the idea of your misunderstanding each other annoys me extremely. Why, you were made for each other. He would tone you down and keep you straight, and you would stimulate him and keep him awake."

"I don't want to be toned down or kept straight," I remonstrated. "I hate prigs who keep their wives in leading strings. I do not mean to marry anyone; but if I should be left to such a piece of folly, it must be to one who will take me for better or for worser, just as I am, and not as a wild plant for him to prune till he has got it into a shape to suit him. And now, Aunty, promise me one thing. Never mention Dr. Elliott's name to me again."

"I shall make no such promise," she replied, laughing. "I like him, and I like to talk about him, and the more you hate and despise him, the more I shall love and admire him. I only wish my Lucy were old enough to be his wife and that he could fancy her; but he never could!"

"On the contrary, I should think that little model of propriety would just suit him," I exclaimed.

"Don't make fun of Lucy," Aunty said, shaking her head. "She is a dear, good child, after all."

"After all" means this (for what with my own observation and what Aunty had told me, Lucy's portrait is easy to paint): The child is the daughter of a man who died from a lingering illness caused by an accident. She entered her family at a most inauspicious moment, two days after this accident. From the outset she comprehended the situation and took the ground that a character of irregular dignity and propriety became an infant coming at such a time. She never cried, never put improper objects into her mouth, never bumped her head or scratched herself. Once put to bed at night, you knew nothing more of her till such time next day as you found it convenient to attend to her. If you forgot her existence, as was not seldom the case under the circumstances, she vegetated on, unmoved. It is possible that pangs of hunger sometimes assailed her, and it is a fact that she teethed, had the measles and the whooping cough. But these minute ripples on her infant life only showed the more clearly what a waveless, placid little sea it was. She got her teeth in the order laid down in *Dewees on Children;* her measles came out on the appointed day, like well-behaved measles as they were, and retired decently and in order, as measles should. Her whooping cough had a well-bred, methodical air and left her conqueror of the field. As the child passed out of her babyhood, she remained still her mother's appendage and glory, a monument of pure white marble, displaying to the human race one instance at least of perfect parental training. Those smooth, round hands were always magically clean; the dress immaculate and uncrumpled; the hair dutifully shining and tidy. She was a model child, as she had been a model baby. No slamming of doors, no litter of carpets, no pattering of noisy feet on the stairs, no headless dolls, no soiled or torn books indicated her presence. Her dolls were subject to a methodical training not unlike her own. They rose, they were dressed, they took air, they retired for the night with clock-like regularity. At the advanced age of eight, she ceased occupying herself with such trifles and began a course of instructive reading. Her lessons were received in mute sub-mission, like medicine, so many doses, so many times a day. An agreeable interlude of needlework was afforded, and Dorcas-like, many were the garments that resulted for the poor. Give her the very eyes out of your head, cut off your right hand for her if you choose, but don't expect a gush of enthusiasm that would crumple your collar; she would as soon strangle herself as run headlong to embrace you. If she has any passions or emotions, they are kept under; but who asks for passion in blancmange or seeks emotion in a comfortable apple pudding?

When her father had been dead a year, her mother married a man with a large family of children and a very small purse. Lucy had a hard time of it, especially as her stepfather, a quick, impulsive man, took a dislike to her. After a time, Aunty had no difficulty in persuading them to give the child to her. She took her from the purest motives, and it does seem as if she ought to have more reward than she gets. She declares, however, that she has all the reward she could ask in the conviction that God accepts this attempt to please Him.

Lucy is now nearly fourteen, very large for her age, with a dead white skin, pale blue eyes, and a little light hair. To hear her talk is most edifying. Her babies are all "babes"; she never begins anything but "commences" it; she never cries, she "weeps"; she never gets up in the morning but "rises." But what am I writing all this for? Why, to escape my own thoughts, which are anything but agreeable companions, and to put off answering the question that must be answered, "Have I really made a mistake in refusing Dr. Elliott? Could I not, in time, have come to love a man who has so honored me?"

–*July 5*–

Here I am again, safely at home, and very pleasant it seems to be with dear Mother again. I have told her about Dr. E. She says very little about it one way or the other.

Mother sees that I am restless and out of sorts. "What is it, dear?" she asked this morning. "Has Dr. Elliott anything to do with the unsettled state you are in?"

"Why, no, Mother," I answered. "My going away has broken up all my habits; that's all. Still, if I knew Dr. Elliott did not care much and was beginning to forget it, I dare say I should feel better."

"If you were perfectly sure that you never could return his affection," she said, "you were quite right in telling him so at once. But if you had any misgivings on the subject, it would have been better to wait and to ask God to direct you."

Yes, it would. But at the moment, I had no misgivings. In my usual headlong style I settled one of the most weighty questions of my life without reflection, without so much as one silent appeal to God to tell me how to act. And now I have forever repelled and thrown away a heart that truly loved me. He will go his way and I shall go mine. He never will know what I am only just beginning to know myself, that I yearn after his love with unutterable yearning.

But I am not going to sit down in sentimental despondency to weep over this irreparable past. No human being could forgive such folly as mine; but God can. In my sorrowfulness and loneliness I fly to Him and find what is better than earthly felicity, the sweetest peace. He allowed me to bring upon myself, in one hasty moment, a shadow out of which I shall not soon pass; but He pities and He forgives me, and I have had many precious moments when I could say sincerely and joyfully, "Whom have I in heaven but Thee, and there is none upon earth that I desire besides

Thee" (Ps. 73:25).

With a character still so undisciplined as mine, I seriously doubt whether I could have made him happy who has honored me with his unmerited affection. Sometimes I think I am as impetuous and as quick-tempered as ever; I get angry with dear Mother and with James, even, if they oppose me; how unfit, then, I am to become the mistress of a household and the wife of a good man!

How came he to love me? I cannot, cannot imagine!

–*August 31*–

The last day of the very happiest summer I ever spent. If I had only been willing to believe the testimony of others I might have been just as happy long ago. But I wanted to have all there was in God and all there was in the world at once; and there was a constant, painful struggle between the two. I hope that struggle is now over. I deliberately choose and prefer God. I have found a sweet peace in trying to please Him such as I never conceived of. I would not change it for all the best things this world can give.

But I have a great deal to learn. I am like a child who cannot run to get what he wants but approaches it step by step, slowly, timidly—and yet approaches it. I am amazed at the patience of my blessed Master and Teacher, but how I love His school!

–*September*–

This, too, has been a delightful month in a certain sense. Amelia's marriage, at which I had to be present, upset me a little, but it was but a little ruffle on a deep sea of peace.

I saw Dr. Cabot today. He is quite well again and speaks of Dr. Elliott's skill with rapture. He asked about my Sunday scholars and my poor folks, etc., and I could not help letting out a little of the joy that has taken possession of me.

"This is as it should be," he said. "I should be sorry to see a person of your temperament enthusiastic in everything save religion. Do not be discouraged if you still have some ups and downs. 'He that is down need fear no fall'; but you are away up on the heights and may have a fall now and then."

This made me a little uncomfortable. I don't want any falls. I want to go on to perfection.

–*Oct. 1*–

Laura Cabot came to see me today and seemed very affectionate.

"I hope we may see more of each other than we have done," she began. "My father wishes it, and so do I."

Katy, mentally—"Ah! He sees how unworldly, how devoted I am, and so wants Laura under my influence.

Katy, aloud—"I am sure that is very kind."

Laura—"Not at all. He knows it will be profitable to me to be with you. I get a good deal discouraged at times and want a friend to strengthen and help me."

Katy, to herself—"Yes, yes, he thinks me quite experienced and trustworthy."

Katy, aloud—"I shall never dare to try to help you."

Laura—"Oh, yes, you must. I am so far behind you in Christian experience."

But I am ashamed to write down any more. After she had gone I felt delightfully puffed up for a while. But when I came up to my room this evening and knelt down to pray, everything looked dark and chaotic. God seemed far away, and I took no pleasure in speaking to Him. I felt sure that I had done something or felt something wrong and asked Him to show me what it is. There then flashed into my mind the remembrance of the vain, conceited thoughts I had had during Laura's visit and ever since.

How perfectly contemptible! I have had a fall, indeed!

I think now my first mistake was in telling Dr. Cabot my secret, sacred joys as if some merit of mine had earned them for me. That gave Satan a fine chance to triumph over me! After this I am determined to maintain the utmost reserve in respect to my religious experiences. Nothing is gained by running to tell them, and much is lost.

I feel depressed and comfortless.

CHAPTER IX

Oct. 10

*W*e have very sad news from Aunty. She says my uncle is quite broken down with some obscure disease that has been creeping stealthily along for months. All his physicians agree that he must give up his business and try the effect of a year's rest. Dr. Elliott proposes his going to Europe, which seems to me about as formidable as going to the next world. Aunty makes the best she can of it, but she says the thought of being separated from Uncle a whole year is dreadful. I pray for her day and night that this wild project may be given up. Why, he would be on the ocean ever so many weeks, exposed to all the discomforts of narrow quarters and poor food, and that just as winter is drawing nigh!

–Oct. 12–

Aunty writes that the voyage to Europe has been decided on and that Dr. Elliott is to accompany Uncle, travel with him, amuse him, and bring him home a well man. I hope Dr. E's power to amuse may exist somewhere, but I must own it was in a most latent form when I had the pleasure of knowing him. Poor Aunty! How much better it would be for her to go with Uncle! There are all the children, to be sure. Well, I hope Uncle may be the better for this great undertaking, but I don't like the idea of it.

–Oct. 15–

Another letter from Aunty and new plans! The Dr. is to stay at home, Aunty is to go with Uncle, and we—Mother and myself—are to take possession of the house and the children during their absence! In other words, all this is to be if we say amen. Could anything be more frightful? To refuse would be selfish and cruel. If we consent, I thrust myself under Dr. Elliott's very nose.

–Oct. 16–

Mother is surprised that I can hesitate one instant. She seems to have forgotten all about Dr. E. She says we can easily find a family to take this house for a year and that she is delighted to do anything for Aunty that can be done.

–Nov. 4–

Here we are, the whole thing settled. Uncle and Aunty started a week ago, and we are monarchs of all we survey, and this is a great deal. I am determined that Mother shall not be worn out with these children, although, of course, I could not manage them without her advice and help. It is to be hoped they won't all have the measles in a body or anything of that sort; I am sure it would be annoying to Dr. E. to come here now.

–Nov. 25–

Of course the baby must go on teething if only to have

the doctor sent for to lance his gums. I told Mother I was sure I could not be present when this was being done, so, though she looked surprised and said people should accustom themselves to such things, she volunteered to hold the baby herself.

—*Nov. 26*—

The baby was afraid of Mother, not being used to her, so she sent for me. As I entered the room, she gave him to me with an apology for doing so since I shrank from witnessing the operation. What must Dr. E. think I am made of if I can't bear to see a child's gums lanced? However, it is my own fault that he thinks me such a coward for I made Mother think me one. It was very embarrassing to hold baby and have the doctor's face so close to mine. I really wonder Mother should not see how awkwardly I am situated here.

—*Nov. 27*—

We have a good many visitors, friends of Uncle and Aunty. How uninteresting most people are! They all say the same thing, namely, how strange that Aunty had courage to undertake such a voyage and to leave her children, etc., etc., etc., and what was Dr. Elliott thinking of to let them go, etc., etc., etc.

Dr. Embury called today with a pretty little fresh creature, his new wife, who hangs on his arm like a work bag. He is Dr. Elliott's intimate friend and spoke of him very warmly, and so did his wife, who says she has known him always, as they were born and brought up in the same small village. I wonder he did not marry her himself instead of leaving her for Dr. Embury!

She says he, Dr. Elliott I mean, was the most devoted

son she ever saw and that he deserves his present success because he has made such sacrifices for his parents. I never met anyone whom I like so well on so short acquaintance—I mean Mrs. Embury, though you might fancy, you poor deluded Journal you, that I meant somebody else.

–Nov. 30–

I have so much to do that I have little time for writing. The way the children wear out their shoes and stockings, the speed with which their hair grows, the way they bump their heads and pinch their fingers, and the insatiable demand for stories is something next to miraculous. Not a day passes that somebody doesn't need something bought, that somebody else doesn't choke itself, and that I don't have to tell stories till I feel my intellect reduced to the size of a pea. If ever I was alive and wide awake, however, it is just now, and in spite of some vague shadows of I don't know what, I am very happy indeed. So is dear Mother. She and the doctor have become bosom friends. He keeps her making beef tea, scraping lint, and boiling calves' feet for jelly till the house smells like a hospital.

I suppose he thinks me a poor, selfish, frivolous girl, whom nothing would tempt to raise a finger for his invalids. But, of course, I do not care what he thinks.

–Dec. 4–

Dr. Elliott came this morning to ask Mother to go with him to see a child who had met with a horrible accident. She turned pale and pressed her lips together but went at once to get ready. Then my long-suppressed wrath burst out.

"How can you ask poor Mother to go and see such sights?" I cried. "You must think her nothing but a stone if you suppose that after the way in which my father died—"

"It was indeed most thoughtless of me," he interrupted. "But your Mother is such a rare woman, so decided and self-controlled, yet so gentle, so full of tender sympathy, that I hardly know where else to look for just the help I need today. If you could see this poor child, even you would justify me."

"Even you!" you monster of selfishness, heart of stone, floating bubble, "even you would justify it!"

How cruel, how unjust, how unforgiving he is!

I rushed out of the room and cried until I was tired.

–*Dec. 6*–

Mother says she feels really grateful to Dr. E. for taking her to see that child and to help soothe and comfort it while he went through with a severe, painful operation that she would not describe because she fancied I looked pale. I said I should think the child's mother the most proper person to soothe it on such an occasion.

"The poor thing has no mother," she said, reproachfully. "What has got into you, Kate? You do not seem at all like yourself."

"I should think you had enough to do with this great house to keep in order, so many mouths to fill, and so many servants to oversee without wearing yourself out with nursing all Dr. Elliott's poor folks," I said gloomily.

"The more I have to do, the happier I am," she replied. "Dear Katy, the old wound isn't healed yet, and I like to be with those who have wounds and bruises of their own. And Dr. Elliott seems to have divined this by instinct."

I ran and kissed her dear, pale face, which grows more beautiful every day. No wonder she misses Father so! He loved and honored her beyond description and never forgot one of those little courtesies that must have a great deal to do with a wife's happiness. People said of him that he was a gentleman of the old school, and that race is dying out.

I feel a good deal out of sorts myself. Oh, I do so wish to get above myself and all my childish, petty ways and to live in a region where there is no temptation and no sin!

–Dec. 22–

I have been to see Mrs. Embury today. She did not receive me as cordially as usual, and I very soon resolved to come away. She detained me, however.

"Would you mind my speaking to you on a certain subject?" she asked with some embarrassment.

I felt myself flush up.

"I do not want to meddle with affairs that don't concern me," she went on, "but Dr. Elliott and I have been intimate friends all our lives. And his disappointment has really distressed me."

One of my moods came on, and I couldn't speak a word.

"You are not at all the sort of a girl I supposed he would fancy," she continued. "He always has said he was waiting to find someone just like his mother, and she is one of the gentlest, meekest, sweetest, and fairest among women."

"You ought to rejoice then that he has escaped the snare," I said, in a husky voice, "and is free to marry his ideal, when he finds her."

"But that is just what troubles me. He is not free. He does not attach himself readily, and I am afraid that it will be a long, long time before he gets over this unlucky passion for you."

"Passion!" I cried contemptuously.

She looked at me with some surprise and then went on.

"Most girls would jump at the chance of getting such a husband."

"I don't know that I particularly care to be classed with 'most girls,' " I replied loftily.

"But if you only knew him as well as I do. He is so noble, so disinterested, and is so beloved by his patients. I could tell you scores of anecdotes about him that would show just what he is."

"Thank you," I said, "I think we have discussed Dr. Elliott quite enough already. I cannot say that he has elevated himself in my opinion by making you take up the cudgels in his defense."

"You do him injustice when you say that," she cried. "His sister, the only person to whom he confided the state of things, begged me to find out, if I could, whether you had any other attachment and if her brother's case was quite hopeless. But I am sorry I undertook the task, as it has annoyed you so much."

I came away a good deal ruffled. When I got home, Mother said she was glad I had been out, at last, for a little recreation and that she wished I did not confine myself to the children. I said that I did not confine myself more than Aunty did.

"But that is different," Mother objected. "She is their own mother, and love helps to bear her burden."

"So it does me," I returned. "I love the children exactly as if they were my own."

"That," she said, "is impossible."

"I certainly do," I persisted.

Mother would not dispute with me, though I wished she would.

"A mother," she went on, "receives her children one at a time and gradually adjusts herself to gradually increasing burdens. But you take a whole houseful upon you at once, and I am sure it is too much for you. You do not look or act like yourself."

"It isn't the children," I said.

"What is it, then?"

"Why, it's nothing," I said pettishly.

"I must say, dear," said Mother, not noticing my manner, "that your wonderful devotion to the children, aside from its effect on your health and temper, has given me great delight."

"I don't see why," I said.

"Very few girls of your age would give up their whole time as you do to such work."

"That is because very few girls are as fond of children as I am. There is no virtue in doing exactly what one likes to do."

"There, go away, you contrary child," said Mother, laughing. "If you won't be praised, you won't."

So I came up here and moped a little. I don't see what ails me.

But there is an undercurrent of peace that is not entirely disturbed by any outside event. In spite of my follies and my shortcomings, I do believe that God loves and pities me and will yet perfect that which concerneth me. It is a great mystery. But so is everything.

DR. ELLIOTT TO MRS. CROFTON:

. . . And now, my dear friend, having issued my usual bulletin of health, you may feel quite at ease about your dear children, and I come to a point in your letter which I would gladly pass over in silence. But this would be but a poor return for the interest you express in my affairs.

Both ladies are devoted to your little flock, and Miss Mortimer seems not to have a thought but for them. The high opinion I formed of her at the outset is more than justified by all I see of her daily, household life. I know what her faults are, for she seems to take delight in revealing them. But I also know her rare virtues and what a wealth of affection she has to bestow on the man who is so happy as to win her heart. But I shall never be that man. Her growing aversion to me makes me dread a summons to your house, and I have hardly manliness enough to conceal the pain this gives me. I entreat you, therefore, never again to press this subject upon me. After all, I would not, if I could, dispense with the ministry of disappointment and unrest.

MRS. CROFTON, IN REPLY:

. . . So she hates you, does she? I am charmed to hear it. Indifference would be an alarming symptom, but good, cordial hatred, or what looks like it, is a most hopeful sign. The next chance you get to see her alone, assure her that you never shall repeat your first offense. If nothing comes of it, I am not a woman and never was one; nor is she.

–*March 25, 1836*–

The New Year and my birthday have come and gone, and this is the first moment I could find for writing down all that has happened.

The day after my last date I was full of serious, earnest thoughts, of new desires to live, without one reserve, for God. I was smarting under the remembrance of my folly at Mrs. Embury's and with a sense of vague disappointment and discomfort and had to fly closer than ever to Him. In the evening I thought I would go to the usual weekly service. It is true I don't like prayer meetings, and that is a bad sign, I am afraid. But I am determined to go where good people go and see if I can't learn to like what they like.

Mother went with me, of course.

What was my surprise to find that Dr. E. was to preside! I had no idea that he was that sort of a man.

The hymns they sang were beautiful and did me good. So was the prayer. If all prayers were like that, I am sure I should like evening meetings as much as I do dislike them. He so evidently spoke to God in it and as if he were used to such speaking.

He then made a little address on the ministry of disappointment, as he called it. He spoke so cheerfully and hopefully that I began to see, almost for the first time, God's reason for the petty trials and crosses that help to make up every day of one's life. He said there were few who were not constantly disappointed with themselves, with their slow progress, their childishness and weakness; disappointed with their friends who, strangely enough, were never quite perfect enough; and disappointed with the world, which was always promising so much and giving so little. Then he urged a wise and patient consent to this discipline, which, if rightly used, would help to temper and strengthen the soul against the day of sorrow and bereavement. But I am not doing him justice in this meager report; there was something almost heavenly in his expression that words cannot describe.

Coming out, I heard someone ask, "Who was that young clergyman?" and the answer, "Oh, that is only a doctor!"

Well! The next week I went again with Mother. We

had hardly taken our seats when Dr. E. marched in with the sweetest looking creature I ever saw. He was so taken up with her that he did not observe either Mother or myself. As she sat by my side I could not see her full face, but her profile was nearly perfect. Her eyes were of that lovely blue one sees in violets and the skies, with long, soft eyelashes, and her complexion was as pure as a baby's. Yet she was not one of your doll beauties; her face expressed both feeling and character. They sang together from the same book, though I offered her a share of mine. Of course, when people do that it can mean but one thing.

So it seems he has forgotten me and consoled himself with this pretty thing. No doubt she is like his mother, that "gentlest, meekest, sweetest, and fairest among women!"

Now if anybody should be sick and he should come here, I thought, what would become of me? I certainly could not help showing that a love that can so soon take up with a new object could not have been a sentiment of much depth.

It is not pleasant to lose even a portion of one's respect and esteem for another.

The next day Mother went to visit an old friend of hers who has a beautiful place outside the city. While I was home without her, I was sitting in the nursery watching the children, and Lucy came with her books to sit with me She always follows me like my shadow. After a while Mrs Embury called. I hesitated a little about trusting the children to Lucy's care, particularly the baby, for though Lucy's prim ways have given her the reputation of being wise beyond her years, I observe that she is apt to get into trouble that a quick-witted child would either avoid or jump out of in a twinkling. However, children are often left to much younger girls, so, with many cautions, I went down, resolving to stay only a few moments.

But I wanted so much to know all about that pretty little friend of Dr. E's that I let Mrs. Embury stay on and on, though not a ray of light did I get for my pains. At last I heard Lucy's step coming downstairs.

"Cousin Katy," she said, entering the room with her usual propriety, "I was seated by the window, engaged with my studies, and the children were playing about, as usual, when suddenly I heard a shriek, and one of them ran past me all in a blaze and—"

I believe I pushed her out of my way as I rushed upstairs, for I took it for granted I should meet the little figure all in a blaze coming to meet me. But I found it wrapped in a blanket, the flames extinguished. Meanwhile, Mrs. Embury had roused the whole house and everybody came running upstairs.

"Get the doctor, some of you," I cried, clasping the poor little writhing form in my arms.

And then I looked to see which of them it was and found it was Aunty's pet lamb, everybody's pet lamb, our little, loving, gentle Emma.

Dr. Elliott must have come on wings for I had no time to be impatient for his arrival. He was as tender as a woman with Emma. We cut off and tore off her clothes wherever the fire had touched her, and he dressed the burns with his own hands. He did not speak a word to me or I to him. This time he did not find it necessary to advise me to control myself. I was as cold and hard as a stone.

But when poor little Emma's piercing shrieks began to subside and she came a little under the influence of some soothing drops he had given her at the outset, I began to feel that sensation in the back of my neck that leads to conquest over the most stubborn and most heroic. I had just time to get Emma into the doctor's arms and then down I went. I got over it in a minute and was up again before anyone had time to come to the rescue. But Dr. E. gave Emma to Mrs. Embury, who had been crying all the time, and said in a low voice, "I beg you will now leave the room and lie down. And do not feel obliged to see me when I visit the child. That annoyance, at least, you should spare yourself."

"No consideration shall make me neglect little Emma," I replied defiantly.

By this time Mrs. Embury had rocked her to sleep and she lay, pale and with an air of complete exhaustion, in her arms.

"You must lie down now, Miss Mortimer," Dr. Elliott said as he rose to go. "I will return in a few hours to see how you both do."

He stood looking at Emma but did not go. Then Mrs. Embury asked the question I had not dared ask.

"Is the poor child in danger?"

"I cannot say; I trust not. Miss Mortimer's presence of mind in extinguishing the flames at once has, I hope, saved its life."

"It was not my presence of mind, it was Lucy's!" I cried eagerly. Oh, how I envied her for being the heroine and for the surprised, delighted smile with which he went and took her hand, saying, "I congratulate you, Lucy! How your mother will rejoice at this!"

I tried to think of nothing but poor little Emma and of the reward Aunty had had for her kindness to Lucy. But I thought of myself and how likely it was that under the same circumstances I should have been beside myself and done nothing. This and many other emotions made me burst out crying.

"Yes, cry, cry with all your heart," said Mrs. Embury, laying Emma gently down and coming to get me into her arms. "It will do you good, poor child!"

She cried with me till at last I could lie down and try to sleep.

Well, the days and the weeks were very long after that.

Dear Mother had a hard time, what with her anxiety about Emma and my crossness and unreasonableness.

Dr. Elliott came and went, came and went. At last he said all danger was over and that our patient little darling would get well. But his visits did not diminish; he came twice and three times every day. Sometimes I hoped he would tell us about his new flame, and sometimes I felt that I could not hear her mentioned. One day Mother was so unwell that I had to help him dress Emma's burns, and I could not help saying:

"Even a mother's gentlest touch, full of love as it is, is almost rough compared with that of one trained to such careful handling as you are."

He looked gratified but said, "I am glad you begin to find that even stones feel sometimes."

Another time something was said about the fickleness of women. Mrs. Embury began it. I fired up, of course.

He seemed astonished at my attack.

"I said nothing," he declared.

"No, but you looked a good many things. Now the fact is women are not fickle. When they lose what they value most, they find it impossible to replace it. But men console themselves with the first good thing that comes along."

I dare say I spoke bitterly, for I was thinking how soon

Ch—, I mean somebody, replaced me in his shallow heart and how, with equal speed, Dr. Elliott had helped himself to a new love.

"I do not like these sweeping assertions," said Dr. Elliott, looking a good deal annoyed.

"I have to say what I think," I persisted.

"It is well to think rightly, then," he said gravely.

"By and by, have you heard from Helen?" Mrs. Embury most irrelevantly asked.

"Yes, I heard yesterday."

"I suppose you will be writing her, then? Will you enclose a little note from me? Or rather let me have the least corner of your sheet?"

I was shocked at her want of delicacy. Of course this Helen must be the new love, and how could a woman with two grains of sense imagine he would want to spare her a part of his sheet!

I felt tired and irritated. As soon as Dr. Elliott had gone, I began to give her a good setting down.

"I could hardly believe my ears," I said, "when I heard you ask to leave to write on Dr. Elliott's sheet."

"No wonder," she said laughing. "I suppose you never knew what it was to have to count every shilling and to deny yourself the pleasure of writing to a friend because of what it would cost. I'm sure I never did till I was married."

"But to ask him to let you help write his love letters," I objected.

"Ah! Is that the way the wind blows?" she cried, nodding her pretty little head. "Well then, let me relieve your mind, my dear, by informing you that this 'love letter' is to his sister, my dearest friend and the sweetest little thing you ever saw."

"Oh!" I said and immediately felt quite rested and quite like myself.

Like myself? And who is she, pray?

Two souls dwell in my poor little body, and which of them is me and which of them isn't it would be hard to tell. This is the way they behave:

Scene 1st

Katy, to the other creature whom I will call Kate—Your mother looks tired, and you have been very cross. Run and put your arms around her and tell her how you love her.

Kate—Oh I can't; it would look queer. I don't like palaver. Besides, who would not be cross who felt as I do?

Scene 2nd

Katy—Little Emma has nothing to do and ought to be amused. Tell her a story, do.

Kate—I am tired and need to be amused myself.

Katy—But the dear little thing is so patient and has suffered so much.

Kate—Well, I have suffered, too. If she had not climbed up on the fender, she would not have got burned.

Scene 3d

Katy—You are very irritable today. You had better go upstairs to your room and pray for patience.

Kate—One can't be always praying. I don't feel like it.

Scene 4th

Katy—You treat Dr. Elliott shamefully. I should think he would really avoid you as you avoid him.

Kate—Don't let me hear his name. I don't avoid him.

Katy—You do not deserve his good opinion.

Kate—Yes, I do.

Scene 5th

Just awake in the morning.

Katy—Oh, dear! How hateful I am! I am cross and selfish and domineering and vain. I think of myself the whole time; I behave like a heroine when Dr. Elliott is present and like a naughty, spoiled child when he is not. Poor Mother! How can she endure me? As to my piety, it is worse than none.

Kate, a few hours later—Well, nobody can deny that I have a real gift in managing children! And I am very lovable, or Mother wouldn't be so fond of me. I am always pleasant unless I am sick or worried, and my temper is not half so hasty as it used to be. I never think of myself but am all the time doing something for others. As to Dr. E., I am thankful to say that I have never stooped to attract him by putting on airs and graces. He sees me just as I am. And I am very devout. I love to read good books and to be with good people. I pray a great deal. The bare thought of doing wrong makes me shudder. Mother is proud of me, and I don't wonder. Very few girls would have behaved as I did when Emma was burned. Perhaps I am not as sweet as some people. I am glad of it. I hate sweet people. I have great strength of character, which is much better, and am certainly very high-toned.

But, my poor Journal, you can't stand any more such stuff, can you? But tell me one thing, am I Katy or am I Kate?

CHAPTER X

*Y*esterday I felt better than I have done since the accident. I ran about the house quite cheerily, for me. I wanted to see Mother for something and flew singing into the parlor, where I had left her shortly before. But she was not there, and Dr. Elliott was. I started back and was about to leave the room, but he detained me.

"Come in, I beg of you," he said, his voice growing hoarser and hoarser. "Let us put a stop to this."

"To what?" I asked, going nearer and nearer and looking up into his face, which was quite pale.

"To your evident terror of being alone with me, of hearing me speak. Let me assure you, once for all, that nothing would tempt me to annoy you by urging myself upon you, as you seem to fear I may be tempted to do. I cannot force you to love me nor would I if I could. If you ever want a friend, you will find one in me. But do not think of me as your lover or treat me as if I were always lying in wait for a chance to remind you of it. That I shall never do, never."

"Oh, no, of course not!" I broke forth, my face all in a

glow and tears of mortification raining down my cheeks. "I knew you did not care for me! I knew you had got over it!"

I don't know which of us began it, I don't think he did and I am sure I did not, but the next moment I was folded all up in his great long arms, and a new life had begun!

Mother opened the door not long after, and seeing what was going on, trotted away on her dear old feet as fast as she could.

–*April 21*–

I am too happy to write journals. To think how we love each other!

Mother behaves beautifully.

–*April 25*–

One does not feel like saying much about it when one is as happy as I am. I walk the street as one treading on air. I fly about the house as on wings. I kiss everybody I see.

Now that I look at Ernest (for he makes me call him so) with unprejudiced eyes, I wonder I ever thought him clumsy. And how ridiculous it was in me to confound his dignity and manliness with age!

It is very odd, however, that such a cautious, well-balanced man should have fallen in love with me that day at Sunday school. And still stranger that with my headlong, impulsive nature I deliberately walked into love with him!

I believe we shall never get through with what we have to say to each other. I am afraid we are rather selfish to leave Mother to herself every evening.

–*Sept. 5*–

This has been a delightful summer. To be sure, we had

to take the children to the country for a couple of months, but Ernest's letters are almost better than Ernest himself. I have written enough to him to fill a dozen books. We are going back to the city now. In his last letter Ernest says he has been home and that his mother is delighted to hear of his engagement. He says, too, that he went to see an old lady, one of the friends of his boyhood, to tell the news to her.

"When I told her," he goes on, "that I found the most beautiful, the noblest, the most loving of human beings, she only said, 'Of course, of course!'

"Now, you know, dear, that it is not at all of course, but the very strangest, most wonderful event in the history of the world!"

And then he described a scene he had just witnessed at the deathbed of a young girl of my own age, who left this world and every possible earthly joy with delight at going to be with Christ, that made him really eloquent. Oh, how glad I am that God has cast in my lot with a man whose whole business is to minister to others! I am sure this will, of itself, keep him unworldly and unselfish. How delicious it is to love such a character, and how happy I shall be to go with him to sickrooms and to dying beds! He has already taught me that lessons learned in such scenes far outweigh in value what books and sermons, even, can teach.

And now, my dear old Journal, let me tell you a secret that has to do with life and not with death.

I am going to be married!

To think that I am always to be with Ernest! To sit at the table with him every day, to pray with him, to go to church with him, to have him all mine! I am sure that there is not another man on earth whom I could love as I love him. The thought of marrying Ch— I mean of having that silly, schoolgirl engagement end in marriage was always repugnant to me. But I give myself to Ernest joyfully and with all my heart.

How good God has been to me! I do hope and pray that this new, this absorbing love has not detached my soul from Him, will not detach it. If I knew it would, could I, should I have courage to cut it off and cast it from me?

–Jan. 16, 1837–

Yesterday was my birthday and today is my wedding day. We meant to celebrate the one with the other, but Sunday would come this year on the fifteenth.

I am dressed and have turned everybody out of this room, where I have suffered so much mortification and experienced so much joy, that before I give myself to Ernest and before I leave home forever, I may once more give myself away to God. I have been too much absorbed in my earthly love and am shocked to find how it fills my thoughts. But I will belong to God. I will begin my married life in His fear, depending on Him to make me an unselfish, devoted wife.

–Jan. 25–

We had a delightful trip after the wedding was over. Ernest proposed to take me to his own home that I might see his mother and sister. He never has said that he wanted them to see me, but his mother is not well. I am heartily glad of it. I mean, I was glad to escape going there to be examined and criticized. Every one of them would pick at me, I am sure, and I don't like to be picked at.

We have a home of our own, and I am trying to take kindly to housekeeping Ernest is away a great deal more than I expected he would be. I am fearfully lonely. Aunty comes to see me as often as she can and I go there almost every day, but that doesn't amount to much. As soon as I can venture to do it, I shall ask Ernest to let me invite Mother to come and live with us. It is not right for her to be left alone so. I hoped he would do that himself. But men are not like women. We think of everything.

—Feb. 16—

Our honeymoon ends today. There hasn't been quite as much honey in it as I expected. I supposed that Ernest would be at home every evening, at least, and that he would read aloud, and have me play and sing, and that we should have delightful times together. But now he has got me he seems satisfied and goes about his business as if he had been married a hundred years. In the morning he goes off to see his list of patients; he is going in and out all day; after dinner we sit down to have a nice talk together, the doorbell invariably rings, and he is called away. Then in the evening he goes and sits in his office and studies; I don't mean every minute, but he certainly spends hours there. Today he brought me such a precious letter from dear Mother! I could not help crying when I read it, it was so kind and loving. Ernest looked amazed; he threw down his paper and came and took me in his arms and asked, "What is the matter, darling?" Then it all came out. I said I was lonely and hadn't been used to spending my evenings all by myself.

"You must get some of your friends to come and see you, poor child," he said.

"I don't want friends," I sobbed out. "I want you."

"Yes, darling; why didn't you tell me so sooner? Of course I will stay with you if you wish it."

"If that is your only reason, I am sure I don't want you," I pouted.

He looked puzzled.

"I really don't know what to do," he said with a most comical look of perplexity. But he went to his office and brought up a pile of fusty old books.

"Now, dear," he said, "we understand each other, I think. I can read here just as well as downstairs. Get your book and we shall be as cozy as possible."

My heart felt sore and dissatisfied. Am I unreasonable and childish? What is married life? An occasional meeting, a kiss here and a caress there? Or is it the sacred union of the twain who walk together side by side, knowing each other's joys and sorrows and going Heavenward hand in hand?

–*Feb. 17*–

Mrs. Embury has been here today. I longed to compare notes with her and find out whether it really is my fault that I am not quite happy. But I could not bear to open my heart to her on so sacred a subject. We had some general conversation, however, which did me good for the time, at least.

She said she thought one of the first lessons a wife should learn is self-forgetfulness. I wondered if she had seen anything in me to call forth this remark. We meet pretty often, partly because our husbands are such good friends, partly because she is as fond of music as I am; and we like to sing and play together, and I never see her that she does not do or say something elevating, something that strengthens my own best purposes and desires. But she knows nothing of my conflict and dismay and never will. Her gentle nature responds at once to holy influences. I feel truly grateful to her for loving me, for she really does love me, and yet she must see my faults.

I should like to know if there is any reason on earth why a woman should learn self-forgetfulness that does not involve a man?

–Feb. 18–

Uncle says he has no doubt he owes his life to Ernest, who, in the face of opposition to other physicians, insisted on his giving up his business and going off to Europe at just the right moment. For his partner, whose symptoms were very like his own, has been stricken down with paralysis and will not recover.

It is very pleasant to hear Ernest praised, and it is a pleasure I have very often, for his friends come to see me and speak of him with rapture. A lady told me that through the long illness of a sweet young daughter of hers, he prayed with her every day, ministering so skillfully to her soul that all fear of death was taken away and she just longed to go, and did go at last, with perfect delight. I think he spoke of her to me once, but he did not tell me that her preparations for death were his work. I could not conceive of him doing that.

–Feb. 24–

Ernest has been gone a week. His mother is worse and he had to go. I wanted to go, too, but he said it was not worth while, as he should have to return directly. Dr. Embury takes charge of his patients during his absence, and Mrs. E. and Aunty and the children come to see me very often. I like Mrs. Embury more and more. She is not so audacious as I am, but I believe she agrees with me more than she will own.

–*Feb. 25*–

Ernest writes that his mother is dangerously ill and seems in great distress. I am mean enough to want all his love myself, while I should hate him if he gave none to her. Poor Ernest! If she should die, he would be sadly afflicted!

–*Feb. 27*–

She died the very day he wrote. How I long to fly to him and to comfort him! I can think of nothing else. I pray day and night that God would make me a better wife.

A letter came from Mother at the same time with Ernest's. She evidently misses me more than she will own. Just as soon as Ernest returns home, I will ask him to let her come and live with us. I am sure he will; he loves her already; and now that his mother has gone, he will find her a real comfort. I am sure she will only make our home happier.

–*Feb. 28*–

Such a dreadful thing is going to happen! I have cried and called myself names by turns all day. Ernest writes that it has been decided to give up the old homestead and scatter the family about among the married sons and daughters. Our share is to be his father and his sister Martha, and he desires me to have two rooms got ready for them at once.

So all the glory and the beauty is snatched out of my married life at one swoop! And it is done by the hand I love best and that I would not have believed could be so unkind.

I am rent in pieces by conflicting emotions and passions. One moment I am all tenderness and sympathy for poor Ernest and ready to sacrifice everything for his pleasure. The next I am bitterly angry with him for disposing of all my happiness in this arbitrary way. If he had let me make common cause with him and share his interests with him, I know I am not so abominably selfish as to feel as I do now. But he forces two perfect strangers upon me and forever shuts our doors against my darling mother. For of course she cannot live with us if they do.

And who knows what sort of people they are? It is not everybody I can get along with, nor is it everybody can get along with me. Now if Helen were coming instead of Martha, that would be some relief. I could love her, I am sure, and she would put up with my ways. But your Martha I am afraid of. Oh, dear, dear, what a nest of scorpions this affair has stirred up within me! Who would believe I could be thinking of my own misery while Ernest's mother, whom he loved so dearly, is hardly in the grave! But I have no heart; I am stony and cold. It is well to have found out just what I am!

Since I wrote that, I have been trying to tell God all about it. But I could not speak for crying. And I have been getting the rooms ready. How many little things I had planned to put in the best one, which I intended for Mother! I have made myself arrange them just the same for Ernest's father. The stuffed chair I have had in my room and enjoyed so much has been rolled in and the Bible with large print placed on the little table near which I had pictured Mother, with her sweet, pale face, sitting year after year. The only thing I have taken away is a copy of Father's portrait. He won't want that!

When I finished this business, I went and shook my fist at the creature I saw in the glass.

"You're beaten!" I cried. "You didn't want to give up the chair, nor your writing table, nor the Bible in which you expect to record the names of your ten children! But you've had to do it, so there!"

–March 3–

They all got here at 7 o'clock last night, just in time for tea. I was so glad to get hold of Ernest once more that I was gracious to my guests, too. The very first thing, however, Ernest annoyed me by calling me Katherine, though he knows I hate that name and want to be called Katy as if I were a lovable person, as I certainly am (sometimes). Of course his father and Martha called me Katherine, too.

His father is even taller, darker, blacker-eyed, blacker-haired than he.

Martha is a spinster.

I had got up a nice little supper for them, thinking they would need something substantial after their journey. And perhaps there was some vanity in the display of dainties that needed the mortification I felt at seeing my guests both push away their plates in apparent disgust. Ernest, too, looked annoyed and expressed some regret that they could find nothing to tempt their appetites.

Martha said something about not expecting much from young housekeepers, which I inwardly resented, for the light, delicious bread had been sent by Aunty, together with other luxuries from her own table; and I knew they were not the handiwork of a young housekeeper but of old Chloe, who has lived in Aunty's and her mother's family twenty years.

Ernest went out as soon as this unlucky repast was over to hear Dr. Embury's report of his patients, and we passed a dreary evening, as my mind was preoccupied with longing for his return. The more I tried to think of something to say, the more I couldn't.

At last Martha asked at what time we breakfasted.

"At half-past seven, precisely," I answered. "Ernest is very punctual about breakfast. The other meals are more irregular."

"That is very late," she returned. "Father rises early and needs his breakfast at once."

I said I would see that he had it as early as he liked, while I foresaw that this would cost me a battle with Sarah, my cook, the divinity who reigns in the kitchen.

"You need not trouble yourself. I will speak to my brother about it," she said.

"Ernest has nothing to do with it," I said quickly.

She looked at me in a speechless way, and then there was a long silence, during which she shook her head a number of times. A last she inquired, "Did you make the bread we had on the table tonight?"

"No, I do not know how to make bread," I said, smiling at her look of horror.

"Not know how to make bread!" she cried.

The very spirit of mischief got into me and made me ask: "Why, can you?"

Now I know there is but one other question I could have asked her that would have been less insulting, and that is:

"Do you know the Ten Commandments?"

A spinster fresh from a farm not know how to make bread, to be sure!

But in a moment I was ashamed and sorry that I had yielded to myself so far as to forget the courtesy due to her as my guest, and one just come from a scene of sorrow, so I rushed across the room, seized her hand, and said eagerly, "Do forgive me! It slipped out before I thought!"

She looked at me in blank amazement, unconscious that there was anything to forgive.

"How you startled me!" she said. "I thought you had suddenly gone crazy."

I went back to my seat crestfallen enough. All this time Ernest's father had sat grim and grave in his corner without a word. But now he spoke.

"At what hour does my son have family worship? I should like to retire. I feel very weary."

Now family worship at night consists in our kneeling down together hand in hand, the last thing before going to bed, and in our own room. The awful thought of changing this sweet, informal habit into a formal one made me reply quickly, "Oh, Ernest is very irregular about it. He is often out in the evening, and sometimes we are up quite late. I hope you never will feel obligated to wait for him."

"I trust I shall do my duty, whatever it costs," was the answer.

Oh, how I wished they would go to bed!

It was not ten o'clock, and I felt tired and restless. When Ernest is out late, I usually lie on the sofa and wait for him and so am bright and fresh when he comes in. But now I had to sit up, and there was no knowing for how long. I poked at the fire and knocked down the shovel and tongs; now I leaned back in my chair and now I leaned forward; and then I listened for his step. At last he came.

"What, are you not all gone to bed?" he asked. As if I could go to bed when I had scarcely seen him a moment since his return!

I explained why we waited, and then we had prayers and escorted our guest to their rooms. When we got back to the parlor, I was thankful to rest my tired soul in Ernest's arms and to hear what little he had to tell about his mother's last hours.

"You must love me more than ever, now," he said, "for I have lost my best friend."

"Yes," I said, "I will." As if that were possible! All the time we were talking I heard the greatest racket overhead, but he did not seem to notice it. I found, this morning, that Martha or her father or both together had changed the positions of every article of furniture in the room, making it look like a fright.

CHAPTER XI

*T*hings are even worse than I expected. Ernest evidently looked at me with his father's eyes (and this father has got the jaundice, or something) and certainly is cooler toward me than he was before he went home. Martha still declines eating more than enough to keep body and soul together and sits at the table with the air of a martyr. Her father lives on crackers and stewed prunes; and when he has eaten them, fixes his melancholy eyes on me, watching every mouthful with an air of plaintive regret that I will consume so much unwholesome food.

Then Ernest positively spends less time with me than ever and sits in his office reading and writing nearly every evening.

Yesterday I came home from an exhilarating walk and a charming call at Aunty's and at the dinner table gave a lively account of some of the children's exploits. Nobody laughed, and nobody made any response; and after dinner Ernest took me aside and said, kindly enough, but still said it, "My little wife must be careful how she runs on in my

father's presence. He has great dread of everything that might be thought levity."

Then all the vials of my wrath exploded and went off.

"Yes, I see how it is," I cried passionately. "You and your father and your sister have got a box about a foot square that you want to squeeze me into. I have seen it ever since they came. And I can tell you it will take more than three of you to do it. There was no harm in what I said— none, whatever. If you only married me for the sake of screwing me down and freezing me up, why didn't you tell me so before it was too late?"

Ernest stood looking at me like one staring at a problem he had got to solve and didn't know where to begin.

"I am very sorry," he said. "I thought you would be glad to have me give you this little hint. Of course I want you to appear your very best before my father and sister."

"My very best is my real self," I cried. "To talk like a woman of forty is unnatural to a girl of my age. If your father doesn't like me, I wish he would go away and not come here putting notions into your head and making you as cold and hard as a stone. Mother liked to have me 'run on' as you call it, and I wish I had stayed with her all my life."

"Do you mean," he asked, very gravely, "that you really wish that?"

"No," I said, "I don't mean it," for his husky, troubled voice brought me to my senses. "All I mean is that I love you so dearly, and you keep my heart feeling so hungry and restless; and then you went and brought your father and sister here and never asked me if I should like it; and you crowded Mother out, and she lives all alone, and it isn't right! I always said that whoever married me had got to marry Mother, and I never dreamed that you would disappoint me so!"

"Will you stop crying and listen to me?" he said.

But I could not stop. The floods of the great deep were broken up at last, and I had to cry. If I could have told my troubles to someone, I could thus have found vent for them; but there was no one to whom I had a right to speak of my husband.

Ernest walked up and down in silence. Oh, if I could have cried on his breast and felt that he loved and pitied me!

At last, as I grew quieter, he came and sat by me.

"This has come upon me like a thunderclap," he said. "I did not know I kept your heart hungry. I did not know you wished your mother to live with us. And I took it for granted that my wife, with her high-toned, heroic character, would sustain me in every duty and welcome my father and sister to our home. I do not know what I can do now. Shall I send them away?"

"No, no!" I cried. "Only be good to me, Ernest, only love me, only look at me with your own eyes, not with other people's. You knew I had faults when you married me; I never tried to conceal them."

"And did you fancy I had none myself?" he asked.

"N—o," I replied. "I saw no faults in you. Everybody said you were such a noble, good man; and you spoke so beautifully one night at an evening meeting!"

"Speaking beautifully is little to the purpose unless one lives beautifully," he said sadly. "And how is it possible that you and I, a Christian man and a Christian woman, are going on and on with such scenes as this? Are you to wear your life out because I have not your frantic way of loving, and am I to be made weary of mine because I cannot satisfy you?"

"But, Ernest," I said, "you used to satisfy me! Oh, how

happy I was in those first days when we were always to-gether and you seemed so fond of me!" I was down on the floor by this time and looking up into his pale, anxious face.

"Dear child," he said, "I do love you, and that more than you know. But you would not have me leave my work and spend my whole time telling you so?"

"You know I am not so silly," I cried. "It is not fair, it is not right to talk as if I were. I ask for nothing unreasonable. I only want those little daily assurances of your affection that I should suppose would be spontaneous if you felt at all toward me as I do to you."

"The fact is," he returned, "I am absorbed in my work. It brings many grave cares and anxieties. I spend most of my time amid scenes of suffering and at dying beds. This makes me seem abstracted and cold, but it does not make you less dear. On the contrary, the sense it gives me of the brevity and sorrowfulness of life makes you doubly precious since it constantly reminds me that sickbeds and dying beds must sooner or later come to our home as to those of others."

In an agony of terror, I clung to him as he uttered these terrible words.

"Oh, Ernest, promise me, promise me that you will not die first," I pleaded.

"Foolish little thing!" he said and was as silly, for a while, as the silliest heart could ask. Then he became serious again.

"Katy," he said, "if you can once make up your mind to the fact that I am an undemonstrative man, not all fire and fury and ecstasy as you are, yet loving you with all my heart, however it may seem, I think you will spare yourself much needless pain—and spare me also."

"But I want you to be demonstrative," I persisted.

"Then you must teach me. And about my father and sister, perhaps we may find some way of relieving you by and by. Meanwhile, try to bear with the trouble they make, for my sake."

"But I don't mind the trouble! Oh, Ernest, how you do misunderstand me! What I mind is their coming between you and me and making you love me less."

By this time there was a call for Ernest—it is a wonder there had not been forty—and he went.

I feel as heartsore as ever. What has been gained by this tempest? Nothing at all! Poor Ernest! How can I worry him so when he is already full of care?

–*March 20*–

I have had such a truly beautiful letter today from dear Mother! She gives up the hope of coming to spend her last years with us with a sweet patience that makes me cry whenever I think of it. What is the secret of this instant and cheerful consent to whatever God will? Oh, that I had it, too! She begs me to be considerate and kind to Ernest's father and sister and constantly remind myself that my Heavenly Father has chosen to give me this care and trial on the very threshold of my married life. I am afraid I have quite lost sight of that in my indignation with Ernest for bringing them here.

–*April 3*–

Martha is closeted with Ernest in his office day and night. They never give me the least hint of what is going on in these secret meetings. Then this morning, Sarah, my good, faithful cook, bounced into my room to give warning. She said she could not live where there were two mistresses giving contrary directions.

"But, really, there is but one mistress," I urged. Then it came out that Martha went down every morning to look after the soapfat and to scrimp in the housekeeping and see that there was no food wasted. I remembered then that she had inquired whether I attended to these details, evidently ranking such duties with saying one's prayers and reading one's Bible.

I flew to Ernest the moment he was at leisure and poured my grievances into his ear.

"Well, dear," he said, "suppose you give up the housekeeping to Martha. She will be far happier and you will be freed from much annoying, petty care."

I bit my tongue lest it should say something and went back to Sarah.

"Suppose Miss Elliott takes charge of the housekeeping and I have nothing to do with it, will you stay?"

"Indeed, and I won't then. I can't bear her, and I won't put up with her nasty, scrimping, pinching ways!"

"Very well. Then you will have to go," I said with great dignity, though just ready to cry. Ernest, on being applied to for wages, undertook to argue the question himself.

"My sister will take the whole charge," he began.

"And may and welcome for all me!" quoth Sarah. "I don't like her and never shall."

"Your liking or disliking her is of no consequence whatever," said Ernest. "You may dislike her as much as you please. But you must not leave us."

"Indeed, and I'm not going to stay and be put upon by her," persisted Sarah. So she has gone. We had to get dinner ourselves; that is to say, Martha did, for she said I got in her way and put her out with my awkwardness. I have been running hither and thither to find some angel who will consent to live in this ill-assorted household. Oh, how different everything is from what I had planned! I wanted a cheerful home, where I should be the center of every joy; a home like Aunty's, without a cloud. But Ernest's father sits, the personification of silent gloom, like a nightmare on my spirits; Martha holds me in disfavor and contempt; Ernest is absorbed in his profession, and I hardly see him. If he wants advice, he asks it of Martha while I sit humbled, degraded, and ashamed, wondering why he ever married me at all. And then come interludes of wild joy when he appears just as he did in the happy days of our bridal trip, and I forget every grievance and hang on his words and look like one intoxicated with bliss.

–*Oct. 2*–

There has been another explosion. I held in as long as I could and then flew into ten thousand pieces. Ernest had got into the habit of helping his father and sister at the table and apparently forgetting me. It seems a little thing, but it chafed and fretted my already irritated soul till at last I was almost beside myself.

Yesterday they all three sat eating their breakfast, and I, with empty plate, sat boiling over and looking on when Ernest brought things to a crisis by saying to Martha, "If you can find time today, I wish you would go with me for half an hour or so. I want to consult you about—"

"Oh!" I said, rising with my face all in a flame. "Do not trouble yourself to go out in order to escape me. I can leave the room and you can have your secrets to yourselves as you do your breakfast!"

I don't know which struck me most, Ernest's appalled, grieved look or the glance exchanged between Martha and her father.

He did not hinder my leaving the room, and I went upstairs, as pitiable an object as could be seen. I heard him go to his office, then take his hat and set forth on his rounds. What wretched hours I passed, thus left alone! One moment I reproached myself, the next I was indignant at the long series of offenses that had led to this disgraceful scene.

At last Ernest came.

He looked concerned and a little pale.

"Oh, Ernest!" I cried, running to him. "I am so sorry I spoke to you as I did! But, indeed, I cannot stand the way things are going on; I am wearing all out. Everybody speaks of my growing thin. Feel of my hands. They burn like fire."

"I knew you would be sorry, dear," he said. "Yes, your hands are hot, poor child."

There was a long dreadful silence. And yet I was speaking and perhaps he was. I was begging and beseeching God not to let us drift apart, not to let us lose one jot or tittle of our love for each other, to enable me to understand my dear, dear husband and make him understand me.

Then Ernest began.

"What was it vexed you, dear? What is it you can't stand? Tell me. I am your husband, I love you, I want to make you happy."

"Why, you are having so many secrets that you keep from me; and you treat me as if I were only a child, consulting Martha about everything. And of late you seem to have forgotten that I am at the table and never help me to anything!"

"Secrets!" he echoed. "What possible secrets can I have?"

"I don't know," I said, sinking wearily back on the

sofa. "Indeed, Ernest, I don't want to be selfish or exacting, but I am very unhappy."

"Yes, I see it, poor child. And if I have neglected you at the table I do not wonder you are out of patience. I know how it has happened. While you were pouring out the coffee, I busied myself in caring for my father and Martha and so forgot you. I do not give this as an excuse but as a reason. I have really no excuse and am ashamed of myself."

"Don't say that, darling," I cried. "It is I who ought to be ashamed for making such an ado about a trifle."

"It is not a trifle," he said. "And now to the other points. I dare say I have been careless about consulting Martha. But she has always been a sort of oracle in our family, and we all look up to her, and she is so much older than you. Then as to the secrets. Martha comes to my office to help me look over my books. I have been careless about my accounts, and she has kindly undertaken to attend to them for me."

"Could not I have done that?"

"No; why should your little head be troubled about money matters? But to go on. I see that it was thoughtless in me not to tell you what we were about. But I am greatly perplexed and harassed in many ways. Perhaps you would feel better to know all about it. I have only kept it from you to spare you all the anxiety I could."

"Oh, Ernest," I said, "ought not a wife share in all her husband's cares?"

"No," he returned, "but I will tell you all that is annoying me now. My father was in business in our native town and went on prosperously for many years. Then the tide turned—he met with loss after loss till nothing remained but the old homestead, and on that there was a mortgage. We concealed the state of things from my mother; her health was delicate, and we never let her know a trouble we could spare her. Now she has gone, and we have found it necessary to sell our old home and to divide and scatter the family. My father's mental distress when he found others suffering from his own losses threw him into the state in which you see him now. I have, therefore, assumed his debts and with God's help hope in time to pay them to the uttermost farthing. It will be necessary for us to live economically until this is done. There are two pressing cases that I am trying to meet at once. This has given me a preoccupied air, I have no doubt, and made you suspect and misunderstand me. But now you know the whole, my darling."

I felt my injustice and childish folly very keenly and told him so.

"But I think, dear Ernest," I added, "if you will not be hurt at my saying so, that you have led me to it by not letting me share at once in your cares. If you had, at the outset, just told me the whole story, you would have enlisted my sympathies in your father's behalf and in your own. I should have seen the reasonableness of your breaking up the old home and bringing them here, and it would have taken off the edge of my bitter, bitter disappointment about my mother."

"I feel sorry about that," he said. "It would be a real pleasure to have her here. But as things are now, she could not be happy with us."

"There is no room," I put in.

"No, I am truly sorry. And now, my dear little wife must have patience with her stupid, blundering old husband; and we'll start together once more, fair and square. Don't wait, next time, till you are so full that you boil over;

the moment I annoy you by my inconsiderate ways, come right and tell me."

So then I called myself all the horrid names I could think of.

"May I ask one thing more, now we are upon the subject?" I said at last. "Why couldn't your sister Helen have come here instead of Martha?"

He smiled a little.

"In the first place, Helen would be perfectly crushed if she had the care of Father in his present state. She is too young to have such responsibility. In the second place, my brother John, with whom she has gone to live, has a wife who would be quite overwhelmed by my father and Martha. She is one of those little, tender, soft souls one could crush with one's fingers. Now you are not of that sort; you have force of character enough to enable you to live with them while maintaining your own dignity and remaining yourself in spite of circumstances."

"I thought you admired Martha above all things and wanted me to be exactly like her."

"I do admire her, but I do not want you to be like anybody but yourself."

"But you nearly killed me by suggesting that I should take heed how I talked in your father's presence."

"Yes, dear, it was very stupid of me; but my father has a standard of excellence in his mind by which he tests every woman. This standard is my mother. She had none of your life and fun in her and perhaps would not have appreciated your droll way of putting things any better than he and Martha do."

I could not help sighing a little when I thought what sort of people were watching my every word.

"There is nothing amiss to my mind," Ernest continued, "in your gay talk; but my father has his own views as to what constitutes a religious character and cannot understand that real earnestness and real, genuine mirthfulness are consistent with each other."

He had to go now, and we parted as if for a week's separation, this one talk had brought us so near to each other. I understand him now as I never have done and feel that he has given me as real a proof of his affection by unlocking the door of his heart and letting me see its cares as I give him with my wild pranks and caresses and foolish speeches. How truly noble it is in him to take up his father's burden in this way! I must contrive to help to lighten it.

CHAPTER XII

*A*unty has put me in the way of doing that. I could not tell her the whole story, of course, but I made her understand that Ernest needed money for a generous purpose and that I wanted to help him in it. She said the children needed both music and drawing lessons and that she should be delighted if I would take them in hand. Aunty does not care a fig for accomplishments, but I think I am right in accepting her offer as the children ought to learn to sing and to play and to draw. Of course I cannot have them come here as Ernest's father could not bear the noise they would make; besides, I want to take Ernest by surprise and keep the whole thing a secret.

–Nov. 14–

I have seen by the way Martha draws down the corners of her mouth of late that I am unusually out of favor with her. This evening, Ernest, coming home quite late, found me lolling back in my chair, idling after a hard day's work with my little cousins and Martha sewing nervously away at the rate of ten knots an hour, which is the first pun I ever made.

"Why will you sit up and sew at such a rate, Martha?" he asked.

She twitched at her thread, broke it, and began with a new one before she replied.

"I suppose you find it convenient to have a whole shirt to your back."

I saw then that she was making his shirts! It made me both hot and cold at once. What must Ernest think of me?

It is plain enough what he thinks of her for he said, quite warmly for him, "This is really too kind."

What right has she to prowl round among Ernest's things and pry into the state of his wardrobe? If I had not had my time so broken up giving lessons, I should have found out that he needed new shirts and set to work on them. Though I must own I hate shirt making. I could not help showing that I felt aggrieved. Martha defended herself by saying that she knew young people would be young people and would gad about, shirts or no shirts. Now it is not her fault that she thinks I waste my time gadding about, but I am just as angry with her as if it were. Oh, why couldn't I have had Helen to be a pleasant companion and friend to me instead of this old—well, I won't say what.

And really, with so much to make me happy, what would become of me if I had no trials?

–*Nov. 15*–

Today Martha has a house cleaning mania and has dragged me into it. In spite of my resolution not to get under her thumb, I have somehow let her rule and reign over me to such an extent that I can hardly sit up long enough to write this. Does the whole duty of woman consist in keeping her house distressingly clean and prim; in making and baking and preserving and pickling; in climbing to the top shelves of closets lest haply a little dust should lodge there; and getting down on her hands and knees to inspect the carpet? The truth is there is not one point of sympathy between Martha and myself, not one. One would think that our love of Ernest would furnish it. But her love aims at the abasement of her character and mine at its elevation. She thinks I should bow down to and worship him, jump up and offer him my chair when he comes in, feed him with every unwholesome dainty he fancies, and feel myself honored by his acceptance of these services. I think it is for him to rise and offer me a seat because I am a woman and his wife and that a silly subservience on my part is degrading to him and to myself. And I am afraid I make known these sentiments to her in a most unpalatable way.

–Nov. 18–

Oh, I am so happy that I sing for joy! Dear Ernest has given me such a delightful surprise! He says he has persuaded James to come and spend his college days here and finally study medicine with him. Dear, darling old James! He is to be here tomorrow. He is to have the little hall bedroom fitted up for him, and he will be here several years. Next to having Mother, this is the nicest thing that could happen. We love each other so dearly and get along so beautifully together. I wonder how he'll like Martha with her grim ways and Ernest's father with his melancholy ones.

–Nov. 30–

James has come, and the house already seems lighter

and cheerier. He is not in the least annoyed by Martha or her father; and though he is as jovial as the day is long, they actually seem to like him. True to her theory on the subject, Martha invariably rises at his entrance and offers him her seat! He pretends not to see it and runs to get one for her. Then she takes comfort in seeing him consume her good things, since his gobbling them down is a sort of tacit tribute to their merits.

Mrs. Embury was here today. She says there is not much the matter with Ernest's father, that he has only got the hypo. I don't know exactly what this is, but I believe it is thinking something is the matter with you when there isn't. At any rate, I put it to you, my dear old Journal, whether it is pleasant to live with people who behave in this way?

In the first place all he talks about is his fancied disease. He gets book after book from the office and studies and ponders his case till he grows quite yellow. One day he says he has found out the seat of his disease to be the liver and changes his diet to meet that view of the case. Martha has to do him up in mustard, and he takes kindly to blue pills. In a day or two he finds his liver is all right but that his brain is all wrong. The mustard goes now to the back of his neck, and he takes solemn leave of us all with the assurance that his last hour has come. Finding that he survives the night, however, he transfers the seat of his disease to the heart, spends hours in counting his pulse, refuses to take exercise lest he should bring on palpitations, and warns us all to prepare to follow him. Everybody who comes in has to hear the whole story; everyone prescribes something, and he tries each remedy in turn. These all failing to reach his case, he is plunged into tenfold gloom. He complains that God has cast him off forever and that his sins are like the sands of the sea for number. I am such a goose that I listen to all these varying moods and symptoms with the solemn conviction that he is going to die immediately. I bathe his head, and count his pulse, and fan him, and take down his dying depositions for Ernest's solace after he has gone. And I talk theology to him by the hour while Martha bakes and brews in the kitchen or makes mince pies, which, after eating, one might give him the whole Bible at one dose without the smallest effect.

Today I stood by his chair, holding his head and whispering such consoling passages as I thought might comfort him, when James burst in, singing and tossing his cap in the air.

"Come here, young man, and hear my last testimony. I am about to die. The end draws near," were the sepulchral words that made James bring his song to an abrupt close.

"I shall take it very ill of you, sir," quoth James, "if you go and die before giving me that cane you promised me."

Who could die decently under such circumstances? The poor old man revived immediately but looked a good deal injured. After James had gone out, he said, "It is very painful to one who stands on the very verge of the eternal world to see the young so thoughtless."

"But James is not thoughtless," I said. "It is only his merry way."

"Daughter Katherine," he went on, "you are very kind to the old man, and you will have your reward. But I wish I could feel sure of your state before God. I greatly fear you deceive yourself and that the ground of your hope is delusive."

I felt the blood rush to my face. At first I was staggered

a good deal. But is a mortal man who cannot judge of his own state to decide mine? It is true he sees my faults; anybody can who looks. But he does not see my prayers or my tears of shame and sorrow. He does not know how many hasty words I repress, how earnestly I am aiming, all the day long, to do right in all the little details of life. He does not know that it costs my fastidious nature an appeal to God every time I kiss his poor old face and that what would be an act of worship in him is an act of self-denial in me. How should he? The Christian life is a hidden life, known only by the eye that seeth in secret. And I do believe this life is mine.

Up to this time I have contrived to get along without calling Ernest's father by name. I mean now to make myself turn over a new leaf.

—December 7—

James is my perpetual joy and pride. We read and sing together, just as we used to do in our old schooldays. Martha sits by with her work, grimly approving; for is he not a man? And, as if my cup of felicity were not full enough, I am to have my dear old pastor come here to settle over this church, and I shall once more hear his beloved voice in the pulpit. Ernest has managed the whole thing. He says the state of Dr. C.'s health makes the change quite necessary and that he can avail himself of the best surgical advice this city affords, in case his old difficulties recur. I rejoice for myself and for this church, but Mother will miss him sadly.

I am leading a very busy, happy life, only I am, perhaps, working a little too hard. What with my scholars, the extra amount of housework Martha contrives to get out of me, the practicing I must keep up if I am to teach, and the many steps I have to take, I have not only no idle moments, but none too many for recreation. Ernest is so busy himself that he fortunately does not see what a race I am running.

–*January 16, 1838*–

The first anniversary of our wedding day, and like all days, has had its lights and its shades. I thought I would celebrate it in such a way as to give pleasure to everybody and spent a good deal of time in getting up a little gift for each from Ernest and myself. And I took special pains to have a good dinner, particularly for Father. Yes, I had made up my mind to call him by that sacred name for this first time today, cost what it may. But he shut himself up in his room directly after breakfast, and when dinner was ready, refused to come down. This cast a gloom over us all. Then Martha was nearly distracted because a valuable dish has been broken in the kitchen, and she could not recover her equanimity at all. Worst of all, Ernest, who is not in the least sentimental, never said a word about our wedding day and didn't give me a thing! I have kept hoping all day that he would make me some little present, no matter how small, but now it is too late; he has gone out to be gone all night, probably, and thus ends the day, an utter failure.

I feel a good deal disappointed. Besides, when I look back over this, my first year of married life, I do not feel satisfied with myself at all. I can't help feeling that I have been selfish and unreasonable toward Ernest in a great many ways and as contrary to have felt a good deal of secret contempt for his father, with his moods and tenses, his pill boxes and his plasters, his feastings and his fastings. I do not understand how a Christian can make such slow progress as I do and how old faults can hang on so.

If I had made any real progress, should I not be sensible of it?

I have been reading over the early part of this journal, and when I came to the conversation I had with Mrs. Cabot, in which I made a list of my wants, I was astonished that I could ever have had such contemptible ones. Let me think what I really and truly most want now.

First of all, then, if God should speak to me at this moment and offer to give just one thing and that alone, I should say without hesitation, Love to Thee, O my Master!

Next to that, if I could have one thing more, I would choose to be a thoroughly unselfish, devoted wife. Down in my secret heart I know there lurks another wish, which I am ashamed of. It is that in some way or other, some right way, I could be delivered from Martha and her father. I shall never be any better while they are here to tempt me!

—February 1—

Ernest spoke today of one of his patients, a Mrs. Campbell, who is a great sufferer but whom he describes as the happiest, most cheerful person he ever met. He rarely speaks of his patients. Indeed, he rarely speaks of anything. I felt strangely attracted by what he said of her and asked so many questions that at last he proposed to take me to see her. I caught at the idea very eagerly and have just come home from the visit greatly moved and touched. She is confined to her bed and is quite helpless, and at times her sufferings are terrible. She received me with a sweet smile, however, and led me on to talk more of myself than I ought to have done. I wish Ernest had not left me alone with her so that I should have had the restraint of his presence.

–Feb. 14–

I am so fascinated with Mrs. Campbell that I cannot help going to see her again and again. She seems to me like one whose conflict and dismay are all over and who looks on other human beings with an almost divine love and pity. To look at life as she does, to feel as she does, to have such a personal love for Christ as she has, I would willingly go through every trial and sorrow. When I told her so, she smiled a little sadly.

"Much as you envy me," she said, "my faith is not yet so strong that I do not shudder at the thought of a young enthusiastic girl like you going through all I have done in order to learn a few simple lessons which God was willing to teach me sooner and without the use of a rod, if I had been ready for them."

"But you are so happy now," I said.

"Yes, I am happy," she replied, "and such happiness is worth all it costs. If my flesh shudders at the remembrance of what I have endured, my faith sustains God through the whole. But tell me a little more about yourself, my dear. I should so love to give you a helping hand if I might."

"You know," I began, "dear Mrs. Campbell, that there are some trials that cannot do us any good. They only call out all there is in us that is unlovely and severe."

"I don't know of any such trials," she replied.

"Suppose you had to live with people who were perfectly uncongenial, who misunderstood you, and who were always getting into your way as stumbling blocks?"

"If I were living with them and they made me unhappy, I would ask God to relieve me of this trial if He thought it best. If He did not think it best, I would then try to find out the reason. He might have two reasons. One would be the good they might do me. The other, the good I might do them."

"But in the case I was supposing, neither party can be of the least use to the other."

"You forget perhaps the indirect good one may gain by living with uncongenial, tempting persons. First such people do good by the very self-denial and self-control their mere presence demands. Then, their making one's home less homelike and perfect than it would be in their absence may help to render our real home in heaven more attractive."

"But suppose one cannot exercise self-control and is always flying out and flaring up?" I objected.

"I should say that a Christian who was always doing that," she replied, gravely, "was in pressing need of just the trial God sent when He shut that person up to such a life of hourly temptation. We only know ourselves and what we really are when the force of circumstances brings us out."

"It is very mortifying and painful to find how weak one is."

"That is true. But our mortifications are some of God's best physicians and do much toward healing our pride and self-conceit."

"Do you really think, then, that God deliberately appoints to some of His children a lot where their worst passions are excited, with a desire to bring good out of this seemingly evil? Why, I have always supposed the best thing that could happen to me, for instance, would be to have a home exactly to my mind; a home where all were forbearing, loving, and good-tempered, a sort of little heaven below."

"If you have not such a home, my dear, are you sure it is not partly your own fault?"

"Of course it is my own fault. Because I am very

quick-tempered, I want to live with good-tempered people."

"That is very benevolent in you," she said archly. I colored but went on.

"Oh, I know I am selfish. And therefore I want to live with those who are not so. I want to live with persons to whom I can look for an example and who will constantly stimulate me to something higher."

"But if God chooses quite another lot for you, you may be sure that He sees that you need something totally different from what you want. You said just now that you would gladly go through any trial in order to attain a personal love for Christ that should become the ruling principle of your life. Now as soon as God sees this desire in you, is He not king, is He not wise in appointing such trials as He knows will lead to this end?"

I meditated long before I answered. Was God really asking me not merely to let Martha and her father live with me on sufferance, but to rejoice that He had seen fit to let them harass and embitter my domestic life?

"I thank you for your suggestion," I said at last.

"I want to say one thing more," Mrs. Campbell resumed after another pause. "We look at our fellow men too much from the standpoint of our own prejudices. They may be wrong, they may have their faults and foibles, they may call out all the meanest and most hateful in us. But they are not all wrong; they have their virtues, and when they excite our bad passions by their own, they may be as ashamed and sorry as we are irritated. And I think some of the best, most contrite, most useful of men and women, whose prayers prevail with God and bring down blessings into the homes in which they dwell, often possess unlovely traits that furnish them with their best discipline. The very fact that they are ashamed of themselves drives them to God; they feel safe in His presence. And while they lie in the very dust of self-confusion at His feet, they are dear to Him and have power with Him."

"That is a comforting word, and I thank you for it," I said. My heart was full, and I longed to stay and hear her talk on. But I had already exhausted her strength. On the way home I felt as I suppose people do when they have caught a basket full of fish. I always am delighted to catch a new idea. I thought I would get all the benefit out of Martha and her father; and as I went down to tea after taking off my things, I felt like a holy martyr who had as good as won a crown.

I found, however, that the butter was horrible. Martha had insisted that she alone was capable of selecting that article and had ordered a quantity from her own village that I could not eat myself and was ashamed to have on my table. I pushed back my plate in disgust.

"I hope, Martha, that you have not ordered much of this odious stuff!" I cried.

Martha replied that it was of the very first quality and appealed to her father and Ernest, who both agreed with her, which I thought very unkind and unjust. I rushed into a hot debate on the subject, during which Ernest maintained that ominous silence that indicates his not being pleased, and that irritated and led me on. I would far rather he should say, "Katy, you are behaving like a child, and I wish you would stop talking."

"Martha," I said, "you will persist that the butter is good because you ordered it. If you will only own that, I won't say another word."

"I can't say it," she returned. "Mrs. Jones's butter is

invariably good. I never heard it found fault with before. The trouble is you are so hard to please."

"No, I am not. And you can't convince me that if the buttermilk is not perfectly worked out, the butter could be fit to eat."

This speech I felt to be a masterpiece. It was time to let her know how learned I was on the subject of butter, though I wasn't brought up to make it or see it made.

But here Ernest put in a little oil.

"I think you are both right," he said. "Mrs. Jones makes good butter, but just this once she failed. I dare say it won't happen again, and meanwhile this can be used for making seedcakes and we can get a new supply."

This was his masterpiece! A whole firkin of butter made up into seedcakes!

Martha turned to encounter him on the head, and I slipped off to my room to look, with a miserable sense of disappointment, at my folly and weakness in making so much ado about nothing. I find it hard to believe that it can do me good to have people live with me who like rancid butter and who disagree with me in everything else.

CHAPTER XIII

*A*unty sent for us all to dine with her today to celebrate Lucy's fifteenth birthday. Ever since Lucy behaved so heroically in regard to little Emma, really saving her life, Ernest says, Aunty seems to feel that she cannot do enough for her. The child has taken the most unaccountable fancy to me, strangely enough, and when we got there she came to meet me with something like cordiality.

"Mamma permits me to be the bearer of agreeable news," she said, "because this is my birthday. A friend of whom you are very fond has just arrived and is impatient to embrace you."

"To embrace me?" I cried. "You foolish child!" And the next moment I found myself in my mother's arms!

The despised Lucy had been the means of giving this pleasure. It seems that Aunty had told her she should choose her own birthday treat and that after solemn meditation, she had decided that to see dear Mother again would be the most agreeable thing she could think of. I have never told you, dear Journal, why I did not go home last summer and never shall. If you choose to fancy that I couldn't afford it, you can!

Well! Wasn't it nice to see Mother and to read in her dear, loving face that she was satisfied with her poor, wayward Katy and fond of her as ever! I only longed for Ernest's coming, that she might see us together and see how he loved me.

He came; I rushed out to meet him and dragged him in. But it seemed as if he had grown stupid and awkward. All through the dinner I watched for one of those loving glances that would proclaim to Mother the good understanding between us, but I watched in vain.

"It will come by and by," I thought. "When we get by ourselves, Mother will see how fond of me he is." But "by and by" it was just the same. I was preoccupied, and Mother asked me if I were well. It was all very foolish, I dare say, and yet I did want to have her know that with all my faults he still loves me. Then, besides the disappointment, I have to reproach myself for misunderstanding poor Lucy as I have done. Because she was not all fire and fury like myself, I need not have assumed that she had no heart. It is just like me; I hope I shall never be so severe in my judgment again.

–*April 30*–

Mother has just gone. Her visit has done me a world of good. She found out something to like in Father at once and then something good in Martha. She says Father's sufferings are real, not fancied, that his error is not knowing where to locate his disease, and is starving one week and overeating the next. She charged me not to lay up future misery for myself by misjudging him now and to treat him as a daughter ought without the smallest regard to his appreciation of it. Then as to Martha, she declares that I have no idea how much she does to reduce our expenses, to keep the house in order, and relieve us from care. "But, Mother," I said, "did you notice what horrid butter we have? And it is all her doing."

"But the butter won't last forever," she replied. "Don't make yourself miserable about such a trifle. For my part, it is a great relief to me to know that with your delicate health you have this tower of strength to lean on."

"But my health is not delicate, Mother."

"You certainly look pale and thin."

"Oh, well," I said, whereupon she fell to giving me all sorts of advice about getting up on step ladders, and climbing on chairs, and sewing too much, and all that.

–*June 15*–

The weather, or something, makes me rather languid and stupid. I begin to think that Martha is not an entire nuisance in the house. I have just been to see Mrs. Campbell. In answer to my routine lamentations, she took up a book and read me what was called, as nearly as I can remember, "Four steps that lead to peace."

"Be desirous of doing the will of another, rather than thine own."

"Choose always to have less, rather than more."

"Seek always the lowest place, and to be inferior to every one."

"Wish always, and pray, that the will of God may be wholly fulfilled in thee."

I was much struck with these directions; but I said despondently, "If peace can only be found at the end of such hard roads, I am sure I shall always be miserable."

"Are you miserable now?" she asked.

"Yes, just now I am. I do not mean that I have no happiness; I mean that I am in a disheartened mood, weary of going round and round in circles, committing the same sins, uttering the same confessions, and making no advance."

"My dear," she said after a time, "have you a perfectly distinct, settled view of what Christ is to the human soul?"

"I do not know. I understand, of course, more or less perfectly that my salvation depends on Him alone; it is His gift."

"But do you see with equal clearness that your sanctification must be as fully His gift as your salvation is?"

"No," I said after a little thought. "I have had a feeling that He has done His part and now I must do mine."

"My dear," she said with much tenderness and feeling, "then the first thing you have to do is to learn Christ."

"But how?"

"On your knees, my child, on your knees!" She was tired, and I came away; and I have indeed been on my knees.

–July 1–

I think that I do begin, dimly it is true, but really, to understand that this terrible work that I was trying to do myself is Christ's work and must be done and will be done by Him. I take some pleasure in the thought and wonder why it has all this time been hidden from me, especially after what Dr. C. said in his letter. But I get hold of this idea in a misty, unsatisfactory way. If Christ is to do all, what am I to do? And have I been told over and over again that the Christian life is one of conflict and that I am to fight like a good soldier?

–August 5–

Dr. Cabot has come just as I need him most. I long for one of those good talks with him that always used to strengthen me so. I feel a perfect weight of depression that makes me a burden to myself and to poor Ernest, who, after visiting sick people all day, needs to come home to a cheerful wife. But he comforts me with the assurance that this is merely physical despondency and that I shall get over it by and by. How kind, how even tender he is! My heart is getting all it wants from him, only I am too stupid to enjoy him as I ought. Father, too, talks far less about his own bad feelings and seems greatly concerned at mine. As to Martha, I have done trying to get sympathy or love from her. She cannot help it, I suppose, but she is very hard and dry toward me; and I feel such a longing to throw myself on her mercy and to have one little smile to assure me that she has forgiven me for being Ernest's wife and so different from what she would have chosen for him.

DR. ELLIOTT TO MRS. MORTIMER

October 4, 1838

My dear Katy's Mother:—You will rejoice with us when I tell you that we are the happy parents of a very fine little boy. My dearest wife sends "an ocean of love" to you and says she will write herself tomorrow. That I shall not be very likely to allow, as you will imagine. She is doing extremely well, and we have everything to be grateful for.

Your affectionate Son,
J.E. Elliott

MRS. CROFTON TO MRS. MORTIMER:

I am sure, my dear sister, that the doctor has not written you more than five lines about the great event that has made such a stir in our domestic circle. So I must try to supply the details you will want to hear . . . I need not add that our darling Katy behaved nobly. Her self-forgetfulness and consideration for others were really beautiful throughout the whole scene. The doctor may well be proud of her, and I took care to tell him so in presence of that dreadful sister of his. I never met so angular, so uncompromising a person as she is in all my life. She does not understand Katy and never can, and I find it hard to realize that living with such a person can furnish a wholesome discipline, which is even more desirable than the most delightful home. And yet I know that this is true in the abstract, but I see that it is so in the actual fact. Katy is acquiring both self-control and patience, and her Christian character is developing in a way that amazes me. I cannot but hope that God will, in time, deliver her from this trial; indeed, I feel sure that when it had done its beneficent work, He will do so. Martha Elliott is a good woman, but her goodness is without grace or beauty. She takes excellent care of Katy, keeps her looking as if she had just come out of a bandbox, as the saying is, and always has her room in perfect order. But one misses the loving word, the reassuring smile, the delicate, thoughtful little forbearance that ought to adorn every sickroom and light it up with genuine sunshine. There is one comfort about it, however, and that is that I can spoil dear Katy to my heart's content.

As to the baby, he is a fine little fellow, and his mother is so happy in him that she can afford to do without some other pleasures. I shall write again in a few days. Meanwhile, you may rest assured that I love your Katy almost as well as you do and shall be with her most of the time till she is quite herself again.

JAMES TO HIS MOTHER:

Of course there never was such a baby before on the face of the earth. Katy is so nearly wild with joy that you can't get her to eat or sleep or do any of the proper things that her charming sister-in-law thinks becoming under the circumstances. You never saw anything so pretty in your life as she is now. I hope the doctor is as much in love with her as I am. He is the best fellow in the world and Katy is just the wife for him.

–*Nov. 4*–

My darling baby is a month old today. I never saw such a splendid child. I love him so that I lie awake nights to watch him. Martha says, in her dry way, that I had better show my love by sleeping and eating for him, and Ernest says I shall as soon as I get stronger. But I don't get strong, and that discourages me.

–*Nov. 26*–

I begin to feel rather more myself and as if I could write with less labor. I have had in these few past weeks such a revelation of suffering and such a revelation of joy as mortal mind can hardly conceive of. The world I live in now is a new world, a world full of suffering that leads to unutterable felicity. Oh, this precious, precious baby! How can I thank God enough for giving him to me!

I see now why He has put some thorns into my domestic life; but for them I should be too happy to live. It does now seem just the moment to complain, and yet, as I can speak to no one, it is a relief, a great relief, to write about my trials. During my whole sickness, Martha has been so hard, so cold, so unsympathizing that sometimes it has seemed as if my cup of trial could not hold another drop. She routed me out of bed when I was so languid that everything seemed a burden and when sitting up made me faint away. I heard her say to herself that I had no constitution and had no business to be married. The worst of all is that during that dreadful night before baby came, she kept asking Ernest to lie down and rest and was sure he would kill himself and all that, while she had not one word of pity for me. But, oh, why need I let this rankle in my heart! Why cannot I turn my thoughts entirely to my darling baby, my dear husband, and all the other sources of joy that make my home a happy one in spite of this one discomfort! I hope I am learning some useful lessons from my joys and from my trials and that both will serve to make me in earnest and to keep me so.

–Dec. 4–

We have had a great time about poor baby's name. I expected to call him Raymond, for my own dear father, as a matter of course. It seemed a small gratification for Mother in her loneliness. Dear Mother! How little I have known all these years what I cost her! But it seems there has been a Jotham in the family ever since the memory of man, each eldest son handing down his father's name to the next in descent, and Ernest's real name is Jotham Ernest—of all the extraordinary combinations! His mother would add the latter name in spite of everything. Ernest behaved very well through the whole affair and said he had no feeling about it all. But he was so gratified when I decided to keep up the family custom that I feel rewarded for the sacrifice.

Father is in one of his gloomiest moods. As I sat caressing baby today, he said to me, "Daughter Katherine, I trust you make it a subject of prayer to God that you may be kept from idolatry."

"No, Father," I returned, "I never do. An idol is something one puts in God's place, and I don't put baby there."

He shook his head and said the heart is deceitful above all things and desperately wicked.

"I have heard Mother say that we might love an earthly object as much as we pleased if we only love God better." I might have added, but of course I didn't, that I prayed every day that I might love Ernest and baby better and better. Poor Father seemed puzzled and troubled by what I did say, and after musing awhile, went on thus: "The Almighty is a great and terrible Being. He cannot bear a rival; He will have the whole heart or none of it. When I see a young woman so absorbed in a created being as you are in that infant and in your other friends, I tremble for you, I tremble for you!"

"But, Father," I persisted, "God gave me this child, and He gave me my heart, just as it is."

"Yes; and that heart needs renewing."

"I hope it is renewed," I replied. "But I know there is a great work still to be done in it. And the more effectually it is done, the more loving I shall grow. Don't you see, Father? Don't you see that the more Christ-like I become, the more I shall be filled with love for every living thing?"

He shook his head but pondered long, as he always does, on whatever he considers audacious. As for me, I am vexed with my presumption in disputing with him and am sure, too, that I was trying to show off what little wisdom I have picked up. Besides, my mountain does not stand so strong as it did. Perhaps I am making idols out of Ernest and the baby.

–*January 16, 1839*–

This is our second wedding day. I did not expect much from it after last year's failure. Father was very gloomy at breakfast and retired to his room directly after it. No one could get in to make his bed, and he would not come down to dinner. I wonder Ernest lets him go on so. But his rule seems to be to let everybody have their own way. He certainly lets me have mine. After dinner he gave me a book I have been wanting for some time and had asked him for— *The Imitation of Christ.* Ever since that day at Mrs. Campbell's, I have felt that I should like it, though I did think, in old times, that it preached too hard a doctrine. I read aloud to him the "Four steps to peace"; he said they were admirable and then took it from me and began reading to himself here and there. I felt the precious moments when I had got him all to myself were passing away and was becoming quite out of patience with him when the words, "Constantly seek to have less, rather than more," flashed into my mind. I suppose this direction had reference to worldly goods, but I despise money and despise people who love it. The riches I crave are not silver and gold, but my husband's love and esteem. And of these must I desire to have less rather than more? I puzzled myself over this question in vain, but when I silently prayed to be satisfied with just what God chose to give me of the wealth I crave, yes, hunger and thirst for, I certainly felt a sweet content, for the time at least, that was quite resting and quieting. And just as I had reached that acquiescent mood, Ernest threw down his book and came and caught me in his arms.

"I thank God," he said, "my precious wife, that I married you this day. The wisest thing I ever did was when I fell in love with you and made a fool of myself!"

What a speech for my silent old darling to make! Whenever he says and does a thing out of character and takes me all by surprise, how delightful he is! Now the world is a beautiful world, and so is everybody in it. I met Martha on the stairs after Ernest had gone and caught her and kissed her. She looked perfectly astonished.

"What spirits the child has!" I heard her whisper to herself. "No sooner down than up again."

And she sighed. Can it be that under that stern and hard crust, there lie hidden affections and perhaps hidden sorrows?

I ran back and asked as kindly as I could, "What makes you sigh, Martha? Is anything troubling you? Have I done anything to annoy you?"

"You do the best you can," she said and pushed past me to her own room.

CHAPTER XIV

*W*ho would have thought I would have anything more to do with poor old Susan Green?
Dr. Cabot came to see me today and told me the strangest
thing! It seems that the nurse who performed the last offices
for her was taken sick about six months ago and that Dr.
Cabot visited her from time to time. Her physician said she
needed nothing but rest and good, nourishing food to restore
her strength, yet she did not improve at all; and at last it
came out that she was not taking the food the doctor ordered
because she could not afford to do so, having lost what little money she had contrived to save. Dr. Cabot, on learning
this, gave her enough out of Susan's legacy to meet her case
and in doing so told her about that extraordinary will. The
nurse then assured him that when she reached Susan's room
and found the state that she was in and that I was praying
with her, she had remained waiting in silence, fearing to
interrupt me. She saw me faint and sprang forward just in
time to catch me and keep me from falling.

"I take great pleasure, therefore," Dr. Cabot continued,

"in making over Susan's little property to you, to whom it belongs; and I cannot help congratulating you that you have had the honor and the privilege of perhaps leading that poor, benighted soul to Christ, even at the eleventh hour."

"Oh, Dr. Cabot!" I cried, "what a relief it is to hear you say that! For I have always reproached myself for the cowardice that made me afraid to speak to her of her Savior. It takes less courage to speak to God than to man."

"It is my belief," replied Dr. Cabot, "that every prayer offered in the name of Jesus is sure to have its answer. Every such prayer is dictated by the Holy Spirit and therefore finds acceptance with God; and if your cry for mercy on poor Susan's soul did not prevail with Him in her behalf, as we may hope it did, then He has answered it in some other way."

These words impressed me very much. To think that every one of my poor prayers is answered! Every one!

Dr. Cabot then returned to the subject of Susan's will, and in spite of all I could say to the contrary, insisted that he had no legal right to this money and that I had. He said he hoped that it would help to relieve us from some of the petty economics now rendered necessary by Ernest's struggle to meet his father's liabilities. Instantly my idol was rudely thrown down from his pedestal. How could he reveal to Dr. Cabot a secret he had pretended cost him so much to confide to me, his wife? I could hardly restrain tears of shame and vexation but did control myself so far as to say that I would sooner die than appropriate Susan's hard earnings for such a purpose and that I should use it for the poor, as I was sure he would have done. He then advised me to invest the principle and use the interest from year to year as occasions presented themselves. So I shall have more than a hundred dollars to give away each year, as long as I live! How perfectly delightful. I can hardly conceive of anything that could give me so much pleasure! Poor old Susan! How many hearts she shall cause to sing for joy!

–Feb. 25–

Things have not gone on well of late. Dearly as I love Ernest, he has lowered himself in my eye by telling that to Dr. Cabot. It would have been far nobler to be silent concerning his sacrifices; and he certainly grows harder, graver, sterner, every day. He is all shut up within himself, and I am growing afraid of him. It must be that he is bitterly disappointed in me and takes refuge in this awful silence. Oh, if I could only please him and could know that I pleased him, how different my life would be!

Baby does not seem well. I have often plumed myself on the thought that having a doctor for his father would be such an advantage to him, as he would be ready to attack the first symptoms of disease. But Ernest hardly listens to me when I express anxiety about this or that; and if I ask a question he replies, "Oh, you know better than I do. Mothers know by instinct how to manage babies." But I do not know by instinct or in any other way, and I often wish that the time I spent over my music had been spent in learning how to meet all the little emergencies that are constantly arising since baby came. How I used to laugh in my sleeve at those anxious mothers who lived near us and always seemed to be in hot water. Martha will take baby when I have other things to attend to, and she keeps him every Sunday afternoon that I may go to church, but she knows no more about his physical training than I do. If my dear mother were only here! I feel a good deal worn out.

What with the care of baby, who is restless at night, and with whom I walk about lest he should keep Ernest awake, the depressing influence of Father's presence, Martha's disdain, and Ernest's keeping so aloof from me, life seems to me little better than a burden that I have not strength to carry and would gladly lay down.

–March 13–

If it were not for James I believe I should sink. He is so kind and affectionate, so ready to fill up the gaps Ernest leaves empty, and is so sunshiny and gay that I cannot be entirely sad. Baby, too, is a precious treasure; it would be wicked to cloud his little life with my depression. I try to look to him always with a smiling face, for he already distinguishes between a cheerful and a sad countenance.

I am sure that there is something in Christ's gospel that would soothe and sustain me amid these varied trials if I only knew what it is and how to put forth my hand and take it. But as it is I feel very desolate. Ernest often congratulates me on having had such a good night's rest, when I have been up and down every hour with baby, half asleep and frozen and exhausted. But he shall sleep at any rate.

–April 5–

The first rays of spring make me more languid than ever. Martha cannot be made to understand that nursing such a large, voracious baby, losing sleep, and confinement within doors are enough to account for this. She is constantly speaking in terms of praise of those who keep up even when they do feel a little out of sorts and says she always does. In the evening, after baby goes to sleep, I feel fit for nothing but to lie on the sofa, dozing; but she sees in this only a lazy habit, which ought not to be tolerated and is constantly devising ways to rouse and set me at work. If I had more leisure for reading, meditation, and prayer, I might still be happy. But all the morning I must have baby till he takes his nap; and as soon as he gets to sleep, I must put my room in order; and by that time all the best part of the day is gone. And at night I am so tired that I can hardly feel anything but my weariness. That, too, is my only chance of seeing Ernest; and if I lock my door and fall upon my knees, I keep listening for his steps, ready to spring to welcome him should he come. This is wrong, I know, but how can I live without one loving word from him, and every day I am hoping it will come.

–May 2–

Aunty was here today. I had not seen her for some weeks. She exclaimed at my looks in a tone that seemed to upbraid Ernest and Martha, though of course she did not mean to do that.

"You are not fit to have the whole care of that great boy at night," said she, "and you ought to begin to feed him, both for his sake and your own."

"I am willing to take the child at night," Martha said, a little stiffly. "But I supposed his mother preferred to keep him herself."

"And I do, I do," I cried. "I should be perfectly miserable if I had to give him up just as he is getting teeth and so wakeful."

"What are you taking to keep up your strength, dear?" asked Aunty.

"Nothing in particular," I said.

"Very well, it is time the doctor looked after that," she

cried. "It really never will do to let you run down in this way. Let me look at baby. Why, my child, his gums need lancing."

"So I have told Ernest half a dozen times," I declared. "But he is always in a hurry and says another time will do."

"I hope baby won't have convulsions while he is waiting for that other time," said Aunty, looking almost savagely at Martha. I never saw Aunty so nearly out of humor.

At dinner Martha began.

"I think, Brother, the baby needs attention. Mrs. Crofton has been here and says so. And she seems to find Katherine run down. I am sure if I had known it, I should have taken her in hand and built her up. But she did not complain."

"She never complains," Father here put in, calling all the blood I had into my face, my heart so leaped for joy at his kind word.

Ernest looked at me and caught the illumination on my face.

"You look well, dear," he said. "But if you do not feel so, you ought to tell us. As to baby, I will attend to him directly."

So Martha's one word prevailed where my twenty fell to the ground.

Baby is much relieved and has fallen into a sweet sleep. And I have had time to carry my tired, oppressed heart to my compassionate Savior and to tell Him what I cannot utter to any human ear. How strange it is that when, through many years of leisure and strength, prayer was only a task, it is now my chief solace if I can only snatch time for it.

Mrs. Embury has a little daughter. How glad I am for

her! She is going to give it my name! That is a real pleasure.

–*July 4*–

Baby is ten months old today and in spite of everything is bright and well. I have come home to Mother. Ernest waked up at last to see that something must be done, and when he is awake he is very wide awake. So he brought me home. Dear Mother is perfectly delighted, only she will make an ado about my health. But I feel a good deal better and think I shall get nicely rested here. How pleasant it is to feel myself watched by friendly eyes, my faults excused and forgiven and what is best in me called out. I have been writing to Ernest and have told him honestly how annoyed and pained I was at learning that he had told his secret to Dr. Cabot.

–*July 12*–

Ernest writes that he has had no communication with Dr. Cabot or anyone else on a subject that, touching his father's honor as it does, he regards as a sacred one.

"You say, dear," he said, "you often say that I do not understand you. Are you sure that you understand me?"

Of course I don't. How can I? How can I reconcile his marrying me and professing to do it with delight with his indifference to my society, his reserve, his carelessness about my health?

But his letters are very kind and really warmer than he is. I can hardly wait for them; and then, though my pride bids me to be reticent as he is, my heart runs away with me, and I pour out upon him such floods of affection that I am sure he is half drowned.

Mother says baby is splendid!

–August 1–

When I took leave of Ernest I was glad to get away. I thought he would perhaps find after I was gone that he missed something out of his life and would welcome me home with a little of the old love. But I did not dream that he would not find it easy to do without me till summer was over; and when, this morning, he came suddenly upon us, carpetbag in hand, I could do nothing but cry in his arms like a tired child.

And now I had the silly triumph of having Mother see that he loved me!

'How could you get away?" I asked at last. "And what made you come? And how long can you stay?"

"I could get away because I would," he replied. "And I came because I wanted to come. And I can stay three days."

Three days of Ernest all to myself!

–August 5–

He has gone, but he has left behind him a happy wife with the memory of three happy days.

After the first joy of our meeting was over, we had time for just such nice long talks as I delight in. Ernest began by upbraiding me a little for my injustice in fancying he had betrayed his father to Dr. Cabot.

"That is not all," I interrupted, "I even thought you had made a boast of the sacrifices you were making!"

"That explains your coldness," he returned.

"My coldness! Of all the ridiculous things in the world!" I cried.

"You were cold, for you, and I felt it. Don't you know that we undemonstrative men prefer loving winsome little women like you just because you are our own opposites?

And when the pet kitten turns into a cat with claws—"

"Now, Ernest, that is really too bad! To compare me to a cat!"

"You certainly did say some sharp things to me about that time."

"Did I, really? Oh, Ernest, how could I?"

"And it was at a moment when I particularly need your help. But do not let us dwell upon it. We love each other; we are both trying to do right in all the details of life. I do not think we shall ever get very far apart."

"But, Ernest—tell me—are you very, very much disappointed in me?"

"Disappointed? Why, Katy!"

"Then what made you seem so indifferent? What made you so slow to observe how miserably I was as to health?"

"Did I seem indifferent? I am sure I never loved you better. As to your health, I am ashamed of myself. I ought to have seen how feeble you were. But the truth is, I was deceived by your bright ways with baby. For him you were all smiles and gaiety."

"That was from principle," I said and felt a good deal elated as I made the announcement.

He fell into a fit of musing, and none of my usual devices for arousing him had any effect. I pulled his hair and his ears and shook him, but he remained unmoved.

At last he began again.

"Perhaps I owe it to you, dear, to tell you that when I brought my father and sister home to live with us, I did not dream how trying a thing it would be for you. I did not know that he was a confirmed invalid or that she would prove to possess a nature so entirely antagonistic to yours. I thought my father would interest himself in reading, visiting, etc., as he used to do. And I thought Martha's judgment would be of service to you, while her household skill would relieve you of some care. But the whole thing has proved a failure. I am harassed by the sight of my father sitting there in his corner so penetrated with gloom; I reproach myself for it, but I almost dread coming home. When a man has been all day encompassed with sounds and sights of suffering, he naturally longs for cheerful faces and cheerful voices in his own house. Then Martha's pertinacious—I won't say hostility to my little wife—what shall I call it?"

"It is only want of sympathy. She is too really good to be hostile to anyone."

"Thank you, my darling," he said. "I believe you do her justice."

"I am afraid I have not been as forbearing with her as I ought," I said. "But, oh Ernest, it is because I have been jealous of her all along!"

"That is really too absurd."

"You certainly have treated her with more deference than you have me. At least it seemed so."

"My dear child, you have misunderstood the whole thing. I gave Martha just what she wanted most; she likes to be looked up to. And I gave you what I thought you wanted most—my tenderest love. And I expected that I should have your sympathy amid the trials with which I am burdened and that with your strong nature I might look to you to help me bear them. I know you have the worst of it, dear child, but then you have twice my strength. I believe women almost always have more than men."

"I have, indeed, misunderstood you. I thought you liked to have them here and that Martha's not fancying me influenced you against me. But now I know just what you want of me, and I can give it, darling."

After this all our cloud melted away. I only long to go home and show Ernest that he shall have one cheerful face about him and have one cheerful voice.

–*August 12*–

I have had a long letter from Ernest today. He says he hopes he has not been selfish and unkind in speaking of his father and sister as he has done, because he truly loves and honors them both and wants me to do so, if I can. His father had called them up twice to see him die and to receive his last messages. This always happens when poor Ernest has been up all the previous night; there seems a fatality about it.

CHAPTER XV

*H*ome again and with my dear Ernest delighted to see me. Baby is a year old today, and, as usual, Father, who seems to abhor anything like a merry-making, took himself off to his room. Tomorrow he will be all the worse for it and will be sure to have a theological battle with somebody.

—*October 5*—

The somebody was his daughter Katherine, as usual. Baby was asleep in my lap and I reached out for a book, which proved to be a volume of Shakespeare that had done long service as an ornament to the table but that nobody ever read on account of the small print. The battle began thus:

Father—"I regret to see that worldly author in your hands, my daughter."

Daughter—a little mischievously—"Why, were you wanting to talk, Father?"

"No, I am too feeble to talk today. My pulse is very weak."

"Let me read aloud to you, then."

"Not from that profane book."

"It would do you good. You never take any recreation. Do let me read a little."

Father gets nervous.

"Recreation is a snare. I must keep my soul ever fixed on divine things."

"But can you?"

"No, alas, no. It is my grief and shame that I do not."

"But if you would indulge yourself in a little harmless mirth now and then, your mind would get rested and you would return to divine things with fresh zeal. Why should not the mind have its seasons of rest as well as the body?"

"We shall have time to rest in heaven. Our business here on earth is to be sober and vigilant because of our adversary, not to be reading plays."

"I don't make reading plays my business, dear Father. I make it my rest and amusement."

"Christians do not need amusement; they find rest, refreshment, all they want in God."

"Do you, Father?"

"Alas, no. He seems a great way off."

"To me He seems very near. So near that He can see every thought of my heart. Dear Father, it is your disease that makes everything so unreal to you. God is really so near, really loves us so, is so sorry for us! And it seems hard, when you are so good and so intent on pleasing Him, that you get no comfort out of Him."

"I am not good, my daughter. I am a vile worm of the dust."

"Well, God is good at any rate, and He would never have sent His Son to die for you if He did not love you." So then I began to sing. Father likes to hear me sing, and the sweet sense I had that all I had been saying was true and more than true made me sing with joyful heart.

I hope it is not a mere miserable presumption that makes me dare to talk so to poor Father. Of course he is ten times better than I am and knows ten times as much, but his disease, whatever it is, keeps his mind befogged. I mean to begin now to pray that light may shine into his soul. It would be delightful to see the peace of God shining in that pale, stern face!

–*March 28*–

It is almost six months since I wrote that. About the middle of October Father had one of his ill turns one night, and we were all called up. He asked for me particularly, and Ernest came for me at last. I was a good deal agitated and would not stop to half-dress myself; and as I had a slight cold already, I suppose I added to it then. At any rate I was taken very sick, and the worst cough I ever had has racked my poor frame almost to pieces. Nearly six months' confinement to my room; six months of uselessness during which I have been a mere cumberer of the ground. Poor Ernest! What a hard time he has had! Instead of the cheerful welcome home I was to give him whenever he entered the house, here I have lain exhausted, woebegone, and good for nothing. It is the bitterest disappointment I ever had. My ambition is to be the sweetest, brightest, best of wives; and what with my childish follies and my sickness, what a weary life my dear husband has had! But how often I have prayed that God would do His will in defiance, if need be, of mine! I have tried to remind myself of that every day. But I am too tired to write any more now.

–March 30–

This experience of suffering has filled my mind with new thoughts. At one time I was so sick that Ernest sent for Mother. Poor Mother, she had to sleep with Martha. It was a great comfort to have her here, but I knew by her coming how sick I was, and then I began to ponder the question whether I was ready to die. Death looked to me as a most solemn, momentous event, but there was something very pleasant in the thought of being no longer a sinner but a redeemed saint and of dwelling forever in Christ's presence. Father came to see me when I had just reached this point.

"My dear daughter," he asked, "are you prepared to face the Judge of all the earth?"

"No, dear Father," I said, "Christ will do that for me."

"Have you no misgivings?"

I could only smile; I had no strength to talk.

Then I heard Ernest—my dear, calm, self-controlled Ernest—burst out crying and rush out of the room. I looked after him, and how I loved him! But I felt that I loved my Savior infinitely more and that if He now let me come home to be with Him, I could trust Him to be a thousand-fold more to Ernest than I could ever be and to take care of my darling baby and my precious mother far better than I could. The very gates of heaven seemed open to let me in. And then they were suddenly shut in my face, and I found myself a poor, weak, tempted creature here upon the earth. I, who fancied myself an heir of glory, was nothing but a peevish, human creature—very human, indeed; overcome if Martha shook the bed as she always did; irritated if my food did not come at the right moment or was not of the right sort; hurt and offended if Ernest put on a tone less anxious and tender then he had used when I was very ill; and in short, my own poor faulty self once more. Oh, what fearful battles I fought for patience, forbearance, and unselfishness! What sorrowful tears of shame I shed over hasty, impatient words and fretful tones! No wonder I longed to be gone where weakness should be swallowed up in strength and sin give place to eternal perfection!

But here I am, and suffering and work lie before me, for which I feel little physical or mental courage. But "blessed be the will of God."

–April 5–

I was alone with Father last evening, Ernest and Martha both being out, and soon saw by the way he fidgeted in his chair that he had something on his mind. So I laid down the book I was reading and asked him what it was.

"My daughter," he began, "can you bear a plain word from an old man?"

I felt frightened, for I knew I had been impatient to Martha of late, in spite of all my efforts to the contrary. I am still miserably unwell.

"I have seen many deathbeds," he went on, "but I never saw one where there was not some dread of the King of Terrors exhibited, nor one where there was such absolute certainty of having found favor with God as to make the hour of departure entirely free from such doubts and such humility as becomes a guilty sinner about to face his Judge."

"I never saw such a one either," I replied. "But there have been many such deaths, and I hardly know of any scene that so honors and magnifies the Lord."

"Yes," he said slowly, "but they were old, mature, ripened Christians."

"Not always old, dear Father. Let me describe to you a scene Ernest described to me only yesterday."

He waved his hand in token that this would delay his coming to the point he was aiming at.

"To speak plainly," he said, "I feel uneasy about you, my daughter. You are young and in the bloom of life; but when death seemed to be staring you in the face, you expressed no anxiety, asked for no counsel, showed no alarm. It must be pleasant to possess so comfortable a persuasion of our acceptance with God; but is it safe to rest on such an assurance while we know that the human heart is deceitful above all things and desperately wicked?"

"I thank you for the suggestion," I said, "and dear Father, do not be afraid to speak still more plainly. You live in the house with me, see all my shortcomings and my faults, and I cannot wonder that you think me a poor, weak Christian. But do you really fear that I am deceived in believing that notwithstanding this, I do really love my God and Savior and am His child?"

"No," he said, hesitating a little, "I can't say that exactly—I can't say that."

This hesitation distressed me. At first it seemed to me that my life must have uttered a very uncertain sound if those who saw it could misunderstand its language. But then I reflected that it was, at best, a very faulty life and that its springs of action were not necessarily seen by onlookers.

Father saw my distress and perplexity and seemed touched by them.

Just then Ernest came in with Martha; but seeing that

something was amiss, the latter took herself off to her room, which I thought really kind of her.

"What is it, Father? What is it, Katy?" asked Ernest, looking from one troubled face to the other.

I tried to explain.

"I think, Father, you may safely trust my wife's spiritual interests to me," Ernest said with some warmth. "You do not understand her. I do. Because there is nothing morbid about her, because she has a sweet, cheerful confidence in Christ, you doubt and misjudge her. You may depend upon it that people are individual in their piety as in other things and cannot all be shaped in one mould. Katy has a playful way of speaking, I know, and often expresses her strongest feelings with what seems like levity and is, perhaps, a little reckless about being misunderstood in consequence."

He smiled on me as he thus took up the cudgels in my defense, and I never felt so grateful to him in my life. The truth is, I hate sentimentalism so cordially and have besides such an instinct to conceal my deepest, most sacred emotions that I do not wonder people misunderstand and misjudge me.

"I did not refer to her playfulness," Father returned. "Old people must make allowances for the young; they must make allowances. What pains me is that this child, full of life and gaiety as she is, sees death approach without that becoming awe and terror that befits mortal man."

Ernest was going to reply, but I broke in eagerly upon his answer.

"It is true that I expressed no anxiety when I believed death to be at hand. I felt none. I had given myself away to Christ and He had received me, and why should I be afraid to take His hand and go where He led me? And it is true that

I asked for no counsel. I was too weak to ask questions or to like to have questions asked; but my mind was bright and wide awake while my body was so feeble, and I took counsel of God. Oh, let me read to you two passages from the life of Caroline Fry that will make you understand how a poor sinner looks upon death. The first is an extract from a letter written after learning that her days on earth were numbered.

" 'As many will hear and will not understand, why I want no time of preparation, often desired by far holier ones than I, I tell you why, and shall tell others, and so shall you. It is not because I am so holy, but because I am so sinful. The peculiar character of my religious experience has always been a deep, an agonizing sense of sin; the sin of yesterday, of today, confessed with anguish hard to be endured, and cried for pardon that could not be unheard; each day cleansed anew in Jesus' blood, and each day more and more hateful in my own sight; what can I do in death I have not done in life? What do in this week, when I am told I cannot live, other than I did last week, when I knew it not? Alas, there is but one thing undone to serve Him better; and the deathbed is no place for that. Therefore, I say, if I am not ready now, I shall not be by delay, so far as I have to do with it. If He has more to do in me that is His part, I need not ask Him not to spoil His work by too much haste.'

"And these are her dying words, a few days later:

" 'This is my bridal-day, the beginning of my life. I wish there should be no mistake about the reason of my desire to depart and to be with Christ. I confess myself the vilest, chiefest of sinners, and I desire to go to Him that I may be rid of the burden of sin—the sin of my nature—not the past, repented of every day, but the present, hourly, momentary sin, which I do commit, or may commit—the sense of which at times drives me half mad with grief!' "

I shall never forget the expression of Father's face as I finished reading these remarkable words. He rose slowly from his seat and came and kissed me on the forehead. Then he left the room but returned with a large volume, and pointing to a blank page, requested me to copy them there. He complains that I do not write legibly, so I printed them as plainly as I could with my pen.

–June 20–

On the first of May, there came to us, with other spring flowers, our little fair-haired, blue-eyed daughter. How rich I felt when I heard Ernest's voice, as he replied to a question asked at the door, proclaim, "Mother and children all well." To think that we who thought ourselves rich before are made so much richer now!

But she is not large and vigorous as little Ernest was, and we cannot rejoice in her without some misgiving. Yet her very frailty makes her precious to us. Little Ernest hangs over her with an almost loverlike pride and devotion; and should she live, I can imagine what a protector he will be for her. I have had to give up the care of him to Martha. During my illness I do not know what would have become of him but for her. One of the pleasant events of every day at that time was her bringing him to me in such exquisite order, his face shining with health and happiness, his hair and dress so beautifully neat and clean. Now that she has the care of him, she has become very fond of him; and he certainly forms one bond of union between us for we both agree that he is the handsomest, best, most remarkable child that ever lived or ever will live.

–July 6–

I have come home to dear Mother with both my children. Ernest says our only hope for baby is to keep her out of the city during the summer months.

What a petite wee maiden she is. Where does all the love come from? If I had had her always, I do not see how I could be more fond of her. And do people call it living who never had any children?

–July 10–

If this darling baby lives, I shall always believe it is owing to my mother's prayers.

I find little Ernest has a passionate temper and a good deal of self-will. But he has fine qualities. I wish he had a better mother. I am so impatient with him when he is wayward and perverse! What he needs is a firm, gentle hand, moved by no caprice and controlled by the constant fear of God. He never ought to hear an irritable word or a sharp tone; but he does hear them, I must own with grief and shame. The truth is, it is so long since I really felt strong and well that I am not myself and cannot do him justice, poor child. Next to being a perfect wife, I want to be a perfect mother. How mortifying, how dreadful in all things to come short of even one's own standard! What approach, then, does one make to God's standard?

Mother seems very happy to have us here, though we make so much trouble. She encourages me in all my attempts to control myself and to control my dear little boy, and the chapters she gives me out of her own experience are as interesting as a novel and a good deal more instructive.

–August–

Dear Ernest has come to spend a week with us. He is all tired out as there has been a great deal of sickness in the city and Father has had quite a serious attack. He brought with him a nurse for baby as one more desperate effort to strengthen her constitution.

I reproached him for doing it without consulting me, but he said Mother had written to tell him that I was worn out and not in a state to have the care of the children. It has been a terrible blow to me. One by one I am giving up the sweetest maternal duties. God means that I shall be nothing and do nothing, a mere useless sufferer. But when I tell Ernest so, he says I am everything to him and that God's children please Him just as well when they sit patiently with folded hands, if that is His will, as when they are hard at work. But to be at work, to be useful, to be necessary to my husband and children is just what I want; and I do find it hard to be set against the wall, as it were, like an old piece of furniture no longer of any service. I see now that my first desire has not been to please God but to please myself, for I am restless under His restraining hand and find my prison a very narrow one. I would be willing to bear any other trial if I could only have health and strength for my beloved ones. I pray for patience with bitter tears.

CHAPTER XVI

*W*e are all home together once more. The parting with Mother was very painful. Every year that she lives now increases her loneliness and makes me long to give her the shelter of my home. But in the midst of these anxieties, how much I have to make me happy! Little Ernest is the life and soul of the house; the sound of his feet pattering about and all his prattle are the sweetest music to my ear; and his heart is brimful of love and joy so that he shines on us all like a sunbeam. Baby is improving every day and is one of those tender, clinging things that appeal to everybody's love and sympathy. I never saw a more angelic face than hers. Father sits by the hour looking at her. Today he said:

"Daughter Katherine, this lovely little one is not meant for this sinful world."

"This world needs to be adorned with lovely little ones," I said. "And baby was never so well as she is now."

"Do not set your heart too fondly upon her," he returned. "I feel that she is far too dear to me."

"But, Father, we could give her to God if He should ask for her. Surely we love Him better than we love her."

But as I spoke, a sharp pang shot through and through my soul, and I held my little fair daughter closely in my arms as if I could always keep her there. It may be conceit, but it really does seem as if poor Father was getting a little fond of me. Ever since my own sickness, I have felt great sympathy for him; and he feels, no doubt, that I give him something neither Ernest nor Martha can do, since they were never sick one day in their lives. I do wish he could look more at Christ and at what He has done and is doing for us. The way of salvation is to me a wide path, absolutely radiant with the glory of Him who shines upon it. I see my shortcomings; I see my sins; but I feel myself bathed, as it were, in the effulgent glow that proceeds directly from the throne of God and the Lamb. It seems as if I ought to have some misgivings about my salvation, but I can hardly say that I have one. How strange, how mysterious that is! And here is Father, so much older, so much better than I am, creeping along in the dark! I spoke to Ernest about it. He says I owe it to my training, in a great measure, and that my mother is fifty years in advance of her age. But it can't be all that. It was only after years of struggle and prayer that God gave me this joy.

—*November 24*—

Ernest asked me yesterday if I knew that Amelia and her husband had come here to live and that she was very ill.

"I wish you could go to see her, dear," he added. "She is a stranger here and in great need of a friend." I felt extremely disturbed. I have lost my old affection for her, and the idea of meeting her husband was unpleasant.

"Is she very sick?" I asked.

"Yes. She is completely broken down. I promised her that you should go to see her."

"Are you attending her?"

"Yes, her husband came for me himself."

"I don't want to go," I said. "It will be very disagreeable."

"Yes, dear, I know it. But she needs a friend, as I said before."

I put on my things very reluctantly and went. I found Amelia in a richly furnished house but looking untidy and ill cared for. She was lying on a couch in her bedroom; three delicate-looking children were playing about, and their nurse sat sewing at the window.

A terrible fit of coughing made it impossible for her to speak for some moments. At last she recovered herself sufficiently to welcome me by throwing her arms around me and bursting into tears.

"Oh, Katy!" she cried. "Should you have known me if we had met in the street? Don't you find me sadly altered?"

"You are changed," I said, "but so am I."

"Yes, you do not look strong. But then you never did. And you are as pretty as ever, while I—oh, Kate! Do you remember what round white arms I used to have? Look at them now!"

And she drew up her sleeve, poor child. Just then I heard a step in the passage, and her husband sauntered into the room, smoking.

"Do go away, Charles," she said impatiently. "You know how your cigar sets me coughing."

He held out his hand to me with the easy, nonchalant air of one who is accustomed to success and popularity.

I looked at him with an aversion I could not conceal.

The few years since we met have changed him so completely that I almost shuddered at the sight of his already bloated face and at the air that told of a life worse than wasted.

"Do go away, Charles," Amelia repeated.

He threw himself into a chair without paying the least attention to her, and still addressing himself to me again, said, "Upon my word, you are prettier to me than ever, and—"

"I will come to see you at another time, Amelia," I said, putting on all the dignity I could condense in my small frame and rising to take leave.

"Don't go, Katy!" he cried, starting up "Don't go. I want to have a good talk about old times."

Katy, indeed! How dared he? I came away burning with anger and mortification. Is it possible that I ever loved such a man? That to gratify that love I defied and grieved my dear mother through a whole year! Oh, from what hopeless misery God saved me when He snatched me out of the depth of my folly!

–December 1–

Ernest says I can go to see Amelia with safety now, as her husband has sprained his ankle and keeps to his own room. So I am going. But I am sure I shall say something imprudent or unwise and wish I could think it right to stay away. I hope God will go with me and teach me what words to speak.

–Dec. 2–

I found Amelia more unwell than on my first visit, and she received me again with tears.

"How good you are to come so soon," she began. "I did not blame you for running off the other day; Charley's impertinence was shameful. He said, after you left, that he perceived you had not yet lost your quickness to take offense; but I know he felt that you showed a just displeasure and nothing more."

"No, I was really angry," I replied. "I find the road to perfection lies uphill, and I slip back so often that sometimes I despair of ever reaching the top."

"What does the doctor say about me?" she asked. "Does he think me very sick?"

"I dare say he will tell you exactly what he thinks," I returned, "if you ask him. This is his rule with all his patients."

"If I could get rid of this cough I should soon be myself again," she said. "Some days I feel quite bright and well. But if it were not for my poor little children, I should not care much how the thing ended. With the life Charley leads me, I haven't much to look forward to."

"You forget that the children's nurse is in the room," I whispered.

"Oh, I don't mind Charlotte. Charlotte knows how he neglects me, don't you, Charlotte?"

Charlotte was discrete enough to pretend not to hear this question, and Amelia went on:

"It began very soon after we were married. He would go round with other girls exactly as he did before; and when I spoke about it, he would just laugh in his easy, good-natured way but pay no attention to my wishes. Then when I grew more in earnest, he would say that as long as he let me alone, I ought to let him alone. I thought that when our first baby came that would sober him a little, but he wanted a boy and it turned out to be a girl. And my being unhappy and crying so much made the poor thing fretful; it kept him awake at night, so he took another room. After that I saw him less than ever, though now and then he would have a little love-fit, when he would promise to be at home more and treat me with more consideration. We had two more girls—twins—and then a boy. Charley seemed quite fond of him and did certainly seem improved, though he was still out a great deal with a set of idle young men, smoking, drinking wine, and I don't know what else. His uncle gave him too much money, and he had nothing to do but to spend it."

"You must not tell me any more now," I said. "Wait till you are stronger."

The nurse rose and gave her something that seemed to refresh her. I went to look at the little girls, who were all pretty, pale-faced creatures, very quiet and mature in their ways.

"I am rested now," said Amelia, "and it does me good to talk to you because I can see that you are sorry for me."

"I am indeed!" I cried.

"When our little boy was three months old, I took this terrible cold and began to cough. Charley at first remonstrated with me for coughing so much; he said it was a habit I had got and that I ought to cure myself of it. Then the baby began to pine and pine, and the more it wasted, the more I wasted. And at last it died."

Here the poor child burst out again, and I wiped away her tears as fast as they fell, thankful that she could cry.

"After that," she went on after awhile, "Charley seemed to lose his last particle of affection for me. He kept away more than ever; and once when I besought him not to neglect me and my children so, he said he was well paid for not keeping up his engagement with you, that you had some strength of character and—"

"Amelia," I interrupted, "do not repeat such things. They only pain and mortify me."

"Well," she sighed wearily, "this is what he has at last brought me to. I am sick and brokenhearted and care very little what becomes of me."

There was a long silence. I wanted to ask her if, when earthly refuge failed her, she could not find shelter in the love of Christ. But I have what is, I fear, a morbid terror of seeking the confidence of others. I knelt down at last and kissed the poor faded face.

"Yes, I knew you would feel for me," she said. "The only pleasant thought I had when Charley insisted on coming here to live was that I should see you."

"Does your uncle live here, too?" I asked.

"Yes, he came first, and it was that that put it into Charley's head to come. My uncle is very kind to me."

"Yes," I said, "and God is kind, too, isn't He?"

"Kind to let me get sick and disgust Charley? Now, Katy, how can you talk so?"

I replied by repeating two lines from a hymn of which I am very fond:

" '*O Savior, whose mercy, severe in its kindness,*
Hath chastened my wanderings, and guided my way.' "

"I don't much care for hymns," she said. "When one is well and everything goes quite to one's mind, it is nice to go to church and sing with the rest of them. But sick as I am, it isn't too easy to be religious."

"But isn't this the very time to look to Christ for comfort?"

"What's the use of looking anywhere for comfort?" she said peevishly. "Wait till you are sick and heartbroken yourself, and you'll see that you won't feel much like doing anything but just groan and cry your life out."

"I have been sick, and I know what sorrow means," I said. "And I am glad that I do. For I have learned Christ in that school, and I know that He can comfort when no one else can."

"You always were an odd creature," she replied. "I never pretended to understand half you said."

I saw that she was tired and came away. Oh, how I wished that I had been able to make Christ look to her as He did to me all the way home!

–Dec. 24–

Father says he does not like Dr. Cabot's preaching. He thinks that it is not doctrinal enough and that he does not preach enough to sinners. But I can see that it has influenced him already and that he is beginning to think of God as manifested in Christ far more than he used to do. With me he has endless discussions on his and my favorite subjects; and though I can never tell along what path I walked to reach a certain conclusion, the earnestness of my convictions does impress him strangely. I am sure there is a great deal of conceit mixed up with all I say; and then when I compare my life with my own standard of duty, I wonder I ever dare to open my mouth and undertake to help others.

Baby is not at all well. To see such a little, frail, tender thing really suffering tears my soul to pieces. I think it would distress me less to give her to God just as she is now, a vital part of my very heart, than to see her live a mere invalid life. But I try to feel, as I know I say, Thy will be done! Little Ernest is the very picture of health and beauty. He has vitality enough for two children. He and his little sister will make very interesting contrasts as they grow older. His ardor and vivacity will rouse her, and her gentleness will soften him.

–Jan. 1, 1841–

Every day brings its own duty and its own discipline. How is it that I make such slow progress while this is the case? It is a marvel to me why God allows characters like mine to defile His Church. I can only account for it with the thought that if I ever am perfected, I shall be a great honor to His name, for surely worse material for building up a temple of the Holy Ghost was never gathered together before. The time may come when those who know me now, crude, childish, incomplete, will look upon me with amazement, saying, "What hath God wrought!" If I knew such a time would never come, I should want to flee into the holes and caves of the earth.

I have everything to inspire me to devotion. My dear mother's influence is always upon me. To her I owe the habit of flying to God in every emergency and of believing in prayer. Then I am in close fellowship with a true man and a true Christian. Ernest has none of my fluctuations; he is always calm and self-possessed. This is partly his natural character; but he has studied the Bible more than any other book, his convictions of duty are fixed because they are drawn thence, and his constant contact with the sick and the suffering has revealed life to him just as it is. How he has helped me on! God bless him for it!

Then I have James. To be with him one half hour is an inspiration. He lives in such blessed communion with Christ that he is in perpetual sunshine, and his happiness fertilizes even this disordered household; there is not a soul in it that does not catch somewhat of his joyousness.

And there are my children! My darling, precious children! For their sakes I am continually constrained to seek after an amended, a sanctified life; what I want them to become I must become myself.

So I enter on a new year, not knowing what it will bring forth, but surely with a thousand reasons for thanksgiving, for joy, and for hope.

–Jan. 16–

One more desperate effort to make harmony out of the discords of my house and one more failure. Ernest forgot that it was our wedding day, which mortified and pained me, especially as he had made an engagement to dine out. I am always expecting something from life that I never get. Is it so with everybody? I am very uneasy, too, about James. He seems to be growing fond of Lucy's society. I am perfectly sure that she could not make him happy. Is it possible that he does not know what a brilliant young man he is and that he can have whom he pleases? It is easy, in theory, to let God plan our own destiny and that of our friends. But when it comes to a specific case, we fancy we can help His judgment with our poor reason. Well, I must go to Him with this new anxiety and trust my darling brother's future to Him, if I can.

I shall try to win James's confidence. If it is not Lucy, who or what is it that is making him thoughtful and serious yet so wondrously happy?

–*Jan. 17*–

I have been trying to find out whether this is a mere notion of mine about Lucy. James laughs and evades my questions. But he owns that a very serious matter is occupying his thoughts, of which he does not wish to speak at present. May God bless him in it, whatever it is!

–*May 1*–

My delicate little Una's first birthday. Thank God for sparing her to us a year. If He should take her away, I should still rejoice that this life was mingled with ours and has influenced us. Yes, even an unconscious infant is an ever-felt influence in the household. What an amazing thought!

I have given this precious little one away to her Savior and to mine; living or dying, she is His.

–*Dec. 13*–

Writing journals does not seem to be my mission on earth of late. My busy hands find so much else to do! And sometimes when I have been particularly exasperated and tried by the jarring elements that form my home, I have not dared to indulge myself with recording things that ought to be forgotten.

How I long to live in peace with everyone, and how I resent interference in the management of my children! If the time ever comes that I live, a spinster of a certain age in the family of an elder brother, what a model of forbearance, charity, and sisterly lovingkindness I shall be!

CHAPTER XVII

J mean to resume my journal and be more faithful to it this year. How many precious things said by dear Mrs. Campbell and others are lost forever because I did not record them at the time!

I have seen her today. At Ernest's suggestion I have let Susan Green provide her with a comfortable chair, which enables her to sit up during a part of each day. I found her in it, full of gratitude, her sweet, tranquil face shining, as it always is, with a light reflected from heaven itself. She looks like one who has had her struggle with life and conquered it. During last year, I visited her often and gradually learned much of her past history, though she does not love to talk of herself. She has outlived her husband, a houseful of girls and boys, and her ill health is chiefly the result of years of watching by their sickbeds and grief at their loss.

For she does not pretend not to grieve but always says, "It is repining that dishonors God, not grief."

I said to her today:

"Doesn't it seem hard, when you think of the many

happy homes there are in the world, that you should be singled out for such bereavement and loneliness?"

She replied with a smile:

"I am not singled out, dear. There are thousands of God's own dear children scattered over the world suffering far more than I do. And I do not think there are many persons in it who are happier than I am. I was bound to my God and Savior before I knew a sorrow, it is true. But it was by a chain of many links; and every link that dropped away brought me to Him till at last, having nothing left, I was shut up to Him and learned fully what I had only learned partially, how soul-satisfying He is."

"You think then," I said while my heart died within me, "that husband and children are obstacles in our way and hinder our getting near to Christ?"

"Oh, no!" she cried. "God never gives us hindrances. On the contrary, He means, in making us wives and mothers, to put us into the very conditions of holy living. But if we abuse His gifts by letting them take His place in our hearts, it is an act of love on His part to take them away or to destroy our pleasure in them. It is delightful," she added after a pause, "to know that there are some generous souls on earth who love their dear ones with all their hearts yet give those hearts unreservedly to Christ. Mine was not one of them."

I had some little service to render her that interrupted our conversation. The offices I have had to have rendered me in my own long days of sickness have taught me to be less fastidious about waiting upon others. I am thankful that God has at last made me willing to do anything in a sickroom that must be done. She thanked me, as she always does, and then I said:

"I have a great many little trials, but they don't do me

a bit of good. Or, at least, I don't see that they do."

"No, we never see plants growing," she said.

"And do you really think, then, that perhaps I am growing, though unconsciously?"

"I know you are, dear child. There can't be life without growing."

This comforted me. I came home, praying all the way and striving to commit myself entirely to Him in whose school I sit as learner. Oh, that I were a better scholar! But I do not half learn my lessons, I am heedless and inattentive, and I forget what is taught. Perhaps this is the reason that weighty truths float before my mind's eye at times but do not fix themselves there.

–*March 20*–

I have been much impressed by Dr. Cabot's sermons today. While I am listening to his voice and hear him speak of the beauty and desirableness of the Christian life, I feel as he feels that I am willing to count all things but dross that I may win Christ. But when I come home to my worldly cares, I get completely absorbed in them; and it is only by a painful wrench that I force my soul back to God. Sometimes I almost envy Lucy her calm nature, which gives her so little trouble. Why need I throw my whole soul into whatever I do? Why can't I make so much as an apron for little Ernest without ardor and eagerness of a soldier marching to battle? I wonder if people of my temperament ever get toned down and learn to take life coolly?

–*June 10*–

My dear little Una has had a long and very severe illness. It seems wonderful that she could survive such sufferings. And it is almost as wonderful that I could look upon them week after week without losing my senses.

At first Ernest paid little attention to my repeated entreaties that he would prescribe for her, and some precious time was thus lost. But the moment he was fully aroused to see her danger, there was something beautiful in his devotion. He often walked the room with her by the hour together, and it was touching to see her lying like a pale, crushed lily in his strong arms. One morning she seemed almost gone, and we knelt around her with bursting hearts to commend her parting soul to Him in whose arms we were about to place her. But it seemed as if all He asked of us was to come to that point, for then He gave her back to us; and she is still ours, only sevenfold dearer. I was so thankful to see dear Ernest's faith triumphing over his heart and making him so ready to give up even his lamb without a word. Yes, we will give our children to Him if He asks for them. He shall never have to snatch them from us by force.

–*Oct. 4*–

We have had a quiet summer in the country; that is, I have with my darling little ones. This is the fourth birthday of our son and heir, and he has been full of health and vivacity, enjoying everything with all his heart. How he lights up our somber household! Father has been fasting today and is worn out and so nervous in consequence that he could not bear the sound of the children's voices. I wish, if he must fast, he would do it moderately and do it all the time. Now he goes without food until he is ready to sink, and now he eats quantities of improper food. If Martha could only see how mischievous all this is for him. After the children had been hustled out of the way and I had got them both off to bed, he said in his most doleful manner, "I hope, my daughter, that you are faithful to your son. He has now reached the age of four years and is a remarkably intelligent child. I hope you teach him that he is a sinner and that he is in a state of condemnation."

"No, Father, don't," I said. "You are all tired out and do not know what you are saying. I would not have little Ernest hear you for the world."

Poor Father! He fairly groaned.

"You are responsible for the child's soul," he said. "You have more influence over him than all the world beside."

"I know it," I said, "and sometimes I feel ready to sink when I think of the great work God has entrusted to me. But my poor child will learn that he is a sinner only too soon; and before that dreadful day arrives, I want to fortify his soul with the only antidote against the misery that knowledge will give him. I want him to see his Redeemer in all His love and all His beauty and to love Him with all his heart and soul and mind and strength. Dear Father, pray for him, and pray for me, too."

"I do, I will," he said solemnly. And then followed the inevitable long fit of silent musing, when I often wonder what is passing in that suffering soul. For a sufferer he certainly is who sees a great and good and terrible God who cannot look upon iniquity and does not see His risen Son, who has paid the debt we owe, and lives to intercede for us before the throne of the Father.

–Jan. 1, 1842–

James came to me yesterday with a letter he had been writing to Mother.

"I want you to read this before it goes," he said, "for

you ought to know my plans as soon as Mother does."

I did not get time to read it till after tea. Then I came up here to my room and sat down curious to know what was coming.

Well, I thought I loved him as much as one human being could love another already, but now my heart embraced him with a fervor and delight that made me so happy that I could not speak a word when I knelt down to tell my Savior all about it.

He said that he had been led, within a few months, to make a new consecration of himself to Christ and to Christ's cause on earth and that this had resulted in his choosing the life of a missionary instead of settling down, as he had intended to do, as a city physician. Such expressions of personal love to Christ and delight in the thought of serving Him I never read. I could only marvel at what God had wrought in his soul. For me to live to Christ seems natural enough, for I have been driven to Him not only by sorrow but by sin. Every outbreak of my hasty temper sends me weeping and penitent to the foot of the cross, and I love much because I have been forgiven much. But James, as far as I know, has never had a sorrow except my father's death, and that had no apparent religious effect. And his natural character is perfectly beautiful. He is as warmhearted and loving and simple and guileless as a child and has nothing of my intemperance, hastiness, and quick temper. I have often thought that she would be a rare woman who could win him; he is handsome and talented and attractive; everybody is fascinated by him, everybody caresses him; and yet he has turned his back on the world that has dealt so kindly with him and given himself, as Jonathan Edwards says, "clean away to Christ!" Oh, how thankful I am! And yet to let him go! My only brother—Mother's only son! But I know what she will say; she will bid him Godspeed!

Ernest came upstairs looking tired and jaded. I read the letter to him. It impressed him strangely; but he only said:

"This is what we might expect who know James, dear fellow!"

But when we knelt down to pray together, I saw how he was touched and how his soul kindled within him in harmony with that consecrated, devoted spirit. Dear James! It must be Mother's prayers that have done for him this wondrous work that is usually the slow growth of years; and this is the Mother who prays for you, Katy! So take courage!

–Jan. 2–

James means to study theology as well as medicine, it seems. That will keep him with us for some years. Oh, is it selfish to take this view of it? Alas, the spirit is willing to have him go, but the flesh is weak and cries out.

–Oct. 22–

Amelia came to see me today. She has been traveling for her health and certainly looks much improved.

"Charley and I are quite good friends again," she began. "We have jaunted about everywhere and had a delightful time. What a snug little box of a house you have!"

"It is inconveniently small," I said, "for our family is large, and the doctor needs more office room."

"Does he receive patients here? How horrid! Don't you hate to have people with all sorts of ills and aches in the house? It must depress your spirits."

"I dare say it would if I saw them, but I never do."

"I should like to see your children. Your husband says

you are perfectly devoted to them."

"As I suppose all mothers are," I replied, laughing.

"As to that," she returned, "people differ."

The children were brought down. She admired little Ernest, as everybody does, but only glanced at the baby.

"What a sickly looking little thing!" she said. "But this boy is a splendid fellow! Ah, if mine had lived he would have been just such a child! But some people have all the trouble and others all the comfort. I am sure I don't know what I have done that I should have to lose my only boy and have nothing left but girls. To be sure I can afford to dress them elegantly; and as soon as they get old enough, I mean to have them taught all sorts of accomplishments. You can't imagine what a relief it is to have plenty of money!"

"Indeed, I can't!" I said. "It is quite beyond the reach of my imagination."

"My uncle—that is to say, Charley's uncle—has just given me a carriage and horses for my own use. In fact he heaps everything upon me. Where do you go to church?"

I told her, reminding her that Dr. Cabot was the pastor.

"Oh, I forgot! Poor Dr. Cabot! Is he as old-fashioned as ever?"

"I don't know what you mean," I cried. "He is as good as ever, if not better. His health is very delicate, and that one thing seems to be a blessing to him."

"A blessing! Why, Kate Mortimer! Kate Elliott, I mean. It is a blessing I, for one, am very willing to dispense with. But you always do say queer things. Well, I dare say Dr. Cabot is very good and all that, but his church is not a fashionable one, and Charley and I go to Dr. Bellamy's. That is, I go once a day, pretty regularly, and Charles goes when he feels like it. Good-bye. I must go now; I have all my fall shopping to do. Have you done yours? Suppose you jump into the carriage and go with me? You can't imagine how it passes away the morning to drive from shop to shop, looking over the new goods."

"There seem to be a number of things I can't imagine," I replied drily. "You must excuse me this morning."

She took her leave. I looked at her rich dress as she gathered it about her and swept away and recalled all her empty, frivolous talk with contempt.

She and Ch—, her husband, I mean, are well matched. They need their money and their palaces and their fine clothes and handsome equipages, for they have nothing else. How thankful I am that I am as unlike them as ex—

–October 30–

I'm sure I don't know what I was going to say when I was interrupted just then. Something in the way of self-glorification, most likely. I remember the contempt with which I looked after Amelia as she left our house and the pinnacle on which I sat perched for some days when I compared my life with hers. Alas, it was my view of life of which I was lost in admiration, for I am sure that if I ever come under the complete dominion of Christ's gospel, I shall not know the sentiment of disdain. I feel truly ashamed and sorry that I am still so far from being penetrated with that spirit.

My pride has had a terrible fall. As I sat on my throne looking down on all the Amelias in the world, I felt a profound pity at their delight in petty trifles, their love of position, of mere worldly show and passing vanities.

"They are all alike," I said to myself. "They are incapable of understanding a character like mine or the exalted, ennobling principles that govern me. They crave the applause of this world, they are satisfied with fine clothes, fine houses, fine equipages. They think and talk of nothing else; I have not one idea in common with them. I see the emptiness and hollowness of these things. I am absolutely unworldly; my ambition is to attain whatever they, in their blind folly and ignorance, absolutely despise."

Thus communing with myself, I was pleased to hear Dr. Cabot and his wife announced. I hastened to meet them and to display to them the virtues I so admired in myself. They had hardly chance to utter a word. I spoke eloquently of my contempt for worldly vanities and of my enthusiastic longing for a higher life. I even went into particulars about the foibles of some of my acquaintances, though faint misgivings as to the propriety of such remarks on the absent made me half-repent the words I still kept uttering. When they took leave, I rushed to my room with my heart beating, my cheeks all in a glow, and caught up and caressed the children in a way that seemed to astonish them. Then I took my work and sat down to sew. What a horrible reaction now took place! I saw my refined, subtle, disgusting pride, just as I suppose Dr. and Mrs. Cabot saw it! I sat covered with confusion, shocked at myself, shocked at the weakness of human nature. Oh, to get back the good opinion of my friends! To recover my own self-respect! But this was impossible. I threw down my work and walked about my room. There was a terrible struggle in my soul. I saw that instead of brooding over the display I had made of myself to Dr. Cabot, I ought to be thinking solely of my appearance in the sight of God, who could see far more plainly than any earthly eye could all my miserable pride and self-conceit. But I could not do that and chafed about till I was worn out, body and soul. At last I sent the children away and knelt down and told the whole story to Him who knew what I was when He had compassion on me, called me by my name, and made me His own child. And here I found a certain peace. Christian, on his way to the celestial city, met and fought his Apollyons and his giants, too; but he got there at last!

CHAPTER XVIII

This morning Ernest received an early summons to Amelia. I got out of all manner of patience with him because he would take his bath and eat his breakfast before he went and should have driven anyone else distracted by my hurry and flurry.

"She has had a hemorrhage!" I cried. "Do, Ernest, make haste."

"Of course," he returned, "that would come sooner or later."

"You don't mean," I said, "that she has been in danger of this all along?"

"I certainly do."

"Then it was very unkind in you not to tell me so."

"I told you at the outset that her lungs were diseased."

"No, you told me no such thing. Oh, Ernest, is she going to die?"

"I did not know you were so fond of her," he said apologetically.

"It is not that," I cried. "I am distressed at the thought

of the worldly life she has been living—at my never trying to influence her for her good. If she is in danger, you will tell her so? Promise me that."

"I must see her before I make such a promise," he said and went out.

I flew up to my room and threw myself on my knees, sorrowful, self-condemned. I had thrown away my last opportunity of speaking a word to her in season, though I had seen how much she needed one, and now she was going to die! Oh, I hope God will forgive me and hear the prayers I have offered for her!

—Evening—

Ernest says he had a most distressing scene at Amelia's this morning. She insisted on knowing what he thought of her and then burst into bitter complaints and lamentations, charging it to her husband that she had this disease, declaring that she could not and would not die, and insisting that he must prevent it. Her uncle urged for a consultation of physicians, to which Ernest consented, of course, though he says no mortal power can save her now. I asked him how her husband appeared, to which he made the evasive answer that he appeared just as one would expect him to do.

—December—

Amelia was so determined to see me that Ernest thought it best for me to go. I found her looking very feeble.

"Oh, Katy," she began at once, "do make the doctor say that I shall get well!"

"I wish he could say so with truth," I answered. "Dear

Amelia, try to think how happy God's own children are when they are with Him."

"I can't think," she replied. "I do not want to think. I want to forget all about it. If it were not for this terrible cough, I could forget it, for I am really a great deal better than I was a month ago."

I did not know what to say or what to do.

"May I read a hymn or a few verses from the Bible?" I asked at last.

"Just as you like," she said indifferently.

I read a verse now and then, but she looked tired, and I prepared to go.

"Don't go," she cried. "I do not dare to be alone. Oh, what a terrible, terrible thing it is to die! To leave this bright, beautiful world and be nailed up in a coffin and buried up in a cold, dark grave!"

"Nay," I said, "to leave this poor sick body there and to fly to a world ten thousand times brighter, more beautiful than this."

"I had just got to feeling nearly well," she said, "and I had everything I wanted, and Charley was quite good to me, and I kept my little girls looking like fairies just from fairyland. Everybody said they wore the most picturesque costumes when they were dressed according to my taste. And I have got to go and leave them, and Charley will be marrying somebody else and saying to her all the nice things he has said to me."

"I really must go now," I said. "You are wearing yourself all out."

"I declare you are crying," she exclaimed. "You do pity me after all."

"Indeed, I do," I said and came away heartsick.

Ernest says there is nothing I can do for her now but to pray for her, since she does not really believe herself in danger and has a vague feeling that if she can once convince him how much she wants to live, he will use some vigorous measures to restore her. Martha is to watch with her tonight. Ernest will not let me.

–Jan. 18, 1843–

Our wedding day has passed unobserved. Amelia's suffering condition absorbs us all. Martha spends much time with her and prepares almost all the food she eats.

–Jan. 20–

I have seen poor Amelia once more and perhaps for the last time. She has failed rapidly of late and Ernest says may drop away at almost any time.

When I went in, she took me by the hand and with great difficulty and at intervals said something like this:

"I had made up my mind to it, and I know it must come. I want to see Dr. Cabot. Do you think he would be willing to visit me after my neglecting him so?"

"I am sure he would," I cried.

"I want to ask him if he thinks I was a Christian at that time—you know when. If I was, then I need not be so afraid to die."

"But, dear Amelia, what he thinks is very little to the purpose. The question is not whether you ever gave yourself to God, but whether you are His now. But I ought not to talk to you. Dr. Cabot will know just what to say."

"No, but I want to know what you thought about it."

I felt distressed, as I looked at her wasted dying figure, to be called on to help decide such a question. But I knew what I ought to say and said it:

"Don't look back to the past; it is useless. Give your-self to Christ now."

She shook her head.

"I don't know how," she said. "Oh, Katy, pray to God to let me live long enough to get ready to die. I have led a worldly life. I shudder at the bare thought of dying; I must have time."

"Don't wait for time," I said with tears. "Get ready now, this minute. A thousand years would not make you more fit to die."

So I came away weary and heavy laden. On the way home I stopped to tell Dr. Cabot all about it, and by this time he is with her.

–*March 1*–

Poor Amelia's short race on earth is over. Dr. Cabot saw her every few days and says he hopes she did depart in Christian faith, though without Christian joy. I have not seen her since that last interview. That excited me so that Ernest would not let me go again.

Martha has been there nearly the whole time for three or four weeks, and I really think it has done her good. She seems less absorbed in mere outside things and more lenient toward me and my failings.

I do not know what is to become of those motherless little girls. I wish I could take them into my own home, but, of course, that is not even to be thought of at this juncture. Ernest says their father seemed nearly distracted when Amelia died and that his uncle is going to send him off to Europe immediately.

I have been talking with Ernest about Amelia. "What

do you think," I asked "about her last days on earth? Was there really any preparation for death?"

"These scenes are very painful," he returned. "Of course there is but one real preparation for Christian dying, and that is Christian living."

"But the sickroom often does what a prosperous life never did!"

"Not often. Sick persons delude themselves or are deluded by their friends; they do not believe they are really about to die. Besides, they are bewildered and exhausted by disease; and what mental strength they have is occupied with studying symptoms, watching for the doctor, and the like. I do not now recall a single instance where a worldly Christian died a happy, joyful death, in all my patients."

"Well, in one sense it makes no difference whether they die happily or not. The question is, do they die in the Lord?"

"It may make no vital difference to them; but we must not forget that God is honored or dishonored by the way a Christian dies as well as by the way in which he lives. There is great significance in the description given in the Bible of the death by which John should 'Glorify God' (John 21:19); to my mind it implies that to die well is to live well."

"But how many thousands die suddenly or of such exhausting disease that they cannot honor God by even one feeble word."

"Of course I do not refer to such cases. All I ask is that those whose minds are clear, who are able to attend to all other final details should let it be seen what the gospel of Christ can do for poor sinners in the great exigency of life, giving Him the glory. I can tell you, my darling, that standing, as I so often do, by dying beds, this whole subject has become one of great magnitude to my mind. And it gives me positive personal pain to see heirs of the eternal kingdom, made such by the ignominious death of their Lord, go shrinking and weeping to the full possession of their inheritance."

Ernest is right, I am sure; but how shall the world, even the Christian world, be convinced that it may have blessed foretastes of heaven while yet plodding upon earth and faith to go thither joyfully for the simple asking?

Poor Amelia! But she understands it all now. It is a blessed thing to have this great faith, and it is a blessed thing to have a Savior who accepts it when it is but a mere grain of mustard seed!

—May 24—

I celebrated my little Una's third birthday by presenting her with a new brother. Both the children welcomed him with delight that was of itself compensation enough for all it cost me to get up such a celebration. Martha takes a most prosaic view of this proceeding, in which she detects malice prepense on my part. She says I shall now have one mouth the more to fill and two feet the more to shoe, more disturbed nights, more laborious days, and less leisure or visiting, reading, music, and drawing.

Well! This is one side of the story, to be sure, but I look at the other. Here is a sweet, fragrant mouth to kiss; here are two more feet to make music with their pattering about my nursery. Here is a soul to train for God; and the body in which it dwells is worthy all it will cost, since it is the abode of a kingly tenant. I may see less of friends, but I have gained one dearer than them all, to whom, while I minister in Christ's name, I make a willing sacrifice of what little leisure for my own recreation my other darlings had left me. Yes, my precious baby, you are welcome to your mother's heart, welcome to her time, her strength, her health, her tenderest cares, to her lifelong prayers! Oh, how rich I am, how truly, how wondrously blest!

—June 5—

We begin to be woefully crowded. We need a larger house or a smaller household. I am afraid I secretly, down at the bottom of my heart, wish Martha and her father could give place to my little ones. May God forgive me if this is so! It is a poor time for such emotions when He has just given me another darling child for whom I have as rich and ample a love as if I had spent no affection on the other two. I have made myself especially kind to poor Father and to Martha, lest they should perceive how inconvenient it is to have them here and be pained by it. I would not, for the world, despoil them of what little satisfaction they may derive from living with us. But, oh! I am so selfish, and it is so hard to practice the very law of love I preach to my children! Yet I want this law to rule and reign in my home, that it may be a little heaven below; and I will not, no I will not cease praying that it may be such, no matter what it costs me. Poor Father! Poor old man! I will try to make your home so sweet and homelike to you that when you change it for heaven, it shall be but a transition from one bliss to a higher!

—Evening—

Soon after writing that, I went down to see Father, whom I have had to neglect of late, baby has so used up both time and strength. I found him and Martha engaged in what seemed to be an exciting debate, as Martha had a fiery little red spot on each cheek and was knitting furiously. I was about to retreat, when she got up in a flurried way and went off, saying as she went:

"You tell her, Father; I can't."

I went up to him tenderly and took his hand. Ah, how gentle and loving we are when we have just been speaking to God!

"What is it, dear Father?" I asked. "Is anything troubling you?"

"She is going to be married," he replied.

"Oh, Father!" I cried, "how n—" Nice, I was going to say but stopped just in time.

All my abominable selfishness that I thought I had left at my Master's feet ten minutes before now came trooping back in full force.

"She's going to be married; she'll go away and will take her father to live with her! I can have room for my children and room for Mother! Every element of discord will now leave my home, and Ernest will see what I really am!"

These were the thoughts that rushed through my mind and that illuminated my face.

"Does Ernest know?" I asked.

"Yes, Ernest has known it for weeks."

Then I felt injured and inwardly accused Ernest of unkindness in keeping so important a fact a secret. But when I went back to my children, vexation with him took flight at once. The coming of each new child strengthens and deepens my desire to be what I would have it become, makes my fault more odious in my eyes, and elevates my whole character. What a blessed discipline of joy and of pain my married life has been; how thankful I am to reap its fruits even while pricked by its thorns!

–June 21–

It seems that the happy man who has wooed Martha and won her is no less a personage than old Mr. Underhill, Amelia's uncle. His ideal of a woman is one who has no nerves, no sentiment, no backaches, no headaches, who will see that the wheels of his household machinery are kept well oiled, so that he need never hear them creak and who, in addition to her other accomplishments, believes in him and will be kind enough to live forever for his private accommodation. This exposé of his sentiments he has made to me in a loud, cheerful, pompous way; and he has also favored me with a description of his first wife, who lacked all these qualifications and was obliging enough to depart in peace at an early stage in their married life, meekly preferring thus to make way for a worthier successor. Mr. Underhill, with all his foibles, however, is on the whole a good man. He intends to take Amelia's little girls into his home and be a father, as Martha will be a mother, to them. For this reason he hurries on the marriage, after which they will all go at once to his country seat, which is easy of access and which he says he is sure Father will enjoy. Poor old Father! I hope he will; but when the subject is alluded to, he maintains a somber silence, and it seems to me he never spent so many days alone in his room, brooding over his misery, as he has of late. Oh, that I could comfort him.

–July 12–

The marriage was appointed for the first of the month as old Mr. Underhill wanted to get out of town before the Fourth. As the time drew near, Martha began to pack Father's trunk as well as her own and brush in and out of his room till he had no rest for the sole of his foot and seemed as forlorn as a pelican in the wilderness (Psalm 102:6).

I know no more striking picture of desolation than that presented by one of these quaint birds, standing upon a single leg, feeling as the story has it, "den Jammer und das Elend der Welt" (the misery and distress of the world).

On the last evening in June, we all sat together on the piazza enjoying, each in our own way, a refreshing breeze that had sprung up after a sultry day. Father was quieter than usual and seemed very languid. Ernest, who, out of regard for Martha's last evening at home, had joined our little circle, observed this and said cheerfully:

"You will feel better as soon as you are once more out of the city, Father."

Father made no reply for some minutes; and when he did speak, we were all startled to find his voice trembled as if he were shedding tears. We could not understand what he said. I went to him and made him lean his head upon me as he often did when it ached. He took my hand in both his.

"You do love the old man a little?" he asked in the same tremulous voice.

"Indeed, I do!" I cried, greatly touched by his helpless appeal. "I love you dearly, Father. And I shall miss you sadly."

"Must I go away then?" he whispered. "Cannot I stay here till my summons hence? It will not be long, it will not be long, my child."

With the cry of a hurt animal, Martha sprang up and rushed past us into the house. Ernest followed her, and we heard them talking together a long time. At last Ernest joined us.

"Father," he said, "Martha is a good deal wounded and disappointed at your reluctance to go with her. She threatens to break off her engagement rather than to be separated from you. I really think you would be better off with her than with us. You would enjoy country life because it is what you have been accustomed to; you could spend hours of every day in driving about, just what your health requires."

Father did not reply. He took Ernest's arm and tottered into the house. Then we had a most painful scene. Martha reminded him with bitter tears that her mother had committed him to her with her last breath and set before him all the advantages he would have in her house over ours. Father sat pale and inflexible, tear after tear rolling down his cheeks. Ernest looked distressed and ready to sink. As for me, I cried with Martha and with her father by turns and clung to Ernest with a feeling that all the foundations of the earth were giving way. It came time for evening prayers, and Ernest prayed as he rarely does, for he is rarely moved. He quieted us all by a few simple words of appeal to Him who loved us, and Father then consented to spend the summer with Martha if he might call our home his home and be with us through the winter. But this was not till long after the rest of us went to bed and hard battle with Ernest. He says Ernest is his favorite child and that I am his favorite daughter and our children inexpressibly dear to him. I am ashamed to write down what he said of me. Besides, I am sure there is a wicked, wicked triumph over Martha in my secret heart. I am too elated with his extraordinary preference for us to sympathize with her mortification and grief as I ought. Something whispered that she who has never pitied me deserves no pity now. But I do not like this mean and narrow spirit in myself, nay more, I hate and abhor it.

The marriage took place and they went off together, Father's rigid, white face whiter, more rigid than ever. I am to go to Mother's with the children at once. I feel that a great stone has been rolled away from before the door of my heart; the one human being who refused me a kindly smile, a sympathizing word, has gone, never to return. May God go with her and give her a happy home and make her true and loving to those motherless little ones!

CHAPTER XIX

J have had a charming summer with dear Mother; and now I have the great joy, so long deferred, of having her in my own home. Ernest has been very cordial about it, and James has settled up all her worldly affairs so that she has nothing to do now but to love us and let us love her. It is a pleasant picture to see her with my little darlings about her, telling the old sweet story she told me so often and making God and Heaven and Christ such blissful realities. As I listen, I realize that it is to her I owe that early, deep-seated longing to please the Lord Jesus, which I never remember as having a beginning or an ending, though it did have its fluctuations. And it is another pleasant picture to see her sit in her own old chair, which Ernest was thoughtful enough to have brought for her, pondering cheerfully over her Bible and her Thomas à Kempis just as I have seen her do ever since I can remember. And there is still a third pleasant picture, only that is a new one; it is as she sits at my right hand at the table, the living personification of the blessed gospel of good tidings, with

Father, opposite, the fading image of the law given by Moses. For Father has come back; Father and all his ailments, his pill boxes, his fits of despair, and his fits of dying. But he is quiet and gentle and even loving; and as he sits in his corner, his Bible on his knees, I see how much more he reads the New Testament than he used to do and that the fourteenth chapter of St. John almost opens to him of itself.

I must do Martha the justice to say that her absence, while it increases my domestic peace and happiness, increases my cares also. What with the children, the housekeeping, the thought for Mother's little comforts and the concern for Father's, I am like a bit of chaff driven before the wind and always in a hurry. There are so many stitches to be taken, so many things to pass through one's brain! Mother says no mortal woman ought to undertake so much, but what can I do? While Ernest is straining every nerve to pay off those debts, I must do all the needlework; and we must get along with servants whose want of skill makes them willing to put up with low wages. Of course I cannot tell Mother this, and I really believe she thinks I scrimp and pinch and overdo out of mere stinginess.

–*December 30*–

Ernest came to me today with our accounts for the last three months. He looked quite worried, for him, and asked me if there were any expenses we could cut down.

My heart jumped up into my mouth, and I said in an irritated way:

"I am killing myself with overwork now. Mother says so. I sew every night till twelve o'clock, and I feel all jaded out."

"I did not mean that I wanted you to do any more than you are doing now, dear," he said kindly. "I know you are all jaded out, and I look on this state of feverish activity with great anxiety. Are all these stitches absolutely necessary?"

"You men know nothing about such things," I said, while my conscience pricked me as I went on hurrying to finish the fifth tuck in one of Una's little dresses. "Of course I want my children to look decent."

Ernest sighed.

"I really don't know what to do," he said in a hopeless way. "Father's persisting in living with us is throwing a burden on you that with all your other cares is quite too much for you. I see and feel it every day. Don't you think I had better explain this to him and let him go to Martha's?"

"No, indeed!" I said. "He shall stay here if it kills me, poor old man!"

Ernest began once more to look over the bills. "I don't know why it is," he said, "but since Martha left us, our expenses have increased a good deal."

Now the truth is that when Aunty paid me most generously for teaching her children, I did not dare to offer my earnings to Ernest lest he should be annoyed. So I had quietly used it for household expenses, and it had held out till the time of Martha's marriage. Ernest's injustice was just as painful, just as insufferable as if he had known this; and I now burst out with whatever my rasped, overtaxed nerves impelled me to say, like one possessed.

Ernest was annoyed and surprised.

"I thought we had done with these things," he said and gathered up the papers and went off.

I rose and locked my door and threw myself down upon the floor in an agony of shame, anger, and physical exhaustion. I did not know how large a part of what seemed mere childish ill temper was really the cry of exasperated nerves that had been on too strained a tension and silent too long, and Ernest did not know it either. How could he? His profession kept him for hours every day in the open air; there were times when his work was done and he could take entire rest; and his health is absolutely perfect. But I did not make any excuse for myself at the moment. I was overwhelmed with the sense of my utter unfitness to be a wife and a mother.

Then I heard Ernest try to open the door, and finding it locked, he knocked, calling pleasantly, "It is I, darling; let me in."

I opened it reluctantly enough.

"Come," he said, "put on your things and drive about with me on my rounds. I have no long visits to make; and while I am seeing my patients, you will be getting the air, which you need."

"I do not want to go," I said. "I do not feel well enough. Besides, there's my work."

"You can't see to sew with these red eyes," he declared. "Come! I prescribe a drive as your physician."

"Oh, Ernest, how kind, how forgiving you are!" I cried, running into the arms he held out to me. "If you knew how ashamed, how sorry I am!"

"And if you only knew how ashamed and sorry I am!" he returned. "I ought to have seen how you were taxing and overtaxing yourself, doing your own work and Martha's, too. It must not go on so."

By this time, with a veil over my face, he had got me downstairs and out into the air, which fanned my fiery cheeks and cooled my heated brain. It seemed to me that I have had all this tempest about nothing at all and that with a character still so undisciplined, I was utterly unworthy to be either a wife or mother. But when I tried to say so in broken words, Ernest comforted me with the gentleness and tenderness of a woman.

"Your character is not undisciplined, my darling," he said. "Your nervous organization is very peculiar, and you have had unusual cares and trials from the beginning of our married life. I ought not to have confronted you with my father's debts at a moment when you had every reason to look forward to freedom from most petty economies and cares."

"Don't say so," I interrupted. "If you had not told me you had this draft on your resources, I should have always suspected you of meanness. For you know, dear, you have kept me—that is to say—well you could not help it, but I suppose men can't understand how many demands are made upon a mother for money almost every day. I got along very well till the children came, but since then it has been very hard."

"Yes," he said, "I am sure it has. But let me finish what I was going to say. I want you to make a distinction for yourself, which I make for you, between mere ill temper and the irritability that is the result of a goaded state of the nerves. Until you do that, nothing can be done to relieve you from what I am sure distresses and grieves you exceedingly. Now, I suppose that whenever you speak to me or the children in this irritated way, you lose your own self-respect for the time, at least, and feel degraded in the sight of God also."

"Oh, Ernest! There are no words in any language that mean enough to express the anguish I feel when I speak quick, impatient words to you, the one human being in the universe whom I love with all my heart and soul, and to my darling little children who are almost as dear! I pray and mourn over it day and night. God only knows how I hate myself on account of this one horrible sin!"

"It is a sin only as you deliberately and willfully fulfill the conditions that lead to such results. Now I am sure if you could once make up your mind in the fear of God never to undertake more work of any sort than you can carry on calmly, quietly, without hurry or flurry, and the instant you find yourself growing nervous and like one out of breath, would stop and take breath, you would find this simple, commonsense rule doing for you what no prayers or tears could ever accomplish. Will you try it for one month, my darling?"

"But we can't afford it," I cried with almost a groan. "Why, you have told me this very day that our expenses must be cut down, and now you want me to add to them by doing less work. But the work must be done. The children must be clothed, and there is no end to the stitches to be taken for them, and your stockings must be mended—you make enormous holes in them! And you don't like it if you ever find a button wanting to a shirt or your supply of shirts getting low."

"All you say may be very true," he returned, "but I am determined that you shall not be driven to desperation as you have been of late."

By this time we had reached the house where his visit was to be made, and I had nothing to do but lean back and revolve all he had been saying, over and over again, and to see its reasonableness while I could not see what was to be done for my relief. Ah, I have often felt in moments of bitter grief at my impatience with my children that perhaps God pitied more than He blamed me for it! And now my dear husband was doing the same!

When Ernest had finished his visit, we drove on again in silence.

At last I asked, "Do tell me, Ernest, if you worked out the problem all by yourself?"

He smiled a little.

"No, I did not. But I have had a patient for two or three years whose case has interested me a good deal and for whom I finally prescribed just as I have done for you. The thing worked like a charm and she is now physically and morally quite well."

"I dare say her husband is a rich man," I said.

"He is not as poor as your husband, at any rate," Ernest replied. "But rich or poor, I am determined not to sit looking on while you exert yourself so far beyond your strength. Just think, dear, suppose for fifty or a hundred or two hundred dollars a year you could buy a sweet, cheerful, quiet tone of mind, would you hesitate one moment to do so? And you can do it if you will. You are not ill tempered but quick tempered; the irritability that annoys you so is a physical infirmity that will disappear the moment you cease to be goaded into it by the exacting mistress you have hitherto been to yourself."

All this sounded very plausible while Ernest was talking, but the moment I got home, I snatched up my work from mere force of habit.

"I may as well finish this as it is begun," I said to myself, and the stitches flew from my needle like sparks of fire. Little Ernest came and begged for a story, but I put him off. Then Una wanted to sit on my lap, but I told her I was too busy. In the course of an hour, the influence of the fresh air and of Ernest's talk had nearly lost their power over me; my thread kept breaking, the children leaned on and tired me, the baby woke up and cried, and I got all out of patience.

"Do go away, Ernest," I said, "and let Mamma have a little peace. Don't you see how busy I am? Go and play with Una like a good boy." But he would not go and kept teasing Una till she, too, began to cry, and she and baby made a regular concert of it.

"Oh, dear!" I sighed. "This work will never be done!" And I threw it down impatiently, and took the baby impatiently, and began to walk up and down with him impatiently. I was not willing that this little darling, whom I love so dearly, should get through with his nap and interrupt my work; yet I was displeased with myself, and tried by kissing him to make some amends for the hasty, unpleasant tones with which I had grieved him and frightened the other children. This evening Ernest came to me with a larger sum of money than he had ever given me at one time.

"Now every cent of this is to be spent," he said, "in having work done. I know any number of poor women who will be thankful to have all you can give them."

Dear me! It is easy to talk, and I do feel grateful to Ernest for his thoughtfulness and kindness. But I am almost in rags and need every cent of this money to make myself decent. I am positively ashamed to go anywhere, my clothes are so shabby. Besides, supposing I leave off sewing and all sorts of overdoing of a kindred nature, I must still nurse my baby, I suppose, and be up with him nights; and the others will have their cross days and their sick days, and Father will have his. Alas, there can be for me no royal road to a "sweet, cheerful, quiet tone of mind!"

–*Jan. 1, 1844*–

My mother says Ernest is entirely right in forbidding my working so hard. I must own that I already feel better. I have all the time I need to read my Bible and to pray now, and the children do not irritate and annoy me as they did. Who knows but I shall yet become quite amiable?

Ernest made his father very happy today by telling him that the last of those wretched debts is paid. I think that he might have told me that this deliverance was at hand. I did not know but we had years of these struggles with poverty before us. What with the relief from this anxiety, my improved state of health, and Father's pleasure, I am in splendid spirits today. Ernest, too, seems wonderfully cheerful, and we both feel that we may now look forward to a quiet happiness we have never known. With such a husband and such children as mine, I ought to be the most grateful creature on earth. And I have dear old Mother and James besides. I don't quite know what to think about James's relation to Lucy. He is so brimful and running over with happiness that he is also full of fun and of love, and after all he may only like her as a cousin.

–*Feb. 14*–

Father has not been well of late. It seems as if he kept up until he was relieved about those debts and then sunk down. I read to him a good deal and so does Mother, but his mind is still dark and he looks forward to the hour of death with painful misgivings. He is getting a little childish about my leaving him and clings to me exactly as if I were his own child. Martha spends a good deal of time with him and fusses over him in a way that I wonder she does not see is annoying him. He wants to be read to, to hear a hymn sung or a verse repeated, and to be left otherwise in perfect quiet. But she is continually pulling out and shaking up his pillows, bathing his head in hot vinegar, and soaking his feet. It looks so odd to see her in one of the elegant silk dresses old Mr. Underhill makes her wear, with her sleeves rolled up, the skirt hid away under a large apron, rubbing away at poor Father till it seems as if his tired soul would fly out of him.

—Feb. 20—

Father grows weaker every day. Ernest has sent for his other children, John and Helen. Martha is no longer able to come here; her husband is very sick with a fever and cannot be left alone. No doubt he enjoys her bustling way of nursing and likes to have his pillows pushed from under him every five minutes. I am afraid I feel glad that she is kept away and that I have Father all to myself. Ernest never was so fond of me as he is now. I don't know what to make of it.

—Feb. 22—

John and his wife and Helen have come. They stay at Martha's, where there is plenty of room. John's wife is a little soft dumpling of a thing and looks up to him as a mouse would look up at a steeple. He strikes me as a very selfish man. He steers straight for the best seat, leaving her standing, if need be, accepts her humble attentions with the air of one collecting his just debts, and is continually snubbing and setting her right. Yet in some things he is very like Ernest; and perhaps a wife destitute of self-assertion and without much individuality would have spoiled him as Harriet has spoiled John. For I think it must be partly her fault that he dares to be so egotistical. Helen is the dearest, prettiest creature I ever saw. Oh, why would James take a fancy to Lucy! I feel that new delight of having a sister to love and to admire. And she will love me in time; I feel sure of it.

–*March 1*–

Father is very feeble and in great mental distress. He gropes about in the dark and shudders at the approach of death. We can do nothing but pray for him. And the cloud will be lifted when he leaves this world if not before. For I know he is a good, yes, saintly man, dear to God and dear to Christ.

–*March 4*–

Dear Father has gone. We were all kneeling and praying and weeping around him when suddenly he called me to come to him. I went and let him lean his head on my breast as he loved to do. Sometimes I have stood so by the hour together ready to sink with fatigue and only kept up with the thought that if this were my own precious father's bruised head, I could stand and hold it forever.

"Daughter Katherine," he said in his faint, tremulous way, "you have come with me to the very brink of the river. I thank God for all your cheering words and ways. I thank God for giving you to be a helpmeet to my son. Farewell, now," he added in a low, firm voice. "I feel the bottom, and it is good!"

He lay back on his pillow, looking upward with an expression of seraphic peace and joy on his worn, meager face; and so his life passed gently away.

Oh, the affluence of God's payments! What a recompense for the poor love I had given my husband's father and the poor little services I had rendered him! Oh, that I had never been impatient with him, never smiled at his peculiarities, never in my secret heart felt him unwelcome to my home! And how wholly I overlooked, in my blind selfishness, what he must have suffered in feeling himself homeless, dwelling with us on sufferance, but master and head nowhere on earth! May God carry these lessons home to my heart of hearts and make this cloud of mingled remorse and shame that now envelopes me to descend in showers of love and benediction on every human soul that mine can bless!

CHAPTER XX

I have had a new lesson that has almost broke my heart. In looking over his father's papers, Ernest found a little journal, brief in its records indeed; but we learn from it that on all those wedding and birthdays, when I fancied his austere religion made him hold aloof from our merrymaking, he was spending the time in fasting and praying for us and for our children! Oh, shall I ever learn the sweet charity that thinketh no evil and believeth all things! What blessings may not have descended upon us and our children through those prayers! What evils may they not have warded off! Dear old Father! Oh, that I could once more put my loving arms about him and bid him welcome to our home! And how gladly would I now confess to him all my unjust judgments concerning him and entreat his forgiveness! Must life always go on thus? Must I always be erring, ignorant, and blind? How I hate this arrogant sweeping past my brother man, this utter ignoring of his hidden life!

I see now that it is well for Mother that she did not

come to live with me at the beginning of my married life. I should not have borne with her little peculiarities nor have made her half so happy as I can now. I thank God that my varied disappointments and discomforts, my feeble health, my poverty, my mortifications have done me some little good and driven me to Him a thousand times because I could not get along without His help. But I am not satisfied with my state in His sight. I am sure something is lacking, though I know not what it is.

–May–

Helen is going to stay here and live with Martha. How glad, how enchanted I am! Old Mr. Underhill is getting well; I saw him today. He can talk of nothing but his illness, of Martha's wonderful skill in nursing him, declaring that he owed his life to her. I felt a little piqued at this speech because Ernest was very attentive to him and no doubt did his share toward the cure. We have fitted up Father's room for a nursery. Hitherto all the children have had to sleep in our room, which has been bad for them and bad for us. I have been so afraid they would keep Ernest awake if they were unwell and restless. I have secured an excellent nurse, who is as fresh and blooming as the flower whose name she bears. The children are already attached to her, and I feel that the worst of my life is now over.

–June–

Little Ernest was taken sick on the very day I wrote that. The attack was fearfully sudden and violent. He is still very, very ill. I have not forgotten that I said once that I would give my children to God should He ask for them. And I will. But, oh, this agony of suspense! It eats into my soul and eats it away. Oh, my little Ernest! My first-born son! My pride, my joy, my hope! And I thought the worst of my life was over!

—August—

We have come into the country with what God has left us, our two youngest children. Yes, I have tasted the bitter cup of bereavement and drunk it down to its dregs. I gave my darling to God, I gave him, I gave him! But, oh, with what anguish I saw those round, dimpled limbs wither and waste away, the glad smile fade forever from that beautiful face! What a fearful thing it is to be a mother! But I have given my child to God. I would not recall him if I could. I am thankful He has counted me worthy to present Him so costly a gift.

I cannot shed a tear, and I must find relief in writing or I shall lose my senses. My noble, beautiful boy! My first-born son! And to think that my delicate little Una still lives and that death has claimed that bright, glad creature who was the sunshine of our home!

But let me not forget my mercies. Let me not forget that I have a precious husband and two darling children and my kind, sympathizing Mother still left to me. Let me not forget how many kind friends gathered about us in our sorrow. Above all let me remember God's lovingkindness and tender mercy. He has not left us to the bitterness of a grief that refuses and disdains to be comforted. We believe in Him, we love Him, we worship Him as we never did before.

My dear Ernest has felt this sorrow to his heart's core. But he has not for one moment questioned the goodness or the love of our Father in thus taking from us the child who promised to be our greatest earthly joy. Our consent to

God's will has drawn us together very closely; together we bear the yoke in our youth, together we pray and sing praises in the very midst of our tears. "I was dumb with silence because Thou didst it" (Psalm 39:9).

–Sept.–

The old pain and cough have come back with the first cool nights of this month. Perhaps I am going to my darling —I do not know. I am certainly very feeble. Consenting to suffer does not annul the suffering. Such a child could not go hence without rendering and tearing its way out of the heart that loved it. This world is wholly changed to me and I walk in it like one in a dream. And dear Ernest is changed, too. He says little and is all kindness and goodness to me, but I can see that here is a wound that will never be healed.

I am confined to my room now with nothing to do but to think, think, think. I do not believe that God has taken our child in mere displeasure, but I cannot but feel that this affliction might not have been necessary if I had not so chafed and writhed and secretly repined at the way in which my home was invaded and at our galling poverty. God has exchanged the one discipline for the other; and oh, how far more bitter is this cup!

–Oct. 4–

My darling boy would have been six years old today. Ernest still keeps me shut up, but he rather urges my seeing a friend now and then. People say very strange things in the way of consolation. I begin to think that a tender clasp of the hand is about all one can give to the afflicted. One says I must not grieve because my child is better off in heaven. Yes, he is better off; I know it, I feel it, but I miss him none the less. Others say he might have grown up to be a bad man and broken my heart. Perhaps he might, but I cannot make myself believe that likely. One lady asked me if this affliction was not a rebuke of my idolatry of my darling; and another if I had not been in a cold, worldly state, needing this severe blow on that account.

But I find no consolation or support in these remarks. My comfort is in my perfect faith in the goodness and love of my Father, my certainty that He had a reason in thus afflicting me that I should admire and adore if I knew what it was. And in the midst of my sorrow I have had and do have a delight in Him hitherto unknown, so that sometimes this room in which I am a prisoner seems like the very gate of heaven.

–May–

A long winter in my room and all sorts of painful remedies and appliances and deprivations. And now I am getting well and drive out every day. Martha sends her carriage, and Mother goes with me. Dear Mother! How nearly perfect she is! I never saw a sweeter face nor ever heard sweeter expressions of faith in God and love to all about her than hers. She has been my tower of strength all through these weary months, and yet she has shared my sorrow and made it her own.

I can see that Ernest's affliction and this prolonged anxiety about me have been a heavenly benediction to him. I am sure that every mother whose sick child he visits will have a sympathy he could not have given while all our own little ones were alive and well. I thank God that He has thus increased my dear husband's usefulness, as I think that He has mine also. How tenderly I already feel toward all suffering children, and how easy it will be now to be patient with them!

Keene, N.H., July 12–

It is a year ago this day that the brightest sunshine faded out of our lives, and our beautiful boy was taken from us. I have been tempted to spend this anniversary in bitter tears and lamentations. For, oh, this sorrow is not healed by time! I feel it more and more. But I begged God when I first awoke this morning not to let me so dishonor and grieve Him. I may suffer, I must suffer, He means it, He wills it, but let it be without repining, without gloomy despondency. The world is full of sorrow; it is not I alone who taste its bitter draughts, nor have I the only right to a sad countenance. Oh, for patience to bear on, cost what it may!

"Cheerfully and gratefully I lay myself and all I am or own at the feet of Him who redeemed me with His precious blood, engaging to follow Him, bearing the cross He lays upon me." This is the least I can do, and I do it while my heart lies broken and bleeding at His feet.

My dear little Una has improved somewhat in health, but I am never free from anxiety about her. She is my milk-white lamb, my dove, my fragrant flower. One cannot look in her pure face without a sense of peace and rest. She is the sentinel who voluntarily guards my door when I am engaged at my devotions; she is my little comforter when I am sad; my companion and friend at all times. I talk to her of Christ and always have done, just as I think of Him, and as if I expected sympathy from her in my love to Him. It was the same with my darling Ernest. If I required a little self-denial, I said cheerfully, "This is hard, but doing it for our best Friend sweetens it," and their alacrity was pleasant to see. Ernest threw his whole soul into whatever he did and sometimes when engaged in play would hesitate a little when directed to do something else, such as carrying a message for me and the like. But if I said, "If you do this cheerfully and pleasantly, my darling, you do it for Jesus and that will make Him smile upon you," he would invariably yield at once.

Is not this the true, the natural way of linking every little daily act of a child's life with the Divine Love, that Divine Life that gives meaning to all things?

But what do I mean by the vain boast that I have always trained my children thus? Alas! I have done it only at times; for while my theory was sound, my temper of mind was but too often unsound. I was often and often impatient with my dear little boy; often my tone was a worldly one; I was often full of eager interest in mere outside things and forgot that I was living or that my children were living save for the present moment.

It seems now that I have a child in heaven and am bound to the invisible world by such a tie that I can never again be entirely absorbed by this.

I fancy my ardent, eager little boy as having some such employments in his new and happy home as he had here. I see him loving Him who took children in His arms and blessed them with all the warmth of which his nature is capable, and as perhaps employed as one of those messengers whom God sends forth as His ministers. For I cannot think of those active feet, those busy hands as always quiet. Ah, my darling, that I could look upon you for a moment, a single moment, and catch one of your radiant smiles, just one!

–*August 4*–

How full are David's Psalms of the cry of the sufferer! He must have experienced every kind of bodily and mental torture. He gives most vivid illustrations of the wasting, wearing process of disease—for instance, what a contrast is the picture we have of him when he was "ruddy, and withal of a beautiful countenance, and goodly to look to" (1 Samuel 16:12), and the one he paints of himself in after years when he says, "I may tell my bones, they look and stare upon me; my days are like a shadow that declineth, and I am withered like grass. I am weary and groaning; all the night make I my bed to swim; I water my couch with my tears. For my soul is full of troubles; and my life draweth near unto the grave" (Psalm 22:17; 102:11; 6:6; 88:3).

And then what wails of anguish are these!

"I am afflicted, and ready to die from my youth up; while I suffer thy terrors I am distracted. Thy wrath lieth hard upon me and thou hast afflicted me with all thy waves. All thy waves and thy billows have gone over me. Lover and friend has thou put far from me, and mine acquaintance into utter darkness" (Psalm 88:15,7; 42:7; 88:18).

Yet through it all what grateful joy in God, what expressions of living faith and devotion! During my long illness and confinement to my room, the Bible has been almost a new book to me; and I see that God has always dealt with His children as He deals with them now and that no new thing has befallen me. All these weary days so full of languor, these nights so full of unrest have had their appointed mission to my soul. And perhaps I have had no discipline so salutary as this forced inaction and uselessness at a time when youth and natural energy continually cried out for room and work.

–August 15–

I dragged out my drawing materials in a listless way this morning and began to sketch the beautiful scene from my window. At first I could not feel interested. It seemed as if my hand was crippled and lost its cunning when it unloosened its grasp of little Ernest and let him go. But I prayed, as I worked, that I might not yield to the inclination to despise and throw away the gift with which God has Himself endowed me. Mother was gratified and said it restored her to see me act like myself once more. Ah, I have been very selfish and have been far too much absorbed with my sorrow and my illness and my own petty struggles.

–August 19–

I met today an old friend, Maria Kelly, who is married, it seems, and settled down in this pretty village. She asked so many questions about my little Ernest that I had to tell her the whole story of his precious life, sickness, and death. I forced myself to do this quietly and without any great demand on her sympathies. My reward for the constraint I thus put upon myself was the abrupt question:

"Haven't you grown stoical?"

I felt the angry blood rush through my veins as it has not done in a long time. My pride was wounded to the quick, and those cruel, unjust words still rankle in my heart. This is not as it should be. I am constantly praying that my pride may be humbled; and then when it is attacked, I shrink from the pain the blow causes and am angry with the hand that inflicts it. It is just so with two or three unkind things Martha has said to me. I can't help brooding over them and feeling stung with their injustice even while making the most desperate struggle to rise above and forget them. It is well for our fellow creatures that God forgives and excuses them when we fail to do it, and I can easily fancy that poor Maria Kelly is at this moment dearer in His sight than I am who have taken fire at a chance word. And I can see now, what I wonder I did not see at the time, that God was dealing very kindly and wisely with me when He made Martha overlook my good qualities, of which I suppose I have some, as everybody else has, and call out all my bad ones, since the ax was thus laid at the root of self-love. And it is plain that self-love cannot die without a fearful struggle.

–May 26, 1846–

How long it is since I have written in my journal! We have had a winter full of cares, perplexities, and sicknesses. Mother began it by such a severe attack of inflammatory rheumatism as I could not have supposed she could live through. Her sufferings were dreadful, and I might almost say her patience was, for I often thought it would be less painful to hear her groan and complain than to witness such heroic fortitude, such sweet docility under God's hand. I hope I shall never forget the lessons I have learned in her sickroom. Ernest says he never shall cease to rejoice that she lives with us and that he can watch over her health. He has indeed been like a son to her, and this has been a great solace amid all her sufferings. Before she was able to leave the room, poor little Una was prostrated by one of her ill turns and is still very feeble. The only way in which she can be diverted is by reading to her, and I have done little else these two months but hold her in my arms, singing little songs and hymns, telling stories and reading what few books I find that are unexciting, simple, yet entertaining. My precious little darling! She bears the yoke in her youth without a frown, but it is agonizing to see her suffer so. How much easier it would be to bear all her physical infirmities myself! I suppose to those who look on from outside we must appear like a most unhappy family, since we hardly get free from one trouble before another steps in. But I see more and more that happiness is not dependent on health or any other outside prosperity. We are at peace with each other and at peace with God; His dealings with us do not perplex or puzzle us, though we do not pretend to understand them. On the other hand, Martha, with absolutely perfect health, with a husband entirely devoted to her, and with every wish gratified, yet seems always careworn and dissatisfied. Her servants worry her very life out; she misses the homely household duties to which she has been accustomed; and her conscience stumbles at little things and overlooks greater ones. It is very interesting, I think, to study different homes as well as the different characters that form them.

Amelia's girls are quiet, good children to whom their father writes what Mr. Underhill and Martha pronounce "beautiful" letters wherein he always styles himself their "brokenhearted but devoted Father." "Devotion," to my mind, involves self-sacrifice; and I cannot reconcile its use, in this case, with the life of ease he leads while all the care of his children is thrown upon others. But some people, by means of a few such phrases, not only impose upon themselves but upon their friends and pass for persons of great sensibility.

As I have been confined to the house nearly the whole winter, I have had to derive my spiritual support from books; and as Mother gradually recovered, she enjoyed Leighton with me, as I knew she would. Dr. Cabot comes to see us very often, but I do not now find it possible to get the instruction from him I used to do. I see that the Christian life must be individual, as the natural character is, and that I cannot be exactly like Dr. Cabot, or exactly like Mrs. Campbell, or exactly like Mother, though they all three stimulate and are an inspiration to me. But I see, too, that the great points of similarity in Christ's disciples have always been the same. This is the testimony of all the good books, sermons, hymns, and memoirs I read—that God's ways are infinitely perfect; that we are to love Him for what He is and therefore equally as much when He afflicts as when He prospers us; that there is no real happiness but in doing and suffering His will; and that this life is but a scene of probation through which we pass to the real life above.

CHAPTER XXI

*E*rnest asked me to go with him to see one of his patients, as he often does when there is a lull in the tempest at home. We both feel that as we have so little money of our own to give away, it is a privilege to give what services and what cheering words we can. As I took it for granted that we were going to see some poor old woman, I put up several little packages of tea and sugar, with which Susan Green always keeps me supplied, and added a bottle of my own raspberry vinegar, which never comes amiss, I find, to old people. Ernest drove to the door of an aristo-cratic-looking house and helped me to alight in his usual silence.

"It is probably one of the servants we are going to visit," I thought within myself; "but I am surprised at his bringing me. The family may not approve it."

The next thing I knew I found myself being introduced to a beautiful, brilliant young lady who sat in a wheelchair like a queen on a throne in a room full of tasteful ornaments, flowers, and birds. Now I had come away just as I was, when

Ernest called me, and that "was" means a very plain ging-
ham dress wherein I had been darning stockings all morning.
I suppose a saint wouldn't have cared for that, but I did and
for a moment stood the picture of confusion, my hands full
of oddly shaped parcels and my face all in a flame.

"My wife, Miss Clifford," I heard Ernest say; and then
I caught the curious, puzzled look in her eyes, which said
as plainly as words could do, "What has the creature
brought me?"

"I ask your pardon, Miss Clifford," I said, thinking it
best to speak out just the honest truth, "but I supposed the
doctor was taking me to see someone of his old women,
and so I have brought you a little tea, and a little sugar, and
a bottle of raspberry vinegar!"

"How delicious!" cried she. "It really rests me to meet
with a genuine human being at last! Why didn't you make
some stiff, prim speech instead of telling the truth out and
out? I declare I mean to keep all you have brought me just
for the fun of the thing."

This put me at ease, and I forgot all about my dress in
a moment.

"I see you are just what the doctor boasted you were,"
she went on. "But he never would bring you to see me
before. I suppose he has told you why I could not go to see
you?"

"To tell the truth, he never speaks to me of his patients
unless he thinks I can be of use to them."

"I dare say I do not look much like an invalid," she
said, "but here I am, tied to this chair. It is six months since
I could bear my own weight upon my feet."

I saw then that though her face was so bright and full
of color, her hand was thin and transparent. But what a

picture she made as she sat there in her magnificent beauty, relieved by such a background of foliage, flowers, and artistic objects!

"I told the doctor the other day that life was nothing but a humbug, and he said he should bring me a remedy against that false notion the next time he came, and you, I suppose, are that remedy," she continued. "Come, begin; I am ready to take any number of doses."

I could only laugh and try to look daggers at Ernest, who sat looking over a magazine, apparently absorbed in its contents.

"Ah!" she cried, nodding her head sagaciously, "I knew you would agree with me."

"Agree with you in calling life a humbug!" I cried, now fairly aroused. "Death itself is not more a reality!"

"I have not tried death yet," she said more seriously; "but I have tried life twenty-five years, and I know all about it. It is eat, drink, sleep, yawn, and be bored. It is what shall I wear, where shall I go, how shall I get rid of the time; it says, 'How do you do? How is your husband? How are your children?'—it means, 'Now I have asked all the conventional questions, and I don't care a fig what their answer may be.' "

"This may be its meaning to some persons," I replied, "for instance, to mere pleasure seekers. But of course it is interpreted quite differently by others. To some it means nothing but a dull, hopeless struggle with poverty and hardship—and its whole aspect might be changed to them should those who do not know what to do to get rid of the time spend their surplus leisure in making this struggle less brutalizing."

"Yes, I have heard such doctrine, and at one time I

tried charity myself. I picked up a dozen or so of dirty little wretches out of the streets and undertook to clothe and teach them. I might as well have tried to instruct the chairs in my room. Besides, the whole house had to be aired after they had gone, and Mamma missed two teaspoons and a fork and was perfectly disgusted with the whole thing. Then I fell to knitting socks for babies, but they only occupied my hands, and my head felt as empty as ever. Mamma took me off on a journey, as she always did when I took to moping, and that diverted me for a while. But after that everything went on in the old way. I got rid of part of the day by changing my dress and putting on pretty things—it is a great thing to have a habit of wearing one's ornaments, for instance; and then in the evening one could go to the opera or the theater or some other place of amusement, after which one could sleep all through the next morning, and so get rid of that. But I had been used to such things all my life, and they had got to be about as flat as flat can be. If I had been born a little earlier in the history of the world, I would have gone into a convent; but that sort of thing is out of fashion now."

"The best convent," I said, "for a woman is the seclusion of her own home. There she may find her vocation and fight her battles, and there she may learn the reality and the earnestness of life."

"Pshaw!" cried she. "Excuse me, however, for saying that; but some of the most brilliant girls I know have settled down into mere married women and spend their whole time in nursing babies! Think how belittling!"

"Is it more so than spending it in dressing, driving, dancing, and the like?"

"Of course it is. I had a friend once who shone like a

star in society. She married and had four children as fast as she could. Well! What was the consequence? She lost her beauty, lost her spirit and animation, lost her youth, and lost her health. The only earthly things she can talk about are teething, dieting, and the measles!"

I laughed at this exaggeration and looked round to see what Ernest thought of such talk. But he had disappeared.

"As you have spoken plainly to me, knowing me to be a wife and a mother, you must allow me to speak plainly in return," I began.

"Oh, speak plainly, by all means! I am quite sick and tired of having truth served up in pink cotton and scented with lavender."

"Then you will permit me to say that when you speak contemptuously of the vocation of maternity, you dishonor not only the mother who bore you but the Lord Jesus Himself, who chose to be born of woman and to be ministered unto by her through a helpless infancy."

Miss Clifford was a little startled.

"How terribly earnest you are!" she said. "It is plain that to you, at any rate, life is indeed no humbug."

I thought of my dear ones, of Ernest, of my children, of Mother, and of James; and I thought of my love for them and of theirs for me. And I thought of Him who alone gives reality to even such joys as these. My face must have been illuminated by the thought, for she dropped the bantering tone she had used hitherto and asked with real earnestness:

"What is it you know, and that I do not know, that makes you so satisfied while I am so dissatisfied?"

I hesitated before I answered, feeling as I never felt before, how ignorant, how unfit to lead others I really am.

Then I said:

"Perhaps you need to know God, to know Christ?"

She looked disappointed and tired. So I came away, first promising, at her request, to go to see her again. I found Ernest just driving up and told him what had passed. He listened in his usual silence, and I longed to have him say whether I had spoken wisely and well.

—June 1—

I have been to see Miss Clifford again and made Mother go with me. Miss Clifford took a fancy to her at once.

"Ah!" she said after one glance at the dear, loving face, "nobody need tell me that you are good and kind. But I am a little afraid of good people. I fancy they are always criticizing me and expecting me to imitate their perfection."

"Perfection does not exact perfection," was Mother's answer. "I would rather be judged by an angel than by a man." And then Mother led her on, little by little and most adroitly, to talk of herself and of her state of health. She is an orphan and lives in this great, stately house alone with her servants. Until she was laid aside by the state of her health, she lived in the world and of it. Now she is a prisoner, and prisoners have time to think.

"Here I sit," she said, "all day long. I never was fond of staying at home or of reading, and needlework I absolutely hate. In fact, I do not know how to sew."

"Some such pretty, feminine work might beguile you of a few of the long hours of these long days," said Mother. "One can't be always reading."

"But a lady came to see me, a Mrs. Goodhue, one of your good sort, I suppose, and she preached me quite a sermon on the employment of time. She said I had a solemn admonition of Providence and ought to devote myself entirely to religion. I had just begun to be interested in a bit of embroidery, but she frightened me out of it. But I can't bear such dreadfully good people with faces a mile long."

Mother made her produce the collar or whatever it was, showed her how to hold her needle and arrange her pattern, and they both got so absorbed in it that I had leisure to look at some of the beautiful things with which the room was full.

"Make the object of your life right," I heard Mother say at last, "and these little details will take care of themselves."

"But I haven't any object," Miss Clifford objected, "unless it is to get through these tedious days somehow. Before I was taken ill, my chief object was to make myself attractive to the people I met. And the easiest way to do that was to dress becomingly and make myself look as well as I could."

"I suppose," said Mother, "that most girls could say the same. They have an instinctive desire to please, and they take what they conceive to be the shortest and easiest road to that end. It requires no talent, no education, no thought to dress tastefully; the most empty-hearted, frivolous young person can do it, provided she has money enough. Those who can't get the money make up for it by a fearful expenditure of precious time. They plan, they cut, they fit, they rip, they trim till they can appear in society looking exactly like everybody else. They think of nothing, talk of nothing but how this shall be fashioned and that be trimmed; and as to their hair, Satan uses it as his favorite net and catches them in it every day of their lives."

"But I never cut or trimmed," said Miss Clifford.

"No, because you could afford to have it done for you.

But you acknowledge that you spent a great deal of time in dressing because you thought that the easiest way of making yourself attractive. But it does not follow that the easiest way is the best way, and sometimes the longest way round is the shortest way home."

"For instance?"

"Well, let us imagine a young lady living in the world as you say you lived. She has never seriously reflected on any subject one half hour in her life. She has been borne on by the current and let it take her where it would. But at last some influence is brought to bear upon her that leads her to stop to look about her and to think. She finds herself in a world of serious, momentous events. She sees that she cannot live in it, was not meant to live in it forever, and that her whole unknown future depends on what she is, not on how she looks. She begins to cast about for some plan of life and this leads—"

"A plan of life?" Miss Clifford interrupted. "I never heard of such a thing."

"Yet you would smile at an architect who, having a noble structure to build, should begin to work on it in a haphazard way, putting in a brick here and a stone there, weaving in straws and sticks if they come to hand, and when asked on what work he was engaged and what manner of building he intended to erect, should reply he had no plan but thought something would come of it."

Miss Clifford made to reply. She sat with her head resting on her hand, looking dreamily before her, a truly beautiful but unconscious picture. I, too, began to reflect that while I had really aimed to make the most out of life, I had not done it methodically or intelligently.

We are going to try to stay in town this summer.

Hitherto Ernest would not listen to my suggestion of what an economy this would be. He always said this would turn out anything but an economy in the end. But now we have no teething baby; little Raymond is a strong, healthy child and Una remarkably well for her; and money is so slow to come in and so fast to go out. What discomforts we suffer in the country it would take a book to write down, and here we shall have our own home, as usual. I shall not have to be separated from Ernest and shall have leisure to devote to two very interesting people who must stay in town all year round, no matter who goes out of it. I mean dear Mrs. Campbell and Miss Clifford, who both attract me, though in such different ways.

CHAPTER XXII

*W*ell, I had my own way, and I am afraid it has been an unwise one. For though I have enjoyed the leisure afforded by everybody being out of town and the opportunity it has given me to devote myself to the very sweetest work on earth, the care of my darling little ones, the heat and the stifling atmosphere have been trying for me and for them. My pretty Rose went last May to bloom in a home of her own, so I thought I would not look for a nurse but take the whole care of them myself. This would not be much of a task to a strong person, but I am not strong; and a great deal of the time just dressing them and taking them out to walk has exhausted me. Then all the mending and other sewing must be done, and with the overexertion creeps in the fretful tone, the impatient word. Yet I can never be as impatient with the little children as I should be but for the remembrance that I should count it only a joy to minister once more to my darling boy, cost what weariness it might.

But now new cares are at hand, and I have been

searching for a person to whom I can safely trust my children when I am laid aside. Thus far I have had, in this capacity, three different Temptations in human form.

The first, a smart, tidy-looking woman, informed me at the outset that she was perfectly competent to take the whole charge of the children and should prefer my attending to my own affairs while she attended to hers.

I replied that my affairs lay chiefly in caring for and being with my children; to which she returned that she feared I should not suit her, as she had her own views concerning the training of children. She added, with condescension, that at all events she should except in any case of difference (of judgment) between us, that I, being the younger and least experienced of the two, should always yield to her. She then went on to give me her view on the subject of nursery management.

"In the first place," she said, "I never pet or fondle children. It makes them babyish and sickly."

"Oh, I see you will not suit me," I cried. "You need go no further. I consider love the best educator for a little child."

"Indeed, I think I shall suit you perfectly," she replied, nothing daunted. "I have been in the business twenty years and have always suited wherever I lived. You will be surprised to see how much sewing I shall accomplish and how quiet I shall keep the children."

"But I don't want them kept quiet," I persisted. "I want them to be as merry and cheerful as crickets, and I care a great deal more to have them amused than to have the sewing done, though that is important, I confess."

"Very well, ma'am, I will sit and rock them by the hour if you wish it."

"But I don't wish it," I cried, exasperated at the coolness that gave her such an advantage over me. "Let us say no more about it; you do not suit me and the sooner we part, the better. I must be mistress of my own house, and I want no advice in relation to my children."

"I shall hardly leave you before you will regret parting with me," she returned in a placid, pitying way.

I was afraid I had not been quite dignified in my interview with this person with whom I ought to have had no discussion, and my equanimity was not restored by her shaking hands with me in a patronizing way at parting and expressing the hope that I should one day "be green tree in the Paradise of God." Nor was it any too great a consolation to find that she had suggested to my cook that my intellect was not quite sound.

Temptation the second confessed that she knew nothing but was willing to be taught. Yes, she might be willing, but she could not be taught. She could not see why Raymond should not have everything he chose to cry for nor why she should not take the children to the kitchens where her friends abode instead of keeping them out in the air. She could not understand why she must not tell Una every half hour that she was as fair as a lily and that the little angels in heaven cried for such hair as hers. And there was no rhyme or reason, to her mind, why she could not have her friends visit in her nursery, since, as she declared, the cook would hear all her secrets if she received them in the kitchen. Her assurance that she thought me a very nice lady and that there never were two such children as mine failed to move my hard heart, and I was thankful when I got her out of the house.

Temptation the third appeared, for a time, the perfection

of a nurse. She kept herself and the nursery and the children in most refreshing order; she amused Una, when she was more than usually unwell, with a perfect fund of innocent stories; the work flew from her nimble fingers as if by magic. I boasted everywhere of my good luck and sang her praises in Ernest's ears till he believed in her with all his heart. But one night we were out late; we had been spending the evening at Aunty's and came in with Ernest's night key as quietly as possible in order not to arouse the children. I stole softly to the nursery to see if all was going on well there. Bridget, it seems, had taken the opportunity to wash her clothes in the nursery, and they hung all about the room drying, a hot fire raging for the purpose. In the midst of them, with a candle and prayer book on a chair, Bridget knelt fast asleep, the candle within inches of her sleeve. Her assurance when I aroused her that she was not asleep but merely rapt in devotion did not soften my hard heart, nor was I moved by the representation that she was a saint and always wore black on that account. I packed her off in anything but a saintly frame and felt that a fourth Temptation would scatter what little grace I possessed to the four winds. These changes upstairs made discord, too, below. My cook was displeased at so much coming and going and made the kitchen a sort of purgatory that I dreaded to enter. At last, when her temper fairly ran away with her and she became impertinent to the last degree, I said coolly,

"If any lady should speak to me in this way, I should resent it. But no lady would so far forget herself. And I overlook your rudeness on the ground that you do not know better than to make use of such expressions."

This capped the climax! She declared that she had never been told before that she was no lady and did not know how to behave and gave warning at once.

I wish I could help running to tell Ernest all these annoyances. It does no good and only worries him. But how much of a woman's life is made up of such trials and provocations! And how easy it is when on one's knees to bear them aright and how far easier to bear them wrong when one finds the coal going too fast, the butter out just as one is sitting down to breakfast, the potatoes watery, and the bread sour or heavy! And then when one is well nigh desperate, does one's husband fail to say in bland tones, "My dear, if you would just speak to Bridget, I am sure she would improve!"

Oh, that there were indeed magic in a spoken word!

And do what I can, the money Ernest gives me will not hold out. He knows absolutely nothing about the hydra-headed monster, a household. I have had to go back to sewing as furiously as ever. And with the sewing, the old pain in the side has come back, and the sharp, quick speech that I hate and that Ernest hates and that everybody hates. I groan, being burdened, and am almost weary of my life. And my prayers are all mixed up with worldly thoughts and cares. I am appalled at the things that have got to be done before winter and am tempted to cut short my devotions in order to have more time to accomplish what I must accomplish.

How have I got into this slough? When was it that I came down from the Mount where I had seen the Lord and came back to make these miserable, petty things as much my business as ever? Oh, these fluctuations in my religious life amaze me! I cannot doubt that I am really God's child; it would be a dishonor to Him to doubt it. I cannot doubt that I have held as real communion with Him as with any earthly friend—and oh, it has been far sweeter!

–Oct. 20–

I made a parting visit to Mrs. Campbell today and, as usual, have come away strengthened and refreshed. She said all sorts of kind things to cheer and encourage me and stimulated me to take up the burden of life cheerfully and patiently, just as it comes. She assures me that these fluctuations of feeling will by degrees give place to a calmer life, especially if I avoid, so far as I can do it, all unnecessary work, distraction, and hurry. And a few quiet, resting words from her have given me courage to press on toward perfection, no matter how much imperfection I see in myself and others. And now I am waiting for my Father's next gift and the new cares and labors it will bring with it. I am glad it is not left to me to decide my own lot. I am afraid I should never see precisely the right moment for welcoming a new bird into my nest, dearly as I love the rustle of their wings and the sound of their voices when they do come. And surely He knows the right moments who knows all my struggles with a certain sort of poverty, poor health, and domestic care. If I could feel that all the time, as I do at this moment, how happy I should always be!

–January 16, 1847–

This is the tenth anniversary of our wedding day, and it has been a delightful one. If I were called upon to declare what has been the chief element of my happiness, I should say it was not Ernest's love for me or mine for him, or that I am once more the mother of three children, or that my own dear Mother still lives, though I revel in each and all of these. But underneath them all, deeper, stronger than all, lies a peace with God that I can compare to no other joy, which I guard as I would guard hid treasure and which must abide if all things else pass away.

My baby is two months old, and her name is Ethel. The three children together form a beautiful picture that I am never tired of admiring. But they will not give me much time for writing. This little newcomer takes all there is of me. Mother brings me pleasant reports of Miss Clifford, who, under her gentle, wise influence, is becoming an earnest Christian, already rejoicing in the Providence that arrested her where it did and forced her to reflection. Mother says we ought to study God's Providence more than we do, since He has a meaning and a purpose in everything He does. Sometimes I can do this and find it a source of great happiness. Then worldly cares seem mere worldly cares, and I forget that His wise, kind hand is in every one of them.

–February–

Helen has been spending the whole day with me, as she often does, helping me with her skillful needle and with the children in a very sweet way. I am almost ashamed to indulge in writing down how dearly she seems to love me and how disposed she is to sit at my feet as a learner at the very moment I am longing to possess her sweet, gentle temper. But one thing puzzles me in her, and that is the difficulty she finds in getting hold of these simple truths her father used to grope after but never found till just as he was passing out of the world. It seems as if God compensated such turbulent, fiery natures as mine by revealing Himself to them for the terrible hours of shame and sorrow through which their sins and follies cause them to pass. I suffer far more than Helen does, suffer bitterly, painfully, but I enjoy tenfold more. For I know whom I have believed, and I cannot doubt that I am truly united to Him. Helen is naturally very reserved, but by degrees she has come to talk with me quite frankly. Today as we sat together in the nursery, little Raymond snatched a toy from Una, who, as usual, yielded to him without a frown. I called him to me; he came reluctantly.

"Raymond, dear," I said, "did you ever see Papa snatch anything from me?"

He smiled and shook his head.

"Well, then, until you see him do it to me, never do it to your sister. Men are gentle and polite to women, and little boys should be gentle and polite to little girls."

The children ran off to their play, and Helen said, "Now how different that is from my mother's management with us! She always made us girls yield to the boys. They would not have thought they could go up to bed unless one of us got a candle for them."

"That, I suppose, is the reason then that Ernest expected me to wait upon him after we were married," I replied. "I was a little stiff about yielding to him, for besides Mother's precepts, I was influenced by my father's example. He was so courteous, treating her with as much respect as if she were a queen and yet with as much love as if she were always a girl. I naturally expected the like from my husband."

"You must have been disappointed then," she said.

"Yes, I was. It cost me a good many pouts and tears of which I am now ashamed. And Ernest seldom annoys me now with the little neglects that I used to make so much of."

"Sometimes I think there are no 'little' neglects," said Helen. "It takes less than nothing to annoy us."

"And it takes more than everything to please us!" I cried. "But Ernest and I had one stronghold to which we always fled in our troublous times, and that was our love for each other. No matter how he provoked me by his little heedless ways, I had to forgive him because I loved him so. And he had to forgive me my faults for the same reason."

"I had no idea husbands and wives loved each other so," said Helen. "I thought they got over it as soon as their cares and troubles came on and just jogged on together somehow."

We both laughed, and then she went on.

"If I thought I should be as happy as you are, I should be tempted to be married myself."

"Ah, I thought your time would come!" I cried.

"Don't ask me any questions," she said, her pretty face growing prettier with a bright warm glow. "Give me advice instead; for instance, tell me how I can be sure that if I love a man I shall go on loving him through all the wear and tear of married life, and how can I be sure he can and will go on loving me?"

"Well, then, setting aside the fact that you are both lovable and loving, I will say this: Happiness, in other words love, in married life is not a mere accident. When the union has been formed, as most Christian unions are, by God Himself, it is His intention and His will that it shall prove the unspeakable joy of both husband and wife and become more and more so from year to year. But we are imperfect creatures, wayward and foolish as little children, horribly unreasonable, selfish, and willful. We are not capable of enduring the shock of finding, at every turn, that our idol is made of clay and that it is prone to tumble off its pedestal and lie in the dust till we pick it up and set it in its place again. I was struck with Ernest's asking in the very first prayer he offered in my presence, after our marriage, that

God would help us love each other; I felt that love was the very foundation on which I was built and that there was no danger that I should ever fall short in giving to my husband all he wanted in full measure. But as he went on day after day repeating this prayer, and I naturally made it with him, I came to see that this most precious of earthly blessings had been and must be God's gift and that while we both looked at it in that light and felt our dependence on Him for it, we might safely encounter together all the assaults made upon us by the world, the flesh, and the devil. I believe we owe it to this constant prayer that we have loved each other so uniformly and with such growing comfort in each other; so that our little discords always have ended in fresh accord, and our love has felt conscious of resting on a rock—and that rock was the will of God."

"It is plain, then," said Helen, "that you and Ernest are sure of one source of happiness as long as you live, whatever vicissitudes you may meet with. I thank you so much for what you have said. The fact is you have been brought up to carry religion into everything. But I was not. My mother was as good as she was lovely, but I think she felt and taught us to feel that we were to put it on as we did our Sunday clothes and to wear it, as we did them, carefully and reverently but with pretty long, grave faces. But you mix everything up so that when I am with you I never know whether you are most like or most unlike other people And your mother is just so."

"But you forget that it is to Ernest I owe my best ideas about married life; I don't remember ever talking with my mother or anyone else on the subject. And as to carrying religion into everything, how can one help it if one's religion is a vital part of one's self, not a cloak put on to go to church in and hang up out of the way against next Sunday?"

Helen laughed. She has the merriest, yet gentlest little laugh one can imagine. I long to know who it is that has been so fortunate as to touch her heart!

–March–

I know now, and glad I am! The sly little puss is purring at this moment in James's arms; at least I suppose she is, as I have discreetly come up to my room and left them to themselves. So it seems I have had all these worries about Lucy for naught. What made her so fond of James was simply the fact that a friend of his had looked on her with a favorable eye, regarding her as a very proper mother for four or five children who are in need of a shepherd. Yes, Lucy is going to marry a man so much older than herself that on a pinch he might have been her father. She does it from a sense of duty, she says; and to a nature like hers, duty may perhaps suffice and no cry of the heart have to be stifled in its performance. We are all so happy in the happiness of James and Helen that we are not in the mood to criticize Lucy's decision. I have a strange and most absurd envy when I think what a good time they are having at this moment downstairs while I sit here alone, vainly wishing I could see more of Ernest. Just as if my happiness were not a deeper, more blessed one than theirs, which must be purged of much dross before it will prove itself to be like gold. Yes, I suppose I am as happy in my dear precious husband and children as a wife and mother can be in a fallen world, which must not be a real heaven lest we should love the land we journey through so well as to want to pitch our tents in it forever and cease to look and long for the home whither we are bound.

James will be married almost immediately, I suppose, as he sails for Syria early in April. How much a missionary and his wife must be to each other when, severing themselves from all they ever loved before, they go forth, hand in hand, not merely to be foreigners in heathen lands but to be henceforth strangers in their own should they ever return to it!

Helen says, playfully, that she has not a missionary spirit and is not at all sure that she shall go with James. But I don't think that he feels very anxious on that point!

–March–

It does one's heart good to see how happy they are! And it does one's heart good to have one's husband set up an opposition to the goings-on by behaving like a lover himself.

CHAPTER XXIII

*I*t is a great while since I wrote that. "God has been just as good as ever"; I want to say that before I say another word. But He has indeed smitten me very sorely.

While we were in the midst of our rejoicings about James and Helen and the bright future that seemed opening before them, he came home one day very ill. Ernest happened to be in and attended to him at once. But the disease was, at the very outset, so violent and raged with such absolute fury that no remedies had any effect. Everything, even now, seems confused in my mind. It seems as if there was a sudden transition from the most brilliant, joyous health to a brief but fearful struggle for life, speedily followed by the awful mystery and stillness of death. Is it possible, I still ask myself, that four short days wrought an event whose consequences must run through endless years?—Poor Mother! Poor Helen!—When it was all over, I do not know what to say of Mother but that she behaved and quieted herself like a weaned child. Her sweet composure awed me; I dared not give way to my own vehement, terrible sorrow·

in the presence of this Christ-like patience, all noisy demonstrations seemed profane. I thought no human being was less selfish, more loving than she had been for many years, but the spirit that now took possession of her flowed into her heart and life directly from the great Heart of love, whose depths I had never even begun to sound. There was, therefore, something absolutely divine in her aspect, in the tones of her voice, in the very smile on her face. We could compare its expression to nothing but Stephen, when he, being full of the Holy Ghost, looked up steadfastly to heaven and saw the Glory of God and Jesus standing on the right hand of God.

As soon as James was gone, Helen came to our home; there was never any discussion about it, she came naturally to be one of us. Mother's health, already very frail, gradually failed; and encompassed as I was with cares, I could not be with her constantly. Helen took the place with her of a daughter and found herself welcomed like one. The atmosphere in which we all lived was one that cannot be described; the love for all of us and for every living thing that flowed in Mother's words and tones passed all knowledge. The children's little joys and sorrows interested her exactly as if she was one of themselves; they ran to her with every petty grievance and every new pleasure. During the time she lived with us, she had won many warm friends, particularly among the poor and the suffering. As her strength would no longer allow her to go to them, those who could do so came to her; and I was struck to see she had ceased entirely from giving counsel and now gave nothing but the most beautiful, tender compassion and sympathy. I saw that she was failing but flattered myself that her own serenity and our care would prolong her life still for many years. I longed to have my children become old enough to fully appreciate her sanctified character; and I thought she would gradually fade away and be set free,

> *As light winds wandering through groves of bloom,*
> *Detach the delicate blossoms from the tree.*

But God's thoughts are not as our thoughts, nor His ways as our ways. Her feeble body began to suffer from the rudest assaults of pain; day and night, night and day, she lived through a martyrdom in which what might have been a lifetime of suffering was concentrated into a few months. To witness these sufferings was like the sundering of joints and marrow; and once, only once, thank God! my faith in Him staggered and reeled to and fro. "How can He look down on such agonies!" I cried in my secret soul. "Is this work of a God of love, of mercy?" Mother seemed to suspect my thoughts, for she took my hand tenderly in hers and said with great difficulty:

"Though He slay me, yet will I trust Him (Job 13:15). He is just as good as ever." And she smiled. I ran away to Ernest crying, "Oh, is there nothing you can do for her?"

"What should a poor mortal do where Christ has done so much, my darling?" he said, taking me in his arms. "Let us stand aside and see the glory of God with our shoes from off our feet." But he went to her with one more desperate effort to relieve her, yet in vain.

Mrs. Embury, of whom Mother was fond and who is always very kind when we are in trouble, came in just then; and after looking on a moment in tears, she said to me:

"God knows whom He can trust! He would not lay His hand thus on all His children."

Those few words quieted me. Yes, God knows. And now it is all over. My precious, precious mother has been a saint in heaven more than two years and has forgotten all the battles she fought on earth and all her sorrows and all her sufferings in the presence of her Redeemer. She knew that she was going, and the last words she uttered—and they were spoken with somewhat of the playful, quaint manner in which she had spoken all her life and with her own bright smile—still sound in my ears. "I have given God a great deal of trouble, but He is driving me into pasture now!"

And then, with her cheek on her hand, she fell asleep and slept on till just at sundown she awoke to find herself in the green pasture, the driving all over forever and ever.

Who by searching can find out God? My dear father entered heaven after a prosperous life by a path wherein he was unconscious of a pang, and our beloved James went bright and fresh and untarnished by conflict, straight to the Master's feast. But what a long lifetime of bereavement, sorrow, and suffering was my darling mother's pathway to glory! Surely her felicity must be greater than theirs, and the crown she has won by such a struggle must be brighter than the stars. And this crown she is even now, while I sit here choked with tears, casting joyfully at the feet of her Savior!

My sweet sister, my precious little Helen, still nestles in our hearts and in our home. Martha made one passionate appeal to her to return to her, but Ernest interfered:

"Let her stay with Katy," he said. "James would have chosen to have her with the one human being like himself."

Does he think me, with all my faults, the languor of frail health, and the cares and burdens of life weighing upon me, enough like that sparkling, brave boy to be of use and comfort to dear Helen? I take courage at the thought and rouse myself afresh to bear on with fidelity and patience. My steadfast aim now is to follow in my mother's footsteps; to imitate her cheerfulness, her benevolence, her bright, inspiring ways; and never to rest till in place of my selfish nature I become as full of Christ's love as she became. I am glad she is at last relieved from the knowledge of all my cares; and though I often and often yearn to throw myself into her arms and pour out my cares and trials into her sympathizing ears, I would not have her back for all the world. She has got away from all the turmoil and suffering of life; let her stay!

The scenes of sorrow through which we have been passing have brought Ernest nearer to me than ever, and I can see that this varied discipline has softened and sweetened his character. Besides, we have modified each other. Ernest is more demonstrative, more attentive to those little things that make the happiness of married life; and I am less childish, less vehement—I wish I could say less selfish, but here I seem to have come to a standstill. But I do understand Ernest's trials in his profession far better than I did and can feel and show some sympathy in them. Of course the life of a physician is necessarily one of self-denial, spent as it is amid scenes of suffering and sorrow, which he is often powerless to alleviate. But there is besides the wear and tear of years of poverty; his bills are disputed or allowed to run on year after year unnoticed; he is often dismissed because he cannot put himself in the place of Providence and save life; and a truly grateful, generous patient is almost an unknown rarity. I do not speak of these things to complain of them. I suppose they are a necessary part of that whole providential plan by which God molds and fashions and tempers the human soul, just as my petty, but incessant household cares are. If I had nothing to do but love my husband and children and perform for them, without obstacle or hindrance, the sweet ideal duties of wife and mother, how content I should be to live always in this world! But what would become of me if I were not called, in the pursuit of these duties and in contact with real life, to bear "restless nights, ill health, unwelcome news, the faults of servants, contempt, ingratitude of friends, my own failings, lowness of spirits, the struggle in overcoming my corruption, and a score of kindred trials!"

Bishop Wilson charges us to bear all things "as unto God" and "with the greatest privacy." How seldom I have met them save as lions in my way that I would avoid if I could, and how I have tormented my friends by tedious complaints about them! Yet when compared with the great tragedies of suffering I have both witnessed and suffered, how petty they seem!

Our household, bereft of Mother's and James's bright presence, now numbers just as many members as it did before they left us. Another angel has flown into it, though not on wings; and I have four darling children, the baby, who can hardly be called a baby now, being nearly two years old. My hands and my heart are full, but two of the children go to school, and that certainly makes my day's work easier.

The little things are happier for having regular employment, and we are so glad to meet each other again after the brief separation! I try to be at home when it is time to expect them, for I love to hear the eager voices ask, in chorus, the moment the door opens: "Is Mamma at home?" Helen has taken Daisy to sleep with her, which after so many years of ups and downs at night, now with restless babies, now to answer the bell when Ernest is out, is a great relief to me. Poor Helen! She has never recovered her cheerfulness since James's death. It has crushed her energies and left her very sorrowful. This is partly owing to a soft and tender nature, easily borne down and overwhelmed, partly to what seems an almost constitutional inability to find rest in God's will. She assents to all we say to her about submission in a sweet, gentle way, and then comes the invariable, mournful wail, "But it was so unexpected! It came so suddenly!" But I love the little thing, and her affection for us all is one of our greatest comforts.

Martha is greatly absorbed in her own household, its cares and its pleasures. She brings her little Underhills to see us occasionally, when they put my children quite out of countenance by their consciousness of the fine clothes they wear and their knowledge of the world. Even I find it hard not to feel abashed in the presence of so much of the sort of wisdom in which I am lacking. As to Lucy, she is exactly in her sphere: the calm dignity with which she reigns in her husband's house and the moderation and self-control with which she guides his children are really instructive. She has a baby of her own, and though it acts just like other babies and kicks, scratches, pulls, and cries when it is washed and dressed, she goes through that process with a serenity and deliberation that I envy with all my might. Her predecessor in the nursery was all nerve and brain and has left four children made of the same material behind her. But their wild spirits on one day and their depression and languor on the next have no visible effect upon her. Her influence is always quieting; she tones down their vehemence with her own calm decision and practical good sense. It is amusing to see her seated among those four little furies who love each other in such a distracted way that somebody's feelings are always getting hurt and somebody always crying. By a sort of magnetic influence she heals these wounds immediately and finds some prosaic occupation as an antidote to these poetical moods. I confess that I am instructed and reproved whenever I go to see her and wish I were more like her.

But there is no use in trying to engraft an opposite nature on one's own. What I am, that I must be, except as God changes me into His own image. And everything brings me back to that, as my supreme desire. I see more and more than I must be myself what I want my children to be and that I cannot make myself over even for their sakes. This must be His work, and I wonder that it goes on so slowly; that all the disappointments, sorrows, sicknesses I have passed through have left me still selfish, still full of imperfections!

–March 5, 1852–

This is the sixth anniversary of James's death. Thinking it all over after I went to bed last night, his sickness, his death, and the weary months that followed for Mother, I could not get to sleep till long past midnight. Then Una woke, crying with the earache, and I was up till nearly daybreak with her, poor child. I got up jaded and depressed, almost ready to faint under the burden of life and dreading to meet Helen, who is doubly sad on these anniversaries. She came down to breakfast dressed as usual in deep mourning and looking as spiritless as I felt. The prattle of the children relieved the somber silence maintained by the rest of us, each of whom acted depressingly on the others. How things do flash into one's mind! These words suddenly came to mine, as we sat so gloomily at the table God had spread for us and which He had enlivened by the four young faces around it—

> *Why should the children of a King*
> *Go mourning all their days?*

Why, indeed? Children of a King! I felt grieved that I was so intent on my own sorrows as to lose sight of my relationship to Him. And then I asked myself what I could do to make the day less wearisome and sorrowful for Helen. She came, after a time, with her work to my room. The children took their good-bye kisses and went off to school; Ernest took his, too, and set forth on his day's work while Daisy played quietly about the room.

"Helen, dear," I ventured at last to begin, "I want you to do me a favor today."

"Yes," she said languidly.

"I want you to go to see Mrs. Campbell. This is the day for her beef tea, and she will be looking out for one of us."

"You must not ask me to go today," Helen answered.

"I think I must, dear. When other springs of comfort dry up, there is one always left to us. And that, as Mother often said, is usefulness."

"I do try to be useful," she said.

"Yes, you are very kind to me and to the children. If you were my own sister you could not do more. But these little duties do not relieve that aching void in your heart that yearns so for relief."

"No," she said quickly, "I have no such yearning. I just want to settle down as I am now."

"Yes, I suppose that is the natural tendency of sorrow.

But there is great significance in the prayer for 'a heart at leisure from itself, to soothe and sympathize.' "

"Oh, Katy!" she said. "You don't know, you can't know how I feel. Until James began to love me so, I did not know there was such a love as that in the world. You know our family is different from yours. And it is so delightful to be loved. Or rather it was!"

"Don't say was," I said. "You know we all love you dearly, dearly."

"Yes, but not as James did!"

"That is true. It was foolish in me to expect to console you by such suggestions. But to go back to Mrs. Campbell. She will sympathize with you, if you will let her, as very few can for she has lost both husband and children."

"Ah, but she had a husband for a time, at least. It is not as if he were snatched away before they had lived together."

If anybody else had said this I should have felt that it was out of mere perverseness. But dear little Helen is not perverse; she is simply overburdened.

"I grant that your disappointment was greater than hers," I went on, "but the affliction was not. Every day that a husband and wife walk hand in hand together upon this earth makes the twain more and more one flesh. The selfish element that at first formed so large a part of their attraction to each other disappears, and the union becomes so pure and beautiful as to form a fitting type of the union of Christ and His church. There is nothing else on earth like it."

Helen sighed.

"I find it hard to believe," she said, "there can be anything more delicious than the months in which James and I were so happy together."

"Suffering together would have brought you even

nearer," I replied. "Dear Helen, I am very sorry for you; I hope you feel that even when, according to my want, I fall into arguments, as if one could argue a sorrow away!"

"You are so happy," she answered. "Ernest loves you so dearly and is so proud of you, and you have such lovely children! I ought not to expect you to sympathize perfectly with my loneliness."

"Yes, I am happy," I said after a pause; "but you must own, dear, that I had my sorrows, too. Until you become a mother yourself, you cannot comprehend what a mother can suffer, not merely for herself, in losing her children, but in seeing their suffering. I think I may say of my happiness that it rests on something higher and deeper than even Ernest and my children."

"And what is that?"

"The will of God, the sweet will of God. If He should take them all away, I might still possess a peace which would flow on forever. I know this partly from my own experience and partly from that of others. Mrs. Campbell says that the three months that followed the death of her first child were the happiest she had ever known. Mrs. Wentworth, whose husband was snatched from her almost without warning and while using expressions of affection for her such as a lover addresses to his bride, said to me, with tears rolling down her cheeks, yet with a smile, 'I thank my God and Savior that He has not forgotten and passed me by but has counted me worthy to bear this sorrow for His sake.' And hear this passage from the life of Wesley, which I lighted on this morning:

" 'He visited one of his disciples, who was ill in bed, and after having buried seven of her family in six months, had just heard that the eighth, her husband, whom she dearly loved, had been cast away at sea. "I asked her," he says, "do you not fret at any of those things?" She says, with lovely smile, "Oh, no! how can I fret at anything which is the will of God? Let Him take all beside, He has given me Himself. I love, I praise Him every moment.' "

"Yes," Helen objected, "I can imagine people as saying such things in moments of excitement; but afterwards, they have hours of terrible agony."

"They have 'hours of terrible agony,' of course. God's grace does not harden our hearts and make them proof against suffering like coats of mail. They can all say, 'Out of the depths have I cried unto Thee' (Psalm 130:1); and it is they alone who have been down into the depths and had rich experience of what God could be to His children there who can utter such testimonials to His honor as those I have just repeated."

"Katy?" Helen suddenly asked. "Do you always submit to God's will thus?"

"In great things I do," I said. "What grieves me is that I am constantly forgetting to recognize God's hand in the little, everyday trials of life, and instead of receiving them as from Him, find fault with the instruments by which He sends them. I can give up my child, my only brother, my darling mother without a word; but to receive every tiresome visitor as sent expressly and directly to weary me by the Master Himself; to meet every negligence on the part of the servants as His choice for me at the moment; to be satisfied and patient when Ernest gets particularly absorbed in his books, because my Father sees that little discipline suitable for me at the time; all this I have not fully learned."

"All you say discourages me," said Helen in a tone of deep dejection. "Such perfection was only meant for a few favored ones, and I do not dare so much as to aim at it. I am perfectly sure that I must be satisfied with the low state of grace I am in now and always have been."

She was about to leave me, but I caught her hand as she would have passed me and made one more attempt to reach her poor, weary soul.

"But are you satisfied, dear Helen?" I asked as tenderly as I would speak to a little sick child. "Surely you crave happiness as every human soul does!"

"Yes, I crave it," she replied, "but God has taken it from me."

"He has taken away your earthly happiness, I know, but only to convince you what better things He has in store for you. Let me read you a letter that Dr. Cabot wrote me many years ago but which has been an almost constant inspiration to me ever since."

She sat down, resumed her work again, and listened to the letter in silence. As I came to its last sentence, the three children rushed in from school, at least the boys did, and threw themselves upon me like men assaulting a fort. I have formed the habit of giving myself entirely to them at the proper moment and now entered into their frolicsome mood as joyously as if I had never known a sorrow or lost an hour's sleep. At last they went off to their playroom, and Una settled down by my side to amuse Daisy when Helen began again.

"I should like to read that letter myself," she said. "Meanwhile I want to ask you one question. What are you made of that you can turn from one thing to another like lightning? Talking one moment as if life depended on your every word and then frisking about with those wild boys as if you were a child yourself?"

I saw Una look up curiously to hear my answer as I replied, "I have always aimed at this flexibility. I think a mother, especially, ought to learn to enter into the gayer moods of her children at the very moment when her own heart is sad. And it may be as religious an act for her to romp with them at one time as to pray with them at another."

Helen now went away to her room with Dr. Cabot's letter, which I silently prayed might bless her as it had blessed me. And then a jaded, disheartened mood came over me that made me feel that all I had been saying to her was but as sounding brass and a tinkling cymbal, since my life and my professions did not correspond. Hitherto my consciousness of imperfection has made me hesitate to say much to Helen. Why are we so afraid of those who live under the same roof with us? It must be the conviction that those who daily see us acting in a petty, selfish, trifling way must find it hard to conceive that our prayers and our desires take a wider and higher aim. Dear little Helen! May the ice once broken remain broken forever.

Chapter XXIV

*H*elen returned Dr. Cabot's letter in silence this morning but directly after breakfast set forth to visit Mrs. Campbell, with the little bottle of beef tea in her hands, which ought to have gone yesterday. I had a busy day before me; the usual Saturday baking and Sunday dinner to oversee, the children's lessons for tomorrow to superintend and hear them repeat, their clean clothes to lay out, and a basket of stockings to mend. My mind was somewhat distracted with these cares, and I found it a little difficult to keep on with my morning devotions in spite of them. But I have learned, at least, to face and fight such distractions instead of running away from them as I used to do. My faith in prayer and resort to it become more and more the foundation of my life And I believe, with one wiser and better than myself, that nothing but prayer stands between my soul and the best gifts of God; in other words, that I can and shall get what I ask for.

I went down into the kitchen, put on my large baking apron, and began my labors; of course the doorbell rang, and a poor woman was announced. It is very sweet to follow Fenelon's counsel and give oneself to Christ in all these interruptions; but this time I said, "Oh, dear!" before I thought. Then I wished I hadn't and went up with a cheerful face, at any rate, to my unwelcome visitor, who proved to be one of my aggravating poor folks, a great giant of a woman in perfect health and with a husband to support her, if he will. I told her that I could do no more for her; she answered me rudely and kept on urging her claims. I felt ruffled; why should my time be this frittered away, I asked myself. At last she went off, abusing me in a way that chilled my heart. I could only beg God to forgive her and return to my work, which I hardly resumed when Mrs. Embury sent for a pattern I had promised to lend her. Off came my apron, and up two pairs of stairs I ran; after a long search, it came to light. Work resumed; doorbell again. Aunty wanted the children to come to an early dinner. Going to Aunty's is next to going to Paradise to them. Everything was now hurry and flurry. I tried to be patient and not to fret their temper by undue attention to nails, ears, and other susceptible parts of the human frame; but after it was all over and I had kissed all the sweet, dear faces good-bye and returned to the kitchen, I felt sure that I had not been the perfect mother I want to be in all these little emergencies—yes, far from it. Bridget had let the milk I was going to use boil over and finally burn up. I was annoyed and irritated and already tired and did not see how I was to get more, as Mary was cleaning the silver (to be sure, there is not much of it!) and had other extra Saturday work to do. I thought Bridget might offer to run to the corner for it, though it isn't her business; but she is not obliging and seemed as sulky as if I had burned the milk, not she. "After all," I said to myself "what does it signify if Ernest gets no dessert? It isn't good for him, and how much precious time is wasted over just this one thing?" However, I reflected that arbitrarily refusing to indulge him in this respect is not exactly my mission as his wife; he is perfectly well and likes his little luxuries as well as other people do. So I humbled my pride and asked Bridget to go for the milk, which she did, in a lofty way of her own. While she was gone, the marketing came home and I had everything to dispose of. Ernest had sent home some apples, which plainly said, "I want some apple pie, Katy." I looked nervously at the clock and undertook to gratify him. Mary came down, crying, to say that her mother, who lived in Brooklyn, was very sick; could she go to see her? I looked at the clock once more. I told her she should go, of course, as soon as lunch was over; this involved my doing all her absence left undone.

At last I got through with the kitchen, the Sunday dinner being well underway, and ran upstairs to put away the host of little garments the children had left when they took their flight and to make myself presentable at lunch. Then I began to be uneasy lest Ernest should not be punctual and Mary be delayed; but he came just as the clock struck one. I ran joyfully to meet him, very glad now that I had something good to give him. We had just got through lunch and I was opening my mouth to tell Mary she might go, when the doorbell rang once more and Mrs. Fry, of Jersey City, was announced. I told Mary to wait till I found whether she had lunched or not; no, she hadn't. She had come to town to see friends off, was half-famished, and would I do her the favor, etc., etc. She had a fashionable young lady with her, stranger to me, as well as a Miss Somebody else, from Albany, whose name I did not catch. I apologized for having finished lunch; Mrs. Fry said all they wanted was a cup of tea and a bit of bread and butter, nothing else, dear; now don't put yourself out!

"Now be bright and animated and like yourself," she whispered, "for I have brought these girls here on purpose to hear you talk, and they are prepared to fall in love with you on the spot."

This speech sufficed to shut my mouth.

Mary had to get ready for these unexpected guests, whose appetites proved equal to a raid on a good many things besides bread and butter. Mrs. Fry said, after she had devoured nearly half a loaf of cake, that she would really try to eat a morsel more, which Ernest remarked drily was a great triumph of mind over matter. As they talked and laughed and ate leisurely on, Mary stood looking the picture of despair. At last I gave her a glance that said she might go, when a new visitor was announced, Mrs. Winthrop, from Brooklyn, one of Ernest's patients a few years ago when she lived here. She professed herself greatly indebted to him and said she had come at this hour because she should make sure of seeing him. I tried to excuse him, as I knew he would be thankful to have me do, but no, see him she must. He was her "pet doctor"; he had such "sweet, bedside manners"; and "I am such a favorite with him, you know!"

Ernest did not receive his "favorite" with any special warmth, but invited her out to lunch and gallanted her to the table we had just left. Just like a man! Poor Mary! She had to fly round and get up what she could; Mrs. Winthrop devoted herself to Ernest with a persistent ignoring of me that I thought rude and unwomanly. She asked if he had read a certain book; he had not. She then said, "I need not ask then if Mrs. Elliot has done so? These charming dishes, which she gets up so nicely, must absorb all her time."

"Of course," replied Ernest. "But she contrives to read the reports of all the murders of which the newspapers are full."

Mrs. Winthrop took this speech literally, drew away her skirts from me, looked at me through her eyeglass, and said, "Yes?" At last she departed, Helen came home, and Mary went. I gave Helen an account of my morning; she laughed heartily, and it did me good to hear that musical sound once more.

"It is nearly five o'clock," I said as we at last had restored everything to order, "and this whole day has been frittered away in the veriest trifles. It isn't living to live so. Who is the better for my being in the world since six o'clock this morning?"

"I am for one," she said, kissing my hot cheeks. "And you have given a great deal of pleasure to several persons. Yours and Ernest's hospitality is always graceful; I admire it in you both. And this is one of the little ways, not to be despised, of giving real enjoyment." It was nice in her to say that; it quite rested me.

At the dinner table Ernest complimented me on my good housekeeping.

"I was proud of my little wife at lunch," he said.

"And yet you said the outrageous thing about my reading nothing but murders!" I said.

"Oh, well, you understood it," he said laughingly.

"But that dreadful Mrs. Winthrop took it literally."

"What do we care for Mrs. Winthrop?" he returned. "If you could have seen the contrast between you two in my eyes!"

After all, one must take life as it comes; its homely

details are so mixed up with its sweet charities and loves and friendships that one is forced to believe that God has joined them together and does not will that they should be put asunder. It is something that my husband has been satisfied with his wife and his home today; that does me good.

–March 30–

A stormy day and the children home from school, and no little frolicking and laughing going on. It must be delightful to feel well and strong while one's children are young, there is so much to do for them. I do it; but no one can tell the effort it costs me. What a contrast there is between their vitality and the languor under which I suffer! When their noise became intolerable, I proposed to read to them; of course they made ten times as much clamor of pleasure and of course they leaned on me, ground their elbows into my lap, and tired me all out. As I sat with this precious little group around me, Ernest opened the door, looked in gravely and without a word, and instantly disappeared. I felt uneasy and asked him this evening why he looked so? Was I indulging the children too much, or what was it? He took me into his arms and said:

"My precious wife, why will you torment yourself with such fancies? My very best heart was yearning over you at that moment, as it did the first time I saw you surrounded by your little class at Sunday school years ago, and I was asking myself why God had given me such a wife and my children such a mother."

Oh, I am glad I have got this written down! I will read it over when the sense of my deficiencies overwhelms me, while I ask God why He has given me such a patient, forbearing husband.

–April 1–

This has been a sad day for our church. Our dear Dr. Cabot has gone to his eternal home and left us as sheep without a shepherd.

His death was sudden at the last and found us all unprepared for it. But my tears of sorrow are mingled with tears of joy. His heart had long been in heaven, he was ready to go at a moment's warning; never was a soul so constantly and joyously on the wing as his. Poor Mrs. Cabot! She is left very desolate, for all their children are married and settled at a distance. But she bears this sorrow like one who has long felt herself a pilgrim and a stranger on earth. How strange that we ever forget that we are all such!

–April 16–

The desolate pilgrimage was not long. Dear Mrs. Cabot was this day laid away by the side of her beloved husband, and it is delightful to think of them as not divided by death but united by it in a complete and eternal union.

I never saw a husband and wife more tenderly attached to each other, and this is a beautiful close to their long and happy married life. I find it hard not to wish and pray that I may as speedily follow my precious husband, should God call him away first. But it is not for me to choose.

How I shall miss these faithful friends who, from my youth up, have been my stay and my staff in the house of my pilgrimage! Almost all the disappointments and sorrows of my life have had their Christian sympathy, particularly the daily, wasting solicitude concerning my darling Una, for they too watched for years over as delicate a flower and saw it fade and die. Only those who have suffered thus can appreciate the heartsoreness through which, no matter how outwardly cheerful I may be, I am always passing. But what then! Have I not ten thousand times made this my prayer that, in the words of Leighton, my will might become "identical with God's will."

And shall He not take me at my word? Just as I was writing these very words, my canary burst forth with a song so joyous that a song was put also in my mouth. Something seemed to say this captive sings in his cage because it has never known liberty and cannot regret a lost freedom. So the soul of my child, limited by the restrictions of a feeble body, never having known the gladness of exuberant health, may sing songs that will enliven and cheer. Yes and does sing them! What should we do without her gentle, loving presence, whose frailty calls forth our tenderest affections and whose sweet face makes sunshine in the shadiest places! I am sure that the boys are truly blessed by having a sister always at home to welcome them and that their best manliness is appealed to by her helplessness.

What this child is to me I cannot tell. And yet, if the skillful and kind Gardener should house this delicate plant before frosts come, should I dare to complain?

CHAPTER XXV

*M*iss Clifford came to lunch with us on Wednesday. Her remarkable restoration to health has attracted a good deal of attention and has given Ernest a certain reputation that does not come amiss to him. Not that he is ambitious; a more unworldly man does not live; but his extreme reserve and modesty have obscured the light that is now beginning to shine. We all enjoyed Miss Clifford's visit. She is one of the freshest, most original creatures I ever met with and kept us all laughing with her quaint speeches long after every particle of lunch had disappeared from the table. But this mobile nature turns to the serious side of life with marvelous ease and celerity, as perhaps all sound ones ought to do. I took her up to my room where my work basket was, and Helen followed with hers.

"I have brought something to read to you, dear Mrs. Elliott," Miss Clifford began the moment we had seated ourselves, "which I have just lighted on, and I am sure you will like. A nobleman writes to Fenelon asking certain questions. And a part of these questions, with the replies, I want to enjoy with you, as they cover a good deal of the ground we have often discussed together.

I.

How shall I offer my purely indifferent actions to God; walks, visits made and received, dress, little prophecies, such as washing the hands, etc., the reading of books of history, business with which I am charged for my friends, other amusements, such as shopping, having clothes made, and equipages. I want to have some sort of prayer, method of offering each of these things to God.

REPLY.

The most indifferent actions cease to be such and become good as soon as one performs them with the intention of conforming one's self in them to the will of God. They are often better and purer than certain actions that appear more virtuous. 1st, because they are less of our own choice and more in the order of Providence when one is obliged to perform them; 2nd, because they are simpler and less exposed to vain complaisance; 3rd, because if one yields to them with moderation, one finds in them more of death to one's inclinations than in certain acts of fervor in which self-love mingles; finally, because these little occasions occur more frequently and furnish a secret occasion for continually making every moment profitable.

It is not necessary to make great efforts nor acts of great reflection in order to offer what are called indifferent actions. It is enough to lift the soul one instant to God, to make a simple offering of it. Everything which God wishes us to do, and which enters into the course of occupation suitable to our position, can and ought to be offered to God; nothing is unworthy of Him but sin. When you feel that an action cannot be offered to God, conclude that it does not become a Christian; it is at least necessary to suspect it and seek light concerning it. I would not have a special prayer for each of these things; the elevation of the heart at the moment suffices.

As for visits, commissions and the like, as there is danger of following one's own taste too much, I would add to this elevating of the heart a prayer for grace to moderate myself and use precaution.

II.

In prayer I cannot fix my mind, or I have intervals of time when it is elsewhere, and it is often distracted for a long time before I perceive it. I want to find some means of becoming its master.

REPLY.

Fidelity in following the rules that have been given you, and in recalling your mind every time you perceive its distraction, will gradually give you the grace of being more recollect. Meanwhile bear your involuntary distractions with patience and humility; you deserve nothing better. Is it surprising that recollection is difficult to a man so long dissipated and far from God?

III.

I wish to know if it is best to record, on my tablets, the faults and the sins I have committed, in order not to run the risk of forgetting them. I excited in myself to repentance of my faults as much as I can; but I have never felt any real grief on account of them. When I examine myself at night,

I see persons far more perfect than I, complain of more sin; as for me, I seek, I find nothing; and yet it is impossible there should not be many points on which to implore pardon every day of my life.

REPLY.

You should examine yourself every night, but simply and briefly. In the disposition to which God has brought you, you will not voluntarily commit any considerable fault without remembering and reproaching yourself for it. As to little faults scarcely perceived, even if you sometimes forget them, this need not make you uneasy.

As to lively grief on account of your sins, it is not necessary. God gives it when it pleases Him. True and essential conversion of the heart consists in a full will to sacrifice all to God. What I call full will is a fixed, immovable disposition of the will to resume none of the voluntary affections that may alter the purity of the love to God and to abandon itself to all the crosses that it will perhaps be necessary to bear, in order to accomplish the will of God always and in all things. As to sorrow for sin, when one has it, one ought to return thanks for it; when one perceives it to be wanting, one should humble one's self peacefully before God without trying to excite it by vain efforts.

You find in your self-examination fewer faults than persons more advanced and more perfect do; it is because your interior light is still feeble. It will increase, and the view of your infidelities will increase in proportion. It suffices, without making yourself uneasy, to try to be faithful to the degree of light you possess and to instruct yourself by reading and meditation. It will not do to try to forestall the grace that belongs to a more advanced period. It would only serve to trouble and discourage you and even to exhaust you by continual anxiety; the time that should be spent in loving God would be given to forced returns upon yourself, which secretly nourish self-love.

IV.

In my prayers my mind has difficulty in finding anything to say to God. My heart is not in it, or it is inaccessible to the thoughts of my mind.

REPLY.

It is not necessary to say much to God. Oftentimes one does not speak much to a friend whom one is delighted to see; one looks at him with pleasure; one speaks certain short words to him that are mere expressions of feeling. The mind has no part in them, or next to none; one keeps repeating the same words. It is not so much a variety of thoughts that one seeks in intercourse with a friend as a certain repose and correspondence of heart. It is thus we are with God, who does not disdain to be our tenderest, most cordial, most familiar, most intimate friend. A word, a sigh, a sentiment says all to God; it is not always necessary to have transports of sensible tenderness; a will all naked and dry, without life, without vivacity, without pleasure is often purest in the sight of God. In fine, it is necessary to content one's self with giving to Him what He gives it to give, a fervent heart when it is fervent, a heart firm and faithful in its aridity, when He deprives it of sensible fervor. It does not always depend on you to feel; but it is necessary to wish to feel. Leave it to God to choose to make you feel sometimes in order to sustain your weakness and infancy in Christian life; sometimes weaning you from that sweet and consoling sentiment that is the milk of babes, in order to humble you, to make you grow, and to make you robust in the violent exercise of faith, by causing you to eat the bread of the strong in the sweat of your brow. Would you only love God according as He will make you take pleasure in loving Him? You would be loving your own tenderness and feeling, fancying that you were loving God. Even while receiving sensible gifts, prepare yourself by pure faith for the time when you might be deprived of them; and you will suddenly succumb if you had only relied on such support.

I forgot to speak of some practices that may, at the beginning, facilitate the remembrances of the offering one ought to make to God of all the ordinary acts of the day.

1. Form the resolution to do so every morning, and call yourself to account in your self-examination at night.

2. Make no resolutions but for good reasons, either from propriety or the necessity of relaxing the mind, etc. Thus, in accustoming one's self to retrench the useless little by little, one accustoms one's self to offer what is not proper to curtail.

3. Renew one's self in this disposition whenever one is alone in order to be better prepared to recollect it when in company.

4. Whenever one surprises one's self in too great dissipation or in speaking too freely of his neighbor, let him collect himself and offer to God all the rest of the conversation.

5. To flee with confidence to God, to act according to His will when one enters company or engages in some occupation that may cause one to fall into temptation. The sight of danger ought to warn of the need there is to lift the heart toward Him by whom one may be preserved from it.

We both thanked her as she finished reading, and I begged her to lend me the volume that I might make the above copy.

I hope I have gained some valuable hints from this letter and that I shall see more plainly than ever that it is a religion of principle that God wants from us, not one of mere feeling.

Helen remarked that she was most struck by the assertion that one cannot forestall the graces that belong to a more advanced period. She said she had assumed that she ought to experience all that the most mature Christian did and that it rested her to think of God as doing this work for her, making repentance, for instance, a free gift, not a conquest to be won for one's self.

Miss Clifford said that the whole idea of giving one's self to God in such little daily acts as visiting, shopping, and the like was entirely new to her.

"But fancy," she went on, her beautiful face lighted up with enthusiasm, "what a blessed life that must be, when the base things of this world and things that are despised are so many links to the invisible world and to the things God has chosen!"

"In other words," I said, "the top of the ladder that rests on earth reaches to heaven, and we may ascend it as the angels did in Jacob's dream."

"And descend, too, as they did," Helen put in despondently.

"Now you shall not speak in that tone," cried Miss Clifford. "Let us look at the bright side of life and believe that God means us to be always ascending, always getting nearer to Himself, always learning something new about Him, always loving Him better and better. To be sure our souls are sick and of themselves can't keep 'ever on the wing,' but I have had some delightful thoughts of late from just hearing the title of a book, *God's Method with the Maladies of the Soul.* It gives one such a conception of the seeming ills of life: to think of Him as our Physician, the ills all remedies, the deprivations only a wholesome regimen, the losses all gains. Why, as I study this individual case and that, see how patiently and persistently He tries now this remedy now that, and how infallibly He cures the souls that submit to His remedies, I love Him so! I love Him so! And I am so astonished that we are restive under His unerring hand! Think how He dealt with me. My soul was sick unto death, sick with worldliness and self-pleasing folly. There was only one way of making me listen to reason and that was just the way He took. He snatched me right out of the world and shut me up in one room, crippled, helpless, and alone, and set me to thinking, thinking, thinking till I saw the emptiness and shallowness of all in which I had hitherto been involved. And then He sent you and your mother to show me the reality of life and to reveal to me my invisible, unknown Physician. Can I love Him with half my heart? Can I be asking questions as to how much I am to pay towards the debt I owe Him?"

By this time Helen's work had fallen from her hands and tears were in her eyes.

"How I thank you," she said softly, "for what you have said. You have interpreted life to me! You have given me a new conception of my God and Savior."

Miss Clifford seemed quenched and humbled by these words; her enthusiasm faded away, and she looked at Helen with a deprecatory air as she replied, "Don't say that! I never felt so unfit for anything but to sit at the feet of

Christ's disciples and learn of them."

Yet I, so many years one of those disciples, had been sitting at her feet and had learned of her. Never had I so realized the magnitude of the work to be done in this world nor the power and goodness of Him who has undertaken to do it all. I was glad to be alone, to walk my room singing praises to Him for every instance in which, as my Physician, He had "disappointed my hope and defeated my joy" and given me to drink of the cup of sorrow and bereavement.

–May 24–

I read to Ernest the extract from Fenelon that has made such an impression on me.

"Every businessman, in short, every man leading an active life ought to read that," he said. "We should have a new order of things as the result. Instead of fancying that our ordinary daily work was one thing and our religion quite another thing, we should transmute our drudgery into acts of worship. Instead of going to prayer meetings to get into a 'good frame,' we should live in a good frame from morning till night, from night till morning; and prayer and praise would be only another form for expressing the love and faith and obedience we had been exercising amid the pressure of business."

"I only wish I had understood this years ago," I said. "I have made prayer too much of a luxury and have often inwardly chafed and fretted when the care of my children, at times, made it utterly impossible to leave them for private devotion—when they have been sick, for instance, or in other like emergencies. I reasoned this way: 'Here is a special demand on my patience, and I am naturally impatient. I must have time to go away and entreat the Lord to equip me for this conflict.' But I see now that the simple act of cheerful acceptance of the duty imposed and the solace and support withdrawn would have united me more fully to Christ than the highest enjoyment of His presence in prayer could."

"Yes, every act of obedience is an act of worship," he said.

"But why don't we learn that sooner? Why do we waste our lives before we learn how to live?"

"I am not sure," he returned, "that we do not learn as fast as we are willing to learn. God does not force instruction upon us, but when we say as Luther did, 'More light, Lord, more light,' the light comes."

I questioned myself after he had gone as to whether this could be true of me. Is there not in my heart some secret reluctance to know the truth lest that knowledge should call to a higher and a holier life than I have yet tried?

–*June 2*–

I went to see Mrs. Campbell a few days ago and found, to my great joy, that Helen had just been there and that they had had a long and earnest conversation together. Mrs. Campbell has failed a good deal of late, and it is not probable that we shall have her with us much longer. Her every look and word is precious to me when I think of her as one who is so soon to enter the unseen world, and see our Savior, and be welcomed home by Him. If it is so delightful to be with those who are on the way to heaven, what would it be to have fellowship with one who had come thence and could tell us what it is!

She spoke freely about death and said Ernest had promised to take charge of her funeral and to see that she was buried by the side of her husband.

"You see, my dear," she added with a smile, "though I am expecting to be so soon a saint in heaven, I am a human being still, with human weaknesses. What can it really matter where this weary old body is laid away when I have done with it and gone and left it forever? And yet I am leaving directions about its disposal!"

I said I was glad that she was still human, but that I did not think it a weakness to take thought for the abode in which her soul had dwelt so long. I saw that she was tired and was coming away, but she held me and would not let me go.

"Yes, I am tired," she said, "but what of that? It is only a question of days now, and all my tired feelings will be over. Then I shall be as young and as fresh as ever and shall have strength to praise and to love God as I cannot do now. But before I go, I want once more to tell you how good He is, how blessed it is to suffer with Him, how infinitely happy He has made me in the very hottest heat of the furnace. It will strengthen you in your trials to recall this my dying testimony. There is no wilderness so dreary but that His love can illuminate it, no desolation so desolate but that He can sweeten it. I know what I am saying. It is no delusion. I believe that the highest, purest happiness is known only to those who have learned Christ in sickrooms, in poverty, in racking suspense and anxiety, amid hardships, and at the open grave."

Yes, the radiant face, worn by sickness and suffering but radiant still, said in language yet more unspeakably impressive,

"To learn Christ, this is life!"

I came into the busy and noisy streets as one descending from the mount and on reaching home found my darling

Una very ill in Ernest's arms. She had fallen and injured her head. How I had prayed that God would temper the wind to this shorn lamb, and now she had had such a fall! We watched over her till far into the night, scarcely speaking to each other; but I know by the way in which Ernest held my hand clasped in his that her precious life was in danger. He consented at last to lie down, but Helen stayed with me. What a night it was! God only knows what the human heart can experience in a space of time that men call hours. I went over all the past history of the child, recalling her sweet looks and words and my own secret repining at the delicate health that has cut her off from so many of the pleasures that belong to her age. And the more I thought, the more I clung to her on whom, frail as she is, I was beginning to lean and whose influence in our home I could not think of losing without a shudder. Alas, my faith seemed for a time to flee, and I could see just what a poor, weak human being is without it. But before daylight crept into my room, light from on high streamed in my heart, and I gave even this, my ewe lamb, away as my freewill offering to God. Could I refuse Him my child because she was the very apple of my eye? Nay then, but let me give to Him not what I value least, but what I prize and delight in most. Could I not endure heartsickness for Him who had given His only Son for me? And just as I got to that sweet consent to suffer, He who had only lifted the rod to try my faith, laid it down. My darling opened her eyes and looked at us intelligently and with her own loving smile. But I dared not snatch her and press her to my heart; for her sake I must be outwardly calm at least.

–*June 6*–

I am at home with my precious Una, all the rest having

gone to church. She lies peacefully on the bed, sadly disfig ured for the time; but Ernest says he apprehends no danger now, and we are a most happy, a most thankful household. The children have all been greatly moved by the events of the last few days and hover about their sister with great sympathy and tenderness. Where she fell from or how she fell, no one knows; she remembers nothing about it herself, and it will always remain a mystery.

This is the second time that this beloved child has been returned to us after we had given her away to God.

And as the giving cost us tenfold more now than it did when she was a feeble baby, so we receive her now as a fresh gift from our loving Father's hand with tenfold delight. Ah, we have no excuse for not giving ourselves entirely to Him. He has revealed Himself to us in so many sorrows and in so many joys, revealed Himself as He doth not unto the world!

CHAPTER XXVI

May 13

*T*his had been a Sunday to be held in long remembrance. We were summoned early this morning to Mrs. Campbell and have seen her joyful release from the fetters that have bound her so long. Her loss to me is irreparable. But I can truly thank God that one more "tired traveler" has had a sweet "welcome home." I can minister no longer to her bodily wants and listen to her councils no more, but she has entered as an inspiration into my life, and through all eternity I shall bless God that He gave me that faithful, praying friend. How little they know who languish in what seem useless sickrooms or amid the restrictions of frail health, what work they do for Christ by the power of saintly living and by even fragmentary prayers.

Before her words fade out of my memory, I want to write down, from hasty notes made at the time, her answer to some of the last questions I asked her on earth. She had always enjoyed intervals of comparative ease, and it was in one of these that I asked her what she conceived to be the characteristics of an advanced state of grace. She replied, "I think that the mature Christian is always, at all times and in all circumstances, what he was in his best moments in the progressive stages of his life. There were seasons, all along his course, when he loved God supremely; when he embraced the cross joyfully and penitently; when he held intimate communion with Christ and loved his neighbor as himself. But he was always in terror lest under the force of temptation all this should give place to deadness and dullness, when he would chafe and rebel in the hour of trial and judge his fellowman with a harsh and bitter judgment and give way to angry passionate emotions. But these fluctuations cease, after a time, to disturb his peace. Love to Christ becomes the abiding, inmost principle of his life; he loves Him rather for what He is than for what He has done or will do for him individually, and God's honor becomes so dear to him that he feels personally wounded when that is called in question. And the will of God becomes so dear to him that he loves it best when it 'triumphs at his cost.'

"Once he only prayed at times and seasons and idolized good frames and fervent emotions. Now he prays without ceasing, and whether on the mount or down in the depths depends wholly upon his Savior.

"His old self-confidence has now given place to childlike humility that will not let him take a step alone; and the sweet peace that is now habitual to him, combined with the sense of his own imperfections, fills him with love for his fellowman. He hears and believes and hopes and endures all things and thinketh no evil. The tones of his voice, the very expression of his countenance become changed, love now controlling where human passions held sway. In short, he is not only a new creature in Jesus Christ, but has the habitual and blessed consciousness that this is so."

These words were spoken deliberately and with reflection.

"You have described my mother just as she was from the moment her only son, the last of six, was taken from her," I said at last. "I never before quite understood how that final sorrow weaned her, so to say, from herself and made her life all love to God and all love to man. But I see it now. Dear Mrs. Campbell, pray for me that I may yet wear her mantle!"

She smiled with a significance that said she had already done so, and then we parted—parted that she might end her pilgrimage and go to her rest—parted that I might pursue mine, I know not how long, nor amid how many cares and sorrows, nor with what weariness and heartsickness— parted to meet again in the presence of Him we love, with those who have come out of great tribulation, whose robes have been made white in the blood of the Lamb, and who are before the throne of God, and serve Him day and night in His temple, to hunger no more, neither thirst any more, for the Lamb which is in the midst of the throne shall lead them into living fountains of waters; and God shall wipe away all tears from their eyes (Revelation 7:14-17).

–May 25–

We were talking of Mrs. Campbell and of her blessed life and blessed death. Helen said it discouraged and troubled her to see and hear such things.

"The last time I saw her when she was able to converse," said she, "I told her that when I reflected on my want of submission to God's will, I doubted whether I really could be His child. She said, in her gentle, sweet way:

" 'Would you venture to resist His will, if you could?

Would you really have your dear James back again in this world, if you could?'

" 'I would, I certainly would,' I said.

"She returned, 'I sometimes find it a help, when dull and cramped in my devotions, to say to myself: Suppose Christ should now appear before you, and you could see Him as he appeared to His disciples on earth, what would you say to Him? This brings Him near, and I say what I would say if He were visibly present. I do the same when a new sorrow threatens me. I imagine my Redeemer as coming personally to say to me, "For your sake I am a man of sorrows and acquainted with grief; now for My sake give me this child, bear this burden, submit to this loss." Can I refuse Him? Now, dear, He has really come thus to you and asked you to show your love to Him, your faith in Him, by giving Him the most precious of your treasures. If He were here at this moment and offered to restore it to you, would you dare to say, "Yea, Lord, I know far better than Thou dost what is good for him and good for me; I will have him return to me, cost what it may; in this world of uncertainties and disappointments I shall be sure of happiness in his society, and he will enjoy more here on earth with me than he could enjoy in the companionship of saints and angels and of the Lord Himself in heaven." Could you dare to say this?' Oh, Katy, what straits she drove me into! No, I could not dare to say that!"

"Then, my darling little sister," I cried, "you will give up this struggle? You will let God do what He will with His own?"

"I have to let Him," she replied; "but I submit because I must."

I looked at her gentle, pure face as she uttered these

words and could only marvel at the strong will that had no expression there.

"Tell me," she said, "do you think a real Christian can feel as I do? For my part I doubt it. I doubt everything."

"Doubt everything but believe in Christ," I said. "Suppose, for argument's sake, you are not a Christian. You can become one now." The color rose in her lovely face; she clasped her hands together in a sort of ecstacy.

"Yes," she said, "I can."

At last God had sent her the word she wanted.

–*May 28*–

Helen came to breakfast this morning in a simple white dress. I had not time to tell the children not to allude to it, so they began in chorus:

"Why, Aunt Helen! You have put on a white dress!"

"Why, Aunty, how queer you look!"

"Hurrah! if she don't look like other folks!"

She bore it all with her usual gentleness, or rather with a positive sweetness that captivated them as her negative patience had never done. I said nothing to her nor did she to me till late in the day, when she came to me and said:

"Katy, God taught you what to say. All these years I have been tormenting myself with doubts as to whether I could be His child while so unable to say, Thy will be done. If you had said, 'Why yes, you must be His child for you professed yourself one a long time ago and ever since have lived like one,' I should have remained as wretched as ever. As it is, a mountain has been rolled off my heart. Yes, if I was not His child yesterday, I can become one today; if I did not love Him then, I can begin now."

I do not doubt that she was His child yesterday, and

last year, and years ago. But let her think what she pleases. A new life is opening before her; I believe it is to be a life of entire devotion to God and that out of her sorrow there shall spring up a wondrous joy.

–Sept. 2, Sweet Briar Farm–

Ernest spent Sunday with us, and I have just driven him to the station and seen him safely off. Things have prospered with us to such a degree that he has been extravagant enough to give me the use, for the summer, of a bonnie little nag and an antiquated vehicle, and I have learned to drive. To be sure I broke one of the shafts of the poor old thing the first time I ventured forth alone and the other day nearly upset my cargo of children in a pond where I was silly enough to undertake to water my horse. But Ernest, as usual, had patience with me and begged me to spend as much time as possible in driving about with the children. It is a new experience, and I enjoy it quite as much as he hoped I should. Helen is not with us; she has spent the whole summer with Martha, for Martha, poor thing, is suffering terribly from rheumatism and is almost entirely helpless. I am so sorry for her; after so many years of vigorous health, how hard it must be to endure this pain. With this drawback we have had a delightful summer, not one sick day nor one sick night. With no baby to keep me awake, I sleep straight through, as Raymond says, and wake in the morning refreshed and cheerful. We shall have to go home soon; how cruel it seems to bring up children in a great city! Yet what can be done about it? Wherever there are men and women there must be children; what a howling wilderness either city or country would be without them!

The only drawback on my felicity is the separation

from Ernest, which becomes more painful every year to us both. God has blessed our married life; it has had its waves and its billows, but, thanks be unto Him, it has at last settled down into a calm sea of untroubled peace. While I was secretly upbraiding my dear husband for giving so much attention to his profession as to neglect me and my children, he was becoming, every day, more the ideal of a physician, cool, calm, thoughtful, studious, ready to sacrifice his life at any moment in the interests of humanity. How often I have mistaken his preoccupied air for indifference; how many times I have inwardly accused him of coldness when his whole heart and soul were filled with the grave problems of life, aye, and of death likewise!

But we understand each other now, and I am sure that God dealt wisely and kindly with us when He brought together two such opposite natures. No man of my vehement nature could have borne with me as Ernest has done; and if he had married a woman as calm, as undemonstrative as himself, what a strange home his would have been for the nurture of little children! But the heart was in him and only wanted to be waked up, and my life has called forth music from his. Ah, there are no partings and meetings now that leave discords in the remembrance, no neglected birthdays, no forgotten courtesies! It is beautiful to see the thoughtful brow relax in the presence of wife and children and to know that ours is, at last, the happy home I so long sighed for. Is the change all in Ernest? Is it not possible that I have grown more reasonable, less childish and aggravating?

We are at a farmhouse; everything is plain but neat and nice. I asked Mrs. Brown, our hostess, the other day if she did not envy me my four little pets; she smiled, said they

were the best children she ever saw, and that it was well to
have a family if you have means to start them in the world.
For her part, she lived from hand to mouth, as it was, and
was sure she could never stand the worry and care of a
house full of young ones.

"But the worry and care is only half the story," I said.
"The other half is pure joy and delight."

"Perhaps so to people that are well-to-do," she replied; "but to poor folks, driven to death as we are, it's
another thing. I was telling my husband yesterday what a
mercy it was there weren't any young ones round under my
feet, and I could take city boarders and help work off the
mortgage on the farm."

"And what did your husband say to that?"

"Well, he said we were young and hearty, and there was
no such tearing hurry about the mortgage, and that he'd give
his right hand to have a couple of boys like yours."

"Well?"

"Why, I said supposing we had a couple of boys, they
wouldn't be like yours, dressed to look genteel and to have
their genteel ways, but a pair of wild colts, into everything,
tearing their clothes off their backs, and wasting faster than
we could earn. He said 'twasn't the clothes, 'twas the flesh
and blood he wanted, and 'twasn't no use to argufy about it;
a man that hadn't got any children wasn't mor'n half a man.
'Well,' says I, 'supposing you had a pack of 'em, what have
you got to give 'em?' 'Jest exactly what my father and
mother gave me,' says he; 'two hands to earn their bread
with and a welcome you could have heard from Dan to
Beersheba.' "

"I like to hear that!" I said. "And I hope many such
welcomes will resound in this house. Suppose money does
come in while little goes out; suppose you get possession

of the whole farm; what then? Who will enjoy it with you? Who will you leave it to when you die? And in your old age, who will care for you?"

"You seem awful earnest," she said.

"Yes, I am in earnest. I want to see little children adorning every home as flowers adorn every meadow and every wayside. I want to see them welcomed to the homes they enter, to see their parents grow less and less selfish and more and more loving because they have come. I want to see God's precious gifts accepted, not frowned upon and refused."

Mr. Brown came in, so I could say no more. But my heart warmed toward him as I looked at his frank, good-humored face, and I should have been glad to give him the right hand of fellowship. As it was, I could only say a word or two about the beauty of his farm and the scenery of this whole region.

"Yes," he said, gratified that I appreciated his fields and groves, "it is a tormented pretty-laying farm. Part of it was her father's, and part of it was my father's; there ain't another like it in the country. As to the scenery, I don't know as I ever looked at it; city folks talk a good deal about it, but they've nothing to do but look round." Walter came trotting in on two bare, white feet and with his shoes in his hand. He had had his nap, felt as bright and fresh as he looked rosy, and I did not wonder at Mr. Brown's catching him up and clasping his sunburnt arms about the little fellow and pressing him against the warm heart that yearned for nestlings of his own.

–*Sept. 23*–

Home again and full of the thousand cares that follow the summer and precede the winter. But let mothers and wives fret as they will, they enjoy these labors of love and would feel lost without them. For what amount of leisure, ease, and comfort would I exchange husband and children and this busy home?

Martha is better, and Helen has come back to us. I don't know how we have lived without her so long. Her life seems necessary to the completion of every one of ours. Some others have fancied it necessary to the completion of theirs, but she has not agreed with them. We are glad enough to keep her, and yet I hope the day will come when she, so worthy of it, will taste the sweet joys of wifehood and motherhood.

–January 1, 1853–

It is not always so easy to practice as it is to preach. I can see in my wisdom forty reasons for having four children and no more. The comfort of sleeping in peace, of having a little time to read, and to keep on with my music; strength with which to look after Ernest's poor people when they are sick; and, to tell the truth, strength to be bright and fresh and lovable to him—all these little joys have been growing very precious to me, and now I must give them up. I want to do it cheerfully and without a frown. But I find I love to have my own way, and that at that very moment I was asking God to appoint my work for me, I was secretly marking it out for myself. It is mortifying to find my will less in harmony with His than I thought it was and that I want to prescribe to Him how I shall spend the time, and the health, and the strength that are His, not mine. But I will not rest till this struggle is over, till I can say with a smile, "Not my will! Not my will! But Thine!"

We have been, this winter, one of the happiest families

on earth. Our love for each other, Ernest's and mine, though not perfect—nothing on earth is—has grown less selfish, more Christ-like; it has been sanctified by prayer and by the sorrows we have borne together. Then the children have been well and happy and the source of almost unmitigated joy and comfort. And Helen's presence in this home, her sisterly affection, her patience with the children, and her influence over them is a benediction for which I cannot be thankful enough. How delightful it is to have a sister! I think it is not often the case that own sisters have such perfect Christian sympathy with each other as we have. Ever since the day she ceased to torment herself with the fear that she was not a child of God and laid aside the somber garments she had worn so long, she has had a peace that has hardly known a cloud. She says in a note written me about the time:

"I want you to know, my darling sister, that the despondency that made my affliction so hard to bear fled before those words of yours, which, as I have already told you, God taught you to speak. I do not know whether I was really His child at the time or not. I had certainly had an experience very different from yours; prayer had never been much more to me than a duty; and I had never felt the sweetness of that harmony between God and the human soul that I now know can take away all the bitterness from the cup of sorrow. I knew—who can help knowing it that reads God's word?—that He required submission from His children and that His children gave it, no matter what it cost. The Bible is full of beautiful expressions of it; so are our hymns; so are the written lives of all good men and women; and I have seen it in you, my dear Katy, at the very moment you were accusing yourself of the want of it. Entire oneness of the will with the Divine Will seemed to me to be the law and the gospel of the Christian life; and this evidence of a renewed nature I found wanting in myself. At any moment during the three years following James's death, I would have snatched him away from God if I could; I was miserably lonely and desolate without him, not merely because he had been so much to me, but because his loss revealed to me the distance between Christ and my soul. All I could do was to go on praying, year after year, in a dreary, hopeless way that I might learn to say, as David did, 'I opened not my mouth because Thou didst it.' When you suggested that instead of trying to find out whether I had loved God I should begin to love Him now, light broke in upon my soul; I gave myself to Him that instant; and as soon as I could get away by myself, I fell upon my knees and gave myself up to the sense of His sovereignty for the first time in my life. Then, too, I looked at my 'light affliction' and at the 'weight of glory,' side by side, and thanked Him that through the one He had revealed to me the other. Katy, I know the human heart is deceitful above all things, but I think it would be a dishonor to God to doubt that He then revealed Himself to me as He doth not to the world and that the sweet peace I then found in yielding to Him will be more or less mine so long as I live. Oh, if all sufferers could learn what I have learned! That every broken heart could be healed as mine has been healed! My precious sister, cannot we make this one part of our mission on earth, to pray for every sorrow-stricken soul, and whenever we have influence over such, to lead it to honor God by instant obedience to His will, whatever that will may be? I have dishonored Him by years of rebellious, carefully nursed sorrow; I want to honor Him now by years of resignation and grateful joy."

Reading this letter over in my present mood has done

me good. More beautiful faith in God than Helen's I have never seen; let me have it, too. May this prayer, which, under the inspiration of the moment, I can offer without a misgiving, become the habitual, deep-seated desire of my soul.

"Bring into captivity every thought to the obedience of Christ. Take what I cannot give—my heart, body, thoughts, time, abilities, money, health, strength, nights, days, youth, age—and spend them in Thy service, O my crucified Master, Redeemer, God. Oh, let not these be mere words! Whom have I in the heaven but Thee? And there is no one upon earth that I desire in comparison to Thee. My heart is athirst for God, for the living God. When shall I come and appear before God?"

CHAPTER XXVII

I have just written to Mrs. Brown to know whether she will take us for the rest of the summer. A certain little man, not a very old little man, either, has kept us in town till now. Since he has come, we are very glad of him, though he came on his own invitation, brought no wardrobe with him, does not pay for his board, never speaks a word, takes no notice of us, and wants more waiting on than anyone else in the house. The children are full of delicious curiosity about him and overwhelm him with presents of the most heterogeneous character.

—Sweet Briar Farm, Aug. 9—

We got there this afternoon, bag and baggage. I had not said a word to Mrs. Brown about the addition to our family circle, knowing she had plenty of room; and as we alighted from the carriage, I snatched my baby from his nurse's arms and ran gaily up the walk with him in mine. "If this splendid fellow doesn't convert her, nothing will," I said to myself. At that instant, what should I see but Mrs.

Brown, running to meet me with a boy in her arms exactly like Mr. Brown, only not quite six feet long and not yet sunburnt.

"There!" I cried, holding up my little old man.

"There!" she said, holding up hers.

We laughed till we cried; she took my baby and I took hers; after looking at him, I liked mine better than ever; after looking at mine, she was perfectly satisfied with hers.

We got into the house at last; that is to say, we mothers did; the children darted through it and out of the door that led to the fields and woods and vanished in the twinkling of any eye.

Mrs. Brown had always been a pretty woman with bright eyes, shining, well-kept hair, and a color in her cheeks like the rose that had given its name to her farm. But there was now a new beauty in her face; the mysterious and sacred sufferings and joys of maternity had given it thought and feeling.

"I had no idea I should be so fond of a baby," she said, kissing it whenever she stopped to put in a comma. "But I don't know how I ever got along without one. Mr. Brown's off at work nearly the whole day, and when I had got through with mine and had put on my afternoon dress and was ready to sit down, you can't think how lonesome it was. But by now, by the time I am dressed, baby is ready to go out to get the air; he knows the minute he sees me bring out his little hat that he is going to see his father, and he's awful fond of his father. Though that isn't so strange, either, for his father's awful fond of him. All his little ways are so pretty, and he never cries unless he's hungry or tired. Tell Mother a pretty story now; yes, Mother hears, bless his little heart!"

Then when Mr. Brown came home to his supper, his face was a sight to see as he caught sight of me at my open window and came to it with the child's white arm clinging to his neck, looking as happy and as bashful as a girl.

"You see she must needs go to quartering this bouncing young one on to me," he said, "as if I didn't have to work hard enough before. Well, maybe he'll get his feed off the farm; we'll see what we can do."

"Mamma," Una whispered as he went off with his facsimile to kiss it rapturously behind a woodpile, "do you think Mrs. Brown's baby very pretty?"

Which was so mild a way of suggesting the fact of the case, that I kissed her without trying to hide my amusement.

–*Aug. 10*–

After being cooped up in town so large a part of the summer, the children are nearly wild with delight at being in the country once more. Even our demure Una skips about with a buoyancy I have never seen in her; she never has her ill turns when out of the city; and I wish, for her sake, that we could always live here. As to Raymond and Walter, I never pretend to see them except at their meals and their bedtime; they just live out of doors, following the men at their work, asking all sorts of absurd questions, which Mr. Brown reports to me every night with shouts of delighted laughter. Two happy and gladsome boys they are, really good without being priggish; I don't think I could stand that. People ask me how it happens that my children are all so promptly obedient and so happy. As if it chanced that some parents have such children or chanced that some have not! I am afraid it is only too true, as someone has remarked, that "this is the age of obedient parents!" What then will be the future of their children? How can they yield to God who have never been taught to yield to human authority? And how well fitted will they be to rule their own households who have never learned to rule themselves?

–*Aug. 31*–

This has been one of the most cold, dismal, rainy days, which are not infrequent during the month of August. So the children have been obliged to give up the open air, of which they are so fond, and fall back upon what entertainment could be found within the house. I have read to them the little journal I kept during the whole life of the brother I am not willing they should forget. His quaint and sagacious sayings were delicious to them; the history of his first steps, his first words sounded to them like a fairy tale. And the story of his last steps, his last words on earth had for them such a tender charm that there was a cry of disappointment from them all when I closed the little book and told them we should have to wait till we got to heaven before we could know anything more about his precious life.

How thankful I am that I kept this journal and that I have almost as charming ones about most of my other children! What I speedily forgot amid the pressure of cares and of new events is safely written down and will be the source of endless pleasures to them long after the hand that wrote has ceased from it labors and lies inactive and at rest.

Ah, it is a blessed thing to be a mother!

–*September 1*–

This baby of mine is certainly the sweetest and best I ever had. I feel an inexpressible tenderness for it that I cannot quite explain to myself, for I have loved them all dearly, most dearly. Perhaps it is so with all mothers; perhaps they all grow more loving, more forbearing, more patient as they grow older and yearn over these helpless little ones with an ever-increasing, yet chastened delight. One cannot help sheltering their tender infancy who will so soon pass forth to fight the battle of life, each one waging an invisible warfare against invisible foes. How thankfully we would fight it for them, if we might!

—September 20—

The mornings and evenings are very cool now, while in the middle of the day it is quite hot. Ernest comes to see us very often under the pretense that he can't trust me with so young a baby! He is so tender and thoughtful and spoils me so that this world is very bright to me; I am a little jealous of it; I don't want to be so happy in Ernest or in my children as to forget for one instant that I am a pilgrim and a stranger on earth.

—Evening—

There is no danger that I shall. Ernest suddenly made his appearance tonight and, in a great burst of distress quite unlike anything I ever saw in him, revealed to me that he had been feeling the greatest anxiety about me ever since the baby came. It is all nonsense. I cough, to be sure, but that is owing to the varying temperature we always have at this season. I shall get over it as soon as we get home, I dare say.

But suppose I should not; what then? Could I leave this precious little flock uncared for, untended? Have I faith to believe that if God calls me away from them, it will be in love to them? I do not know. The thought of getting away from the sin that still so easily besets me is very delightful, and I have enjoyed so many, many such foretastes of the bliss of heaven and I know I should be happy there; but then, my children, all of them under twelve years old! I will not choose; I dare not.

My married life has been a beautiful one. It is true that sin and folly and sickness and sorrow have marred its perfection, but it has been adorned by a love that has never faltered. My faults have never alienated Ernest; his faults, for like other human beings he has them, have never overcome my love to him. This has been the gift of God in answer to our constant prayer, that whatever other bereavement we might have to suffer, we might never be bereft of this benediction. It has been the glad secret of a happy marriage, and I wish I could teach it to every human being who enters upon a state that must bring with it the depth of misery or life's most sacred and mysterious joy.

–*October 6*–

Ernest has let me stay here to see the autumnal foliage in its ravishing beauty for the first, perhaps for the last, time. The woods and fields and groves are lighting up my very soul! It seems as if autumn had caught the inspiration and the glow of summer, had hidden its floral beauty, its gorgeous sunsets, and its bow of promise in its heart of hearts, and was now flashing it forth upon the world with a lavish and opulent hand. I can hardly tear myself away and return to the prose of city life. But Ernest has come for us and is eager to get us home before colder weather. I laugh at his anxiety about his old wife. Why need he fancy that this trifling cough is not to give way as it often has done before? Dear Ernest! I never knew that he loved me so.

–October 31–

Ernest's fear that he had let me stay too long in the country does not seem to be justified. We went so late that I wanted to indulge the children by staying late. So we have only just got home. I feel about as well as usual; it is true I have a little soreness about the chest, but it does not signify anything.

I never was so happy in my husband and children, in other words, in my home, as I am now. Life looks very attractive. I am glad that I am going to get well.

But Ernest watches me carefully and wants me, as a precautionary measure, to give up music, writing, sewing, and painting—the very things that occupy me!—and lead an idle, useless life for a time. I cannot refuse what he asks so tenderly and as a personal favor to himself. Yet I should like to fill the few remaining pages of my journal; I never like to leave things incomplete.

–June 1, 1860–

I wrote that seven years ago, little dreaming how long it would be before I should use a pen. Seven happy years ago!

I suppose that some who have known what my outward life has been during this period would think of me as a mere object of pity. There has certainly been suffering and deprivation enough to justify the sympathy of my dear husband and children and the large circle of friends who have rallied about us. How little we knew we had so many!

God has dealt very tenderly with me. I was not stricken down by sudden disease, nor were the things I delighted in all taken away at once. There was a gradual loss of strength and gradual increase of suffering, and it was only by degrees that I was asked to give up the employments in which I delighted, my household duties, my visits to the sick and suffering, the society of beloved friends. Perhaps Ernest perceived and felt my deprivations sooner than I did; his sympathy always seemed to outrun my disappointments. When I compare him as he is now with what he was when I first knew him, I bless God for all the precious lessons He has taught him at my cost. There is tenacity and persistence about his love for me that has made these years almost as wearisome to him as they have been to me. As to myself, if I had been told what I was to learn through these protracted sufferings, I am afraid I should have shrunk back in terror and so have lost all the sweet lessons God proposed to teach me. As it is, He has led me on, step by step, answering my prayers in His own way; and I cannot bear to have a single human being doubt that it has been a perfect way. I love and adore it just as it is.

Perhaps suspense has been one of the most trying features of my case. Just as I have unclasped my hand from my dear Ernest's; just as I have let go my almost frantic hold of my darling children; just as heaven opened before me and I fancied my weariness over and my wanderings done; just then almost every alarming sympathy would disappear and life recall me from the threshold of heaven itself. Thus I have been emptied from vessel to vessel, till I have learned that he only is truly happy who has no longer a choice of his own and lies passive in God's hand.

Even now, no one can foretell the issue of this sickness. We live a day at a time, not knowing what shall be on the morrow. But whether I live or die, my happiness is secure, and so, I believe, is that of my beloved ones. This is a true picture of our home:

A sickroom full of the suffering that ravages the body but cannot touch the soul. A worn, wasting mother ministered to by a devoted, saintly husband and by unselfish, Christian children. Some of the peace of God, if not all of it, shines in every face, is heard in every tone. It is a home that typifies and foreshadows the home that is perfect and eternal.

Our dear Helen has been given us for this emergency. Is it not strange that seeing our domestic life should have awakened in her some yearnings for a home and a heart and children of her own. She has said that there was a weary point in her life when she made up her mind that she was never to know these joys. But she accepted her lot gracefully. I do not know any other word that describes so well the beautiful offering she made of her life, first to God and then to us. He accepted it and has given her all the cares and responsibilities of domestic life without the transcendent joys that sustain the wife and the mother. She has been all in all to our children, and God has been all in all to her. And she is happy in His service and in our love.

–June 13–

It took me nearly two weeks to write the above, at intervals, as my strength allowed. Ernest has consented to my finishing my volume, of which so few pages yet remain. And he left me see a dear old friend who came all the way from my native town to see me—Dr. Eaton, our family physician as long as I could remember. He is of an advanced age but full of vigor, his eyes bright, and with a healthful glow on his cheek. But he says he is waiting and longing for his summons home. About that home we had a delightful talk together that did my very heart good. Then he made me tell him about this long sickness and the years of frail health and some of the sorrows through which I had toiled.

"Ah, these lovely children are explained now," he said.

"Do you really think," I asked, "that it has been good for my children to have a feeble, afflicted mother?"

"Yes, I really think so. A disciplined mother—disciplined children."

This comforting thought is one of the last drops in a cup of felicity already full.

–June 20–

Another Sunday and all at church except my darling Una, who keeps watch over her mother. These Sundays, when I have had them each alone in turn, have been blessed days to them and to me. Surely this is some compensation for what they lose in me of health and vigor. I know the state of each soul, as far as it can be known, and have every reason to believe that my children all love my Savior and are trying to live for Him. I have learned, at last, not to despise the day of small things, to cherish the tenderest blossom, and to expect my dear ones to be imperfect before they become perfect Christians.

Una is a sweet, composed young girl, now eighteen years old; and what can I say more of the love her brothers bear her than this: they never tease her. She has long ceased asking why she must have delicate health when so many others her age are full of animal life and vigor, but stands in her lot and place, doing what she can, suffering what she must, with a meekness that makes her lovely in my eyes and that I am sure unites her closely to Christ.

–June 27–

It was Raymond's turn to stay with me today. He opened his heart to me more freely than he had ever done before.

"Mamma," he began, "if Papa is willing, I have made up my mind—that is to say if I ever get decently good—to go on a mission."

I said playfully, "And Mamma's consent is not to be asked?"

"No," he said, getting hold of what there is left of my hand, "I know you wouldn't say a word. Don't you remember telling me once, when I was a little boy, that I might go, and welcome?"

"And don't you remember," I returned, "that you cried for joy and then relieved your mind still further by walking on your hands with your feet in the air?"

We both laughed heartily at this remembrance, and then I said:

"My dear boy, you know your father's plan for you?"

"Yes, I know he expects me to study with him, to take his place in this world."

"And it is a very important place."

His countenance fell, as he fancied I was not entering heartily into his wishes.

"Dear Raymond," I went on, "I gave you to God long before you gave yourself to Him. If He can make you useful in your own or in other lands, I bless His name. Whether I live to see you a man or not, I hope you will work in the Lord's vineyard wherever He calls. I never asked anything for you but usefulness in all my prayers for you; never once." His eyes filled with tears; he kissed me and walked away to the window to compose himself. My poor, dear, lovable, loving boy! He has all his mother's trials and struggles to contend with; but what matter it, if they bring him the same peace?

–*June 30*–

Everybody wonders to see me once more interested in my long-closed journal and becoming able to see the dear friends from whom I have been, in a measure, cut off. We cannot ask the meaning of this remarkable increase of strength.

I have no wish to choose. But I have come to the last page of my journal and, living or dying, shall write in this volume no more. It closes upon a life of much childishness and great sinfulness, whose record makes me blush with shame; but I no longer need to relieve my heart with seeking sympathy in its unconscious pages, nor do I believe it well to go on analyzing it as I have done. I have had large experience of both joy and sorrow; I have seen the nakedness and the emptiness, and I have seen the beauty and sweetness of life. What I have to say now, let me say to Jesus. What time and strength I used to spend in writing here, let me now spend in prayer for all men, for all sufferers, for all who are out of the way, for all whom I love. And their name is Legion, for I love everybody.

Yes, I love everybody! That crowning joy has come to me at last. Christ is in my soul; He is mine; I am as conscious of it as that my husband and children are mine; and His Spirit flows forth from mine in the calm peace of a river whose banks are green with grass and glad with flowers. If I die, it will be to leave a wearied and worn body and a sinful soul to go joyfully to be with Christ, to weary and to sin no more. If I live, I shall find much blessed work to do for Him. So living or dying, I shall be the Lord's.

But I wish, oh, how earnestly, that whether I go or stay, I could inspire some lives with the joy that is now mine. For many years I have been rich in faith, rich in an unfaltering confidence that I was beloved of my God and Savior. But something was wanting; I was ever groping for a mysterious grace the want of which made me often sorrowful in the very midst of my most sacred joy, imperfect when I most long for perfection. It was the personal love of Christ of which my precious mother so often spoke to me, which she often urged me to seek upon my knees. If I had known then, as I know now, what this priceless treasure could be to a sinful human soul, I would have sold all that I had to buy the field wherein it lay hidden. But not till I was shut up to prayer and to study of God's word by the loss of earthly joys, sickness destroying the flavor of them all, did I begin to penetrate the mystery that is learned under the cross. And wondrous as it is, how simple is this mystery! To love Christ and to know that I love Him—this is all!

And when I entered upon the sacred yet often homely duties of married life, if this love had been mine, how would that life have been transfigured! The petty faults of my husband under which I chafed would not have moved me; I should have welcomed Martha and her father to my home and made them happy there, I should have had no conflicts with my servants, shown no petulance to my children. For it would not have been I who spoke and acted, but Christ who lived in me.

Alas! I have had less than seven years in which to atone for a sinful, wasted past and to live a new and a Christ-like life. If I am to have yet more, thanks be to Him who has given me the victory that life will be Love. Not the love that rests in the contemplation and adoration of its object; but the love that gladdens, sweetens, solaces other lives.

O gift of gifts! O grace of faith!
My God! how can it be
That Thou, who has discerning love,
Shouldst give that gift to me?

How many hearts thou mightest have had
More innocent than mine!
How many souls more worthy far
Of that sweet touch of Thine?

Oh, grace! Into unlikeliest hearts
It is thy boast to come,
The glory of Thy light to find
In darkness spots a home.

Oh, happy, happy that I am!
If thou canst be, O faith
The treasure that thou art in life
What wilt thou be in death?

Stepping Westward

While my fellow traveller and I were walking by the side
of Loch Katrine one fine evening after sunset, in our road
to a hut where, in the course of our tour, we had been hospitably entertained some weeks before, we met, in one of
the loneliest parts of that solitary region, two well-dressed
women, one of whom said to us by way of greeting, "What,
you are stepping westward?"

"What, you are stepping westward?" "Yea."

—'Twould be a wildish destiny,
    If we, who thus together roam
In a strange land, and far from home,
    Were in this place the guests of chance:
Yet who would stop, or fear to advance,
    Though home or shelter he had none,
With such a sky to lead him on?
    The dewy ground was dark and cold;
Behind, all gloomy to behold:
    And stepping westward seemed to be
A kind of heavenly destiny:
    I liked the greeting; 'twas a sound

Of something without place and bound;
And seemed to give me spiritual right
To travel through that region bright.
The voice was soft, and she who spake
Was walking by her native lake:
The salutation had to me
The very sound of courtesy:
Its power was felt; and while my eye
Was fixed upon the glowing sky,
The echo of the voice enwrought
A human sweetness with the thought
Of travelling through the world that lay
Before me in my endless way.

WORDSWORTH

Faint not; the miles to heaven are but few and short.

RUTHERFORD

How shall I do to love? Believe. How shall I do to believe? Love.

LEIGHTON

Always add, always walk, always proceed; neither stand still, nor go back, nor deviate; he that standeth still proceedeth not; he goeth back that continueth not; he deviateth that revolteth; he goeth better that creepeth in his way than he that moveth out of his way.

AUGUSTINE

Authors

The following authors are referred to by Elizabeth Prentiss in *Stepping Heavenward*:

RICHARD BAXTER was a seventeenth-century Puritan writer. He wrote *A Treatise on the Blessed State of the Saints, in their Enjoyment of God in Heaven,* which Katy refers to in her entry for March 31, 1835. The book is now available through Soli Deo Gloria Publications.

JOHN BUNYAN, a seventeenth-century author and preacher, wrote *The Pilgrim's Progress*. Katy makes references to this work often throughout her journal.

WILLIAM POTTS DEWEES was an American physician who in 1825 wrote *Treatise on the Physical and Medical Treatment of Children*, a book that nineteenth-century parents looked to for advice on childrearing in the same way twentieth-century parents once looked to Dr. Spock.

JONATHAN EDWARDS was an eighteenth-century American preacher and writer. Collections of his sermons are still available today.

FREDERICK FABER was a nineteenth-century English hymn writer. Mrs. Prentiss was fond of his poems, and Katy closes her journal with one of his hymns.

FRANCOIS FENELON was a seventeenth-century French mystic. He wrote books on the spiritual life such as *Christian Perfection, Royal Way of the Cross, Meditations on the Heart of God,* and *Talking with God.* Most of these are Christian Classics available from Paraclete Press.

CAROLINE FRY lived in the late eighteenth and the early nineteenth centuries. She wrote *Christ Our Example,* available today from Grace Abounding Ministries.

THOMAS À KEMPIS was a fifteenth-century German mystic who wrote the great Christian classic, *The Imitation of Christ.*

ROBERT LEIGHTON was a seventeenth-century archbishop who wrote a commentary on the Book of 1st Peter.

MARTIN LUTHER, the great Protestant reformer, lived from 1483 to 1546. A selection of his writings are available from Templegate Publishers.

HENRY MARTYN was an Anglican missionary to India in the early nineteenth century. His *Memoirs* are still considered to be a classic of devotional literature.

SIR WALTER SCOTT was a nineteenth-century Scottish novelist and poet. *Ivanhoe* is one of his most famous works.

JEREMY TAYLOR was a seventeenth-century English bishop. He wrote *Holy Living and Holy Dying*.

JOHN WESLEY, the eighteenth-century theologian and social reformer, wrote many sermons, letters, and journals, which Zondervan Publishing has compiled into a single volume.

DANIEL WILSON was an Anglican Bishop to India in the first half of the nineteenth century.

Inspirational Library

Beautiful purse/pocket size editions of Christian classics bound in flexible leatherette. These books make thoughtful gifts for everyone on your list, including yourself!

The Bible Promise Book   Over 1000 promises from God's Word arranged by topic. What does God promise about matters like: Anger, Illness, Jealousy, Love, Money, Old Age, and Mercy? Find out in this book!
Flexible Leatherette $3.97

Daily Light   One of the most popular daily devotionals with readings for both morning and evening.
Flexible Leatherette $4.97

Wisdom from the Bible   Daily thoughts from Proverbs which communicate truths about ourselves and the world around us.
Flexible Leatherette $4.97

My Daily Prayer Journal   Each page is dated and features a Scripture verse and ample room for you to record your thoughts, prayers, and praises. One page for each day of the year.
Flexible Leatherette $4.97

Available wherever books are sold.
Or order from:

Barbour Publishing, Inc.
P.O. Box 719
Uhrichsville, OH 44683
http://www.barbourbooks.com

If you order by mail add $2.00 to your order for shipping.
Prices subject to change without notice.